MW00395687

From the notebooks of
Dr. N.

Edited by
Seema Yasmin

Illustrated by
Fahmida Azim

DJINN-OLOGY

An Illuminated Compendium of Spirits and Stories from the Muslim World

CHRONICLE BOOKS
SAN FRANCISCO

Note: The dates in Dr. N.'s manuscript have been styled according to the Holocene Era (HE) calendar, which begins 10,000 years before the start of the Common Era, at roughly the time when human civilization emerged. To convert dates to the Gregorian calendar, simply subtract 10,000. (The exceptions are the primary sources that Dr. N. gathered in her research, which use the Gregorian calendar.)

Library of Congress Cataloging-in-Publication Data
Names: Yasmin, Seema, 1982- author. | Azim, Fahmida, illustrator.
Title: Djinnology : An Illuminated Compendium of Spirits and Stories from the Muslim World / by Seema Yasmin ; illustrated by Fahmida Azim.
Description: San Francisco : Chronicle Books, 2023. | Cover title.
Identifiers: LCCN 2023046265 | ISBN 9781797214818 (hardcover)
Subjects: LCSH: Jinn. | Islamic demonology.
Classification: LCC BP166.89 .Y375 2023 | DDC 297.2/17 23/eng/20231--dc23 LC record available at https://lccn.loc.gov/2023046265

Manufactured in Malaysia.

Design by Jon Glick
Typesetting of Arabic by Cary Han.

10 9 8 7 6 5 4 3 2 1

Chronicle Books LLC
680 Second Street
San Francisco, California 94107
www.chroniclebooks.com

تحذير

A WARNING

You are now entering the realm of the ungraspable:
alam al-ghayb, the dominion of the Unseen.
This journey is not for everyone.
Alam al-ghayb is not only a place—it is a dimension.
Should you choose to embark on this path,
you will discover new ways of seeing and knowing.
You will question all that you witness and believe.
Your grip on what you call "reality" shall loosen.
Your dreams will be altered forever.

DEAR DISTINGUISHED MEMBERS OF THE ACADEMIC COMMITTEE,

I have a confession. For the past twenty-seven years I have been secretly working on an undisclosed project which has taken me far away from the ivory towers of the academy and plunged me deep into the darkness of other worlds. This project began at the behest of a mysterious figure I can refer to only as the Sheikh. The Sheikh urged me to classify and characterize those creatures known as *djinn*. Made of a smokeless flame and haunting humanity since pre-Islamic times, djinn are shape-shifting beasts who grant wishes, inspire poetry, and snatch away innocent children-disappearing them to an entirely different realm.

Of course, I refused. I am Muslim, yes, but I am a tenured scientist-a taxonomist and ontologist who deals with the classification of tangible matter such as marine animals and freshwater flora. The Sheikh was persistent and requested my assistance three times, as is customary. On a fated day all those years ago, I said yes to the Sheikh's third request and watched the course of my life take an astonishing turn.

The scholarly work presented to you here is the culmination of this covert research. While conducting my renowned marine research, I have traveled the world, retrieved long-lost oral histories, translated archival texts from more than two dozen languages, analyzed the Qur'an and prophetic narratives, and become the first scholar to observe and document certain occult rituals regarding djinn. Compiling this compendium has profoundly changed me, and I believe it represents a paradigm shift in taxonomical and ontological research.

However, my safety has been in jeopardy for the last year. While conducting this research, I discovered that the deep pockets from which the Sheikh funded this project were connected to a nefarious agenda. While I was assured that this was a scientific endeavor designed solely for the purpose of advancing knowledge, I came to learn that the true motive for this work was maleficent. The Sheikh's inner circle planned to employ my extensive, first-of-its-kind research, which melded modern scientific methods with ancient rituals, to control djinn and use them to possess and dominate humans and influence geopolitical agendas. As my research gained traction and valuable historic sources revealed themselves, the Sheikh's organization demanded these findings be kept secret. What you hold in your hands is my defiance in the face of that mandate. I firmly believe in epistemic generosity, open access and knowledge sharing-even if these principles now endanger my life and force me into hiding. I urge you to review and publish this manuscript which I have uncoupled from the wishes of the Sheikh's inner circle and completed without their resources.

A note on methodology: *Djinnology* is not simply a retelling of stories that I have heard. My expertise as a taxonomist and ontologist is uniquely complemented by my training as an ethnographer and my lived experiences as a Muslim. This book represents the meticulous analysis, painstaking cultural interpretation, and careful religious contextualization of primary and secondary source materials in a style and format never before published.

For millennia, many of these sources have been plundered, misunderstood, dismissed, and oversimplified by Western scholars. The public understanding of djinn has become tainted by the poor scholarship of researchers ill-equipped to engage with these multidimensional phenomena.

Djinn, whose name derives from the Arabic triliteral root J-N-N, meaning to hide, conceal, or cover, are not the fantastical or demon-like creatures that have been misrepresented, misappropriated, and Disney-fied by colonizers and extractive explorers on their jaunts through the "exotic Middle East." Djinn are essential to the identity of Muslims, both part of a Muslim's faith and integral to a Muslim's relationship to the interconnected and diverse global cultures of Islam. Some djinn *are* Muslim, and to the world's nearly two billion human Muslims, djinn are as real as tax returns and as frightening and captivating as an electrical storm. The Qur'an, the script that guides the lives of Muslims from Sydney to Sarajevo, and from Los Angeles to Lagos, is addressed to humans *and* our shape-shifting compatriots:

وَمَا خَلَقْتُ ٱلْجِنَّ وَٱلْإِنسَ إِلَّا لِيَعْبُدُونِ

And I did not create the djinn and humankind except to worship Me.

—Holy Qur'an 51:56[1]

1 Qur'anic excerpts and translations throughout this manuscript come from the open access source at Quran.com. Numbers in the attribution lines correspond with the surah (chapter) and ayah (verse).

Given my academic accolades and demonstrable track record of publication in prestigious, high-impact journals, you might question my motivation for working on this project, and you might fear for my credibility (at least among the world of Western scientists). I imagine you are thinking: *But she's a scientist who classifies, labels, and organizes sea creatures-actual living, breathing entities that can be seen with the naked eye or under a microscope. What is she doing investigating these . . . otherworldly things?*

Compiling the first ever compendium of djinn might be *the* intellectual challenge of my lifetime. *Djinnology* challenges the norms of Western science, norms that purport to be objective and open-minded but in fact rely on imperialist standards. Western science, based on its hegemony of vision, has granted supremacy to that which can be seen with the eyes. Establishing this "empire of the gaze" comes at the cost of appreciating the other senses and interrogating the Unseen.[2] But in the invisible lies potential. In the Unseen lies possibility.

No other scientific endeavor has stretched, burdened, and taxed my scholarly training, fieldwork methodologies, scientific acumen, and skills of reasoning. Never in my career had I traversed the depths of noetic experiences-until I began to compile this manuscript. I believe this work not only adds to the field of taxonomy but transforms this discipline to include a more honest and inclusive understanding of different ways of knowing.

But here is where *I* have questioned my ability to master this project: not because of any nonsense "anti-science" accusations, but because I have built a reputation and a career off my ability to pin a label on everything. How was I supposed to comprehend and classify entities that cannot be neatly filed into categories and subcategories?

Djinn resist-no, they defy-categorization. They are wily shape-shifters. They are malevolent, beneficent, a capricious combination of both, or otherwise as caught up in the business of being djinn as we are in the business of being human. They are sometimes enthralled by humans but just as often uninterested in our quotidian routines. Djinn may be ancient or young, slow

2 Nils Bubandt, Mikkel Rytter, and Christian Suhr, "A Second Look at Invisibility: Al-Ghayb, Islam, Ethnography," *Contemporary Islam* 13, no. 4 (12019 HE): 1.

or fast, and artistic or mediocre. They are male, female, and genderless; bestial and chimeric and everything in between.

This bestiary is my best attempt to navigate the creatures of the world that lies between our dominion-the terrestrial realm-and the realm above us, the celestial plane. This intermediary and imaginal realm is called al-ghayb, or the Unseen. While djinn mostly occupy this place, they also inhabit the liminal spaces between. Sometimes, as you'll discover in these pages, they become firmly entrenched and at home in our own realm.

Before I proceed, a note on peer review. I have worked on this manuscript surreptitiously, alongside my more formally acceptable-and celebrated-works, and I am unlikely to engage with any of the inevitable eye-rolling, academic grandstanding, or feigned shock that might emerge from the ivory towers regarding this manuscript. I have been a tenured professor for more than a decade, and while "debates" about the compatibility or discordancy of religion and science once piqued my interest, I've become quite bored with "Can a person of faith be a serious scientist?" deliberations.

Islam, science, and the imaginal coexist. This scientist-like millions of Muslim physicians, statisticians, physicists, engineers, and all manner of researchers around the world-is able to balance objectivity and devotion, reconcile her faith and her curiosity, and synthesize her unknowingness and her core beliefs. I belong to an epistemic community that calculates p values *and* prays away malevolent *'ifrits*.

I hope this compendium offers insights and wonderment while smashing apart the norms of our disciplines. I pray that it invites us to explore new ways of knowing. In the name of science, which is, after all, the quest to fathom all that is unknown, I present to the distinguished members of the Committee, *Djinnology: An Illuminated Compendium of Spirits and Stories from the Muslim World*.

Dr. N█████

Name redacted by the academic committee in light of the ongoing investigation into Dr. N.'s disappearance.

Contents

بسم الله الرحمن الرحيم

WELCOME TO THE WORLD OF THE DJINN

Lurking in the corner of your living room, perhaps reading this sentence over your shoulder right now, is an often invisible creature that is everywhere and nowhere, hiding in your dreams or maybe waiting beneath your bed. You can't always see this entity, but you have surely felt its presence: that gust of cool wind in an otherwise warm library or a suspicious blanket of hot air creeping across the back of your neck and settling over your shoulders as you watch television.

Like you, this creature dances and sings, picks fights and offers gifts, marries and divorces, makes babies and cradles its young. It even dies. Death might arrive after thousands of years, but this creature will eventually grow frail and infirm; it will bury its loved ones and grieve for centuries.

Unlike you, this being crisscrosses the globe at lightning speed, materializes the deepest of desires, shape-shifts from humanoid to winged beast to a puff of smoke, and infiltrates the minds of innocent people, provoking them to behave in strange and seemingly inexplicable ways.

Maybe you're a scientist, a rational person who uses inductive reasoning to arrive at conclusions, the kind of thinker who demands facts and figures before you say, "Yes, I believe." But privately, haven't you wondered what could explain the unexplainable? Why you sometimes feel a presence beside you when you are the only person at home? Why you turn on the lights and call out "Hello?" when no other human is there?

You are not alone. At least two billion people around the world believe in djinn. Among them are accountants, chefs, pilots, and entrepreneurs—people who reconcile their belief in the unseen with their reliance on spreadsheets, algorithms, and satellite navigation systems. Many are Muslim—culturally, religiously, or by some other personal definition—who grew up listening to tales of the mystical creatures from ancient, pre-Islamic Arabian folklore, creatures whose origin story, or one version of it, is described in the Qur'an.

Even before the Holy Book codified their existence and described them as born of a smokeless fire, djinn roamed the globe, meddled in human affairs, and were rebuked and exorcised as much as they were revered and invoked for their powerful gifts. Djinn live in the legends of pre-Islamic peoples, for whom they were poetic muses. These peoples believed that djinn could possess and drive mad the most brilliant minds. (The Arabic word for madness, *majnun*, literally means "a person possessed by djinn.") Pagan Arabs armed themselves with necklaces of fox teeth and fragments of animal bones to ward off the most malevolent djinn. Other times they offered gifts and good deeds to lure benevolent or trickster djinn who could make parched land spring with green shoots and make round the bellies of barren women.

Djinn is the plural of *djinni* (masculine) and *djinniyah* (feminine), although djinn defy categorization and morph between genders and forms. The word *djinn* may derive from the Arabic *jann*, meaning "to conceal or transform." Or it may have evolved from the Aramaic *ginnaya*, meaning "guardian" or "minor God." Some linguists say it arrived from the Persian word *jaini*, which describes a (usually female) spirit with malevolent traits.

The Arabic trilateral root ج ن ن (J-N-N), which loosely means to hide, conceal, or cover, is the origin for words that describe what is difficult for human eyes and minds to comprehend. *Jannah* means "heaven"; *janin* is a fetus inside the womb; *majnun* means "insane" or "the covered mind"; *al-janan* is the heart; and *al-janaan* the shroud that conceals a dead body. The same root also gives us the phrase *ajannahu al-layl*, meaning "concealed by the night."

Whether devout or lapsed, culturally Muslim or a firm follower of the Qur'an, whether raised in Kansas City or Khartoum, in Edinburgh or Cartagena, people from Muslim communities share a collective belief in djinn. The specters and sounds of their childhood horror stories differ from one tongue to another and merge with local tales of regional spirits and homegrown deities.

But you don't have to have grown up religious or identify as Muslim to find yourself cowering beneath the sheets to ward off soul-snatching, mind-meddling djinn. You've already met these creatures in Disney films and read about them in classic novels. The wish-granting genie from Aladdin's lamp in *One Thousand and One Nights* (*genie* is the Anglicized version of *djinni*) is one of the most famous examples. This timeless tale, published during Islam's so-called Golden Age,[3] sits alongside stories of vengeful djinn, water-dwelling djinn, and amorous djinn who pry into the lives of lovers, travelers, and humans going about their day-to-day business.

While they can cross into the human universe, djinn mostly reside in an intermediary dominion called *al-ghayb*, or the Unseen, which overlies the human realm of existence. Djinn are dual dimensional and can sporadically cross into the human realm to cause mischief and havoc or take up residence in the home of a human who has captured their heart. Djinn can fall in love with humans, become infatuated and possessive, and snatch away human children and disappear them into the Unseen.

It's not always so extreme, of course. An enamored djinni might try to respect your human boundaries and leave only subtle traces of its desire: a bouquet of fragrant flowers that no (human) lover or friend will admit to sending; that book of poems that you swear you didn't buy but keeps appearing on your coffee table, open to a stanza about moth wings and flames. Or that chill running up your spine just now—maybe the window is ajar, or maybe it's an invisible friend reading over your shoulder, wondering when you will finally believe.

3 The Golden Age is a historiographical invention by Western, particularly Orientalist, scholars which purports that the pinnacle of Islamic excellence in science and technology existed between the eighth and thirteenth centuries. Not only does this construct assess "civilization" using Western standards, but it conveniently allows for the periods before the so-called Golden Age (the Prophetic era) and after the Golden Age (the Ottoman and Mughal eras) to be deemed the decadent or Dark Ages.

TAXONOMIES OF THE LIVING

RANK	HUMANS (AS AN EXAMPLE)
DOMAIN	EUKARYOTE
KINGDOM	ANIMALIA
PHYLUM	CHORDATA
CLASS	MAMMALIA
ORDER	PRIMATES
FAMILY	HOMINIDAE
GENUS	HOMO
SPECIES	SAPIENS

This is how we rank living things and viruses (although I believe viruses are alive . . . but let's not get into that debate now). I can find no such classification system for djinn. Scholars from ancient to medieval times have spoken about djinn tribes, classes, and orders; but did they use these terms in the same way we use them to describe lions, eagles, and orcas? Were rankings understood differently in medieval times, when so much of our current understanding about djinn was recorded in books and scrolls?

Here are some categories that I have found among archival texts:

JANN: the least powerful class of djinn, possibly the first type to exist

DJINN: a catchall term within which roam many different types of creatures

SHAYATEEN: inherently evil djinn or devils who may be descended from the original Shaytan, Iblîs

'IFRIT: malevolent and powerful djinn

MARID: the most evil and powerful djinn

While the Qur'an is addressed to both humans and djinn, one of its 114 chapters is specifically titled "The Djinn." In this chapter, and in other parts of the Holy Book, djinn are referred to most commonly as djinn, but the terms *'ifrit* and *Marid* each appear once.

The Hadith, the sayings of the Prophet (peace be upon him), mention three types of djinn:

1. **WINGED DJINN THAT FLY** (possibly 'ifrit)
2. **SERPENTS AND DOGS** that are djinn in animal form
3. **ROAMING DJINN**

Djinn resist systemization. They seem difficult—practically impossible—to categorize in a neat and traditional (Western) taxonomical methodology. However, they can be classified according to the following attributes: shape-shifting abilities and other powers, interactions with humans, closeness/distance to angels and animals, habitats, preferred time and place to manifest, capabilities, good or evil nature, and many other qualities.

While writing this book, I've explored the djinn classifications offered by scholars who came before me. This process has revealed the ways in which Western taxonomies fail to compute and comprehend the complexities of creatures that exist in an entirely different realm. I find myself remembering that Western "scientists" created classifications and "learned" theologians interpreted biblical stories to justify the enslavement of Africans and others who did not look like them. To hell with these systems of organization!

In addition to offering a historical and taxonomical précis of djinn in the following chapters, I will also draw on firsthand descriptions of their forms and powers, derived from ancient scholars and those who have encountered djinn, and on centuries-spanning stories that reveal how djinn interact with humans.

I have unearthed and retold tales from South Africa, London, Portugal, New Jersey, China, eastern Europe, and beyond; from the ninth century and modern times; from everyday places and from dimensions that are challenging to grasp. These stories were gathered through direct interviews with those affected or witnesses to their ordeals, and through digging deep in the archives. Some stories are printed as they were told to me or lifted from original publication sites such as medical journals and parenting blogs. Other stories are recast in my voice using material aggregated from multiple sources.

It is stories, after all, that reveal the truest nature of djinn. Stories are a portal into the world of the Unseen.

AICHA QANDISA: THE LOVER

Kingdom of Fes, 11541 HE (1541 CE)

She wipes her bloodied mouth with the tail of her long black braid, stands and dusts the sand from her knees. Aicha unties the laces and flings the heavy leather boots to one side, smooths the silk skirt that has creased beneath her legs, and bends to massage her hooves. It is his turn to fall to his knees, his face frozen in an expression of terrific awe as his legs buckle and he tumbles forward onto the beach. His bloodied exposed buttocks attract a circling white-backed vulture. The bird descends as Aicha walks toward her sisters, who are waiting for her where the tide meets the beach.

Soldier's log,

Castelo do Mar (Safi), Morocco

Lt. Santiago Mendes

July 14, 1541
It has been three months since I was detailed to this hellish sandbox. My body is still weary from firing the cannons and cleaning the cannons, repositioning the cannons and firing the cannons once more. But it has been quiet for days. The brown barbarians have kept their distance since our last Mohammedan massacre turned the ocean scarlet as far as the eye could see.

I miss my wife, our shop, our green garden, and our small but comfortable home.

July 15, 1541
It remains quiet. This only makes me miss my dear Sofia more. I feel drawn to take a walk to the caves, beneath the fortress, between the artillery and the sea. The ocean whistles a sweet melody that soothes my soul. The bloody massacre stained these oceanfront rocks that I grip for balance, although the waters themselves have been clear for days, of course. I follow the tinged boulders as they sparkle redder and redder, concentrating on the scrabble of rocks beneath my feet. I must stay fit and healthy. I must remain uninjured.

My ears are filled with the sound of waves crashing, and my mind is focused on keeping steady and not twisting an ankle, so I do not see the women until I am almost upon them. Luckily, they are sitting in a circle and do not spot me. I crouch behind a boulder. There are three of them. Olive-skinned beauties with the longest hair I have ever seen. They sit at the entrance to a cave, perched comfortably on rocks that appear to be wet with blood, dripping even. There is a small inlet where seawater flows into the caverns. The women's long red skirts drape over the rocks, and they seem to be singing and swaying ever so gently. I peek carefully from behind the boulder, but then the one with her back to me turns and smiles. I am paralyzed. I cannot hide, nor can I make sense of this constellation of features: a beauty to rival any queen's. I lift my arm to wave at this mysterious woman, but a force hits me in my side. The wind off the waves, it must have been. My left ankle twists and I fall sideways. I come to on my back, tasting salt, then iron. The long-haired woman eclipses the sun as she leans over my face and kisses my wet lips. I cannot see her features. I close my eyes and taste blood.

July 16, 1541
I wake in the infirmary. My skull aches where it hit the craggy rocks. Still, I must escape the mandatory bed rest and these ugly matrons. I yearn to see my savior again![4] I've always had an eye for olive-skinned beauties, and surely I would have perished without this savage goddess's aid! As soon as the matrons leave to fetch our lunch rations, I escape the fort and clamber down the crumbling rock face, unsteady on my swollen ankle, hopping over the stones. But there are no women here today. Only piles of gray-brown fur surrounding the rocks where they sat. I follow hoofprints, but they lead me to the mouth of a cave that is too dark to enter. I consider waiting at the cavern's entrance but know that one of the hideous matrons will come looking for me.

4 How quickly the lieutenant has forgotten his "dear Sofia."

July 17, 1541
Thirst. But a kind of thirst that envelops the body. First, my tongue is thick and heavy, then my gums bristle like a dusty old rug. Today, my eyelids drag over my sunken eyeballs like gluey sandpaper.

I lie in the infirmary and see the green leaves of the lemon trees in my orchard. The springy moss that covers their roots. I think only about the wetness of water.

The doctors say I have the Affliction.

July 18, 1541
I daydream about a brown-skinned woman, her face obscured by endless waves of black hair. She pours a stream of crystal-clear water into my mouth. As she circles my cot, a floral scent of orange blossoms and rose water wafts over me.

July 19, 1541
Today my savior visited me in the infirmary! She parted the black waves and let me see her face. My heart stopped. Then it opened. Its chambers flooded with blood and love. Dark brown eyes that continue to stare into my soul, even after she has left. A wide mouth that could swallow me whole, and I would allow it. She saved me. Her name is Aicha Qandisa. She sat at the edge of my bed in a scarlet skirt and spoke in a deep voice that erupted into a high-pitched laugh when I asked: "Are you real?" She replied in some babble (maybe a Berber dialect; I don't know and yet I could understand her every word): "Do you taste this water, ya habibi? Are these splashes real?" Then she sprinkled my face with a million droplets of her ocean.

General Pereira barged into the infirmary and said I was babbling.

My love disappeared, taking her sacred waters with her.

July 20, 1541

Aicha lives in the caves between the ocean and this fort. She said this land has always been her father's land; that it remained her father's land even when our soldiers demolished the boulders and built a factory above the waves in 1488. Twenty years later, we erected this fortress and carved holes into the rock face to aim our cannons and artillery at the local guerillas. She speaks of her mother, Lalla Mimuna, who cares for weary travelers, and her father, Sidi Chamharouch,[5] with admiration and frustration. Sidi is a noble judge, once a companion of their prophet, and a leader known to rule over his courts with compassion. But Aicha says that mortal men do not always respect her father's judgments. Her job is to ensure they do.

July 21, 1541

Gen. Pereira sat with me this morning. He confirms what the doctors say: I have the Affliction. That's why my heart pounds so. I want to tell him that my heart pounds and my blood runs thick because I have met true, life-giving love. Her name is Aicha Qandisa. She is a Mohammedan; I have gathered this now. But her love will save me, and my teachings will save her soul.

I keep my parched lips closed. The general wouldn't understand. He says it is a disease of the kidneys and they must exsanguinate me slowly to re-invigorate my organs.

5 I have also seen Aicha's father referred to as Sidi Chamharouch in Sudanese archival materials. In other places the djinn king is referred to as Chaarmarouch, Abu al-Walid Shamhurish, and at-Tayyar (the Flyer). He is also known as Musytary, the King of Jupiter, and the King of Thursday. Aicha seems to tell Lt. Santiago that her father is alive, but at least three historians tell me that Sidi Chamharouch died at the age of one thousand years—perhaps this was after 11541 HE? I visited his green-and-white shrine in Aroumd, Morocco, in the valley of the Atlas mountains and saw worshippers sacrifice goats as they begged the djinn king to help them receive mercy in the human courts they frequent today. What's interesting is that his shrine predates the arrival of Islam in Morocco in the late seventh century. He was venerated as a saint even before that, hence the mausoleum in Aroumd. When Islam came to the Kingdom of Fes (Morocco), a mosque was built next to his shrine, and it was announced that Sidi Chamharouch was actually the Prophet Muhammad's (p.b.u.h.) Qareen, or djinni companion, and that meeting the Holy Prophet (p.b.u.h.) had led Sidi Chamharouch to convert to Islam and take office as a kind and compassionate judge (Qadi).

July 22, 1541
The doctor slashes the vein in the crook of my elbow and squeezes my bicep. The nurse hangs my arm off the side of the bed. Blood drips down my forearm into a metal pan. It is only right that I bleed while my fellow soldiers hemorrhage on the watery battlefields. They are brave souls, seeking to spread the word of our Lord in this land of savagery.

I pray that Aicha will visit tonight. Only she can quench this thirst.

July 23, 1541
Aicha does not come. But I dream she sits by my side and licks clean my bloodied arm. I rouse in the night to find the nurses have bandaged the wound.

There is a new patient in the infirmary. He is pallid and clammy. The nurse says that he, too, has the Affliction. When we are alone he says he is visited by a woman who loves him deeply, deeper than anyone has ever loved. The fevers arose when his heart became intertwined with hers.

I will ask Aicha if she has sisters. How many more lovesick soldiers can this infirmary hold?

July 24, 1541
They slice open the vein in my groin today.

My love visits in a skirt as blue as the rivers she hails from. Aicha prefers the rivers, she says; but for now, she must live by the sea. This is where her business brings her. Aicha's brother, Mutawakkil, will inherit their father's court one day. And even then, she tells me, as she strokes my dry cheeks with her damp and salty fingers, Aicha and her sisters—Ah! So she has sisters!—will help to ensure that justice is served outside of the court, especially when the kindly Qadi's judgments are disrespected.

I tell my love that she is a gallant woman, conducting the business of her father's court. We are not that different, I say. I, a soldier fighting for peace. She, the arbiter of her father's justice. She smiles at me, a wide and sweet smile, and lifts a hand to my head. I burn with such passion that my vision turns black.

July 25, 1541
More blood must be let. The doctor says the Affliction worsens.

July 28, 1541

Our men have been victorious! Hallelujah! The razia was a success and our salto garnered us new ground.[6] My love remains distant. My heart aches to tell her the good news.

July 31, 1541

Aicha visited me in the night while my invalid companion was asleep. I sat up in bed to tell her that we won. We won! More coast is under the King's rule. We will soon conquer all the land and I will take her as my princess! Back to Portugal, where the lush land will water her soul and quench my thirst forever. There is no lake in our part of the country, but there is a well. My love seemed to thrill at the news! She embraced me with such desire that I, intoxicated and overwhelmed by her love, fell into a sleep from which the medics could not wake me for two days and two nights.

August 3, 1541

Aicha wears a red skirt today and wishes to tell me a story. I fall deeper in love with each sentence, each visit, each flick of her hair across my face as she leans in to kiss me. I check that the young soldier cannot see, but tonight he sleeps next to yet another soldier with the disease, both of them inflicted with the deep sleep that robbed me of two eves with my Aicha. My skin burns with anticipation. Tell me, Aicha! Feed me your tales! Here is the story she spun for me.

6 Razia refers to the Portuguese military's raids of Moroccan land. Saltos were land sieges made using amphibian landings. The Portuguese learned these guerilla warfare tactics from observing Moroccan troops in the fifteenth and sixteenth centuries. This occurred long after the Papal Bull of 11341 HE (Gaudeamus et exultemus) granted King Afonso IV the right to conquer the Kingdom of Fes (Morocco). Between the two events, a mysterious plague (what we now call the Black Death) ravaged Portugal and halted colonization for a time. It wasn't until 11415 HE and the Conquest of Ceuta that the Kingdom of Fes was presented to King João I as an easy target. The Portuguese attacked soon after.

IN THE NAME OF ALLAH, MOST GRACIOUS, MOST MERCIFUL.

It has been related (but God alone is omniscient, omnipotent, as well as all-bountiful) that there once was a warrior of great wisdom and physical strength. The warrior's name was Aziz, which means "dear," "darling," and "precious." Aziz was indeed adored and respected. The townspeople knew he would grow up to protect their land, so they cooked special treats for the remarkable boy; the most tender cuts of lamb were braised for him, flaky fillets of white fish were poached with saffron, and sultanas were piled high on ornate plates for the growing boy.

Aziz was raised as a herdsman and hunter, and he grew up to inherit his father's tannery. He skinned enormous beasts, tossing their hides over his broad shoulders like they were flimsy silks.

Before his father died, it was arranged that Aziz would marry the most beautiful woman in the village. Aziz's wife was as intelligent and enterprising as she was bewitching. She helped him run the tannery, taking it from a small venture into a business known across the land.

One day, just as the townspeople had long predicted, Aziz was called away to war to protect their land from merciless invaders. While he was gone, his wife took charge of the family business. Her fingers stayed a deep red from the leather dye in which she bathed the animal hides.

For forty days and forty nights, she slept alone, praying that her love would return home safely, without the lingering wounds that had burdened her uncles and cousins upon their homecoming from war. She kept busy in the tannery by day, fleshing, dehairing, scudding, and frizzing. By night, her hips ached for her darling. She stroked her reddened fingertips along her breastbone and yearned for Aziz's touch, the way he embraced her, pressing his firm hands into the small of her back, making her spine tingle then arch. She awoke drenched in sweat from dreams of her legs wrapped around his waist, of meeting his passion with hers. On his empty pillow, she had lain a copy of one of Aziz's favorite quatrains by Omar Khayyam:

Alike for those who for to-day prepare,
And those that after a to-morrow stare,
A muezzin from the Tower of Darkness Cries,
Fools! your Reward is neither Here nor There!

She memorized poems and vowed to recite them to her darling upon his return. On the forty-first day, Aziz sent word of his battalion's conquest via the imam's son. Alhamdulillah! Subhanallah! Allahu akbar! "May the righteous be protected," the townspeople cried. The wife wept tears of relief. Her love would be home the night of the waxing gibbous moon.

But by the time the full moon gleamed in the night sky, Aziz had not returned, and the wife was still alone with only melancholy quatrains for company. The full moon came and went. She memorized more hopeful poems. She watched the clouds as a waning gibbous moon peeked through, and still, Aziz did not return. The night the crescent moon appeared, the wife crept out of their home in the dead of night and walked to the tannery in search of the tanner's knife (which some call the fleshing knife). She found the double-handed blade and lifted her red skirt to clean the metal of intestines and hair. She went home, placed the gleaming metal under her bed, and softly recited quatrains until she fell into a deep sleep.

The next day, the imam's son came to console the wife.

"It has been sixty-six days," the wife said to the imam's son. "Bring me good news of my Aziz or there will be hell to pay."

The imam's son scuttered away, anguished by the sickening smile on the woman's face as she laid bare her threat. He did not return with good news, or with any news at all. So while he was taking his regular Friday stroll to the butcher, the wife snatched the imam's son into an alleyway, pressed his body between her body and the wall, slid the tanning knife between them, gripped its handles, and thrust the flat blade into his belly, slicing clean the fatty pouch. His guts spilled onto her feet.

She crouched to wipe clean her feet and the blade with the fabric of her pale blue skirt, which was spattered with red. Next, she paid a visit to the imam himself. "You declared this war," she said. "You ordered my husband's battalion to protect this land. You sent all these men away from their wives, mothers, and children with no plan for their return."

The imam stuttered and stalled as he explained to the bloodstained woman that the invaders deserved retaliation.

To which the wife said, "And you deserve this." Pressing his corpulent body between her body and the wall, she opened his belly with the tanner's knife. Outside, she unwound the rope that tied the imam's camel to the fence and galloped toward the battlefield.

What she saw there transmogrified her anger from a passionate rage to an unquenchable thirst for blood. On seventeen stakes stood seventeen heads. One head for each town from which the Muslim men hailed. On the seventh stake, the wife saw Aziz's head, his eyes staring toward the land he loved, the land he had vowed to defend. The wife galloped up to the stakes. She twisted and pulled until she lifted her husband's stake clean out of the ground. She turned her camel on its heels and headed for the enemy's fortress, brandishing her husband's head.

"And then what did she do?" I cry. I cannot bear the mystery. This mad woman on a rampage, crusading across a littered battlefield on camelback with her husband's head in one hand and a machete in the other?! Where did she go? My love flashes a smile—or is it a gleaming blade?—and I experience an excruciating ecstasy that I cannot describe.

August 7, 1541
My blood is drained. Another two-day blackout. Every one of the dozen beds cradles a groaning, sweating soldier. Some clutch their bellies; some pound their chests. They are all, unlike me, unwise enough to tell the truth: Aicha visits them (I believe they mean her sisters) and they yearn for her return. The doctor pinches the space between his eyebrows and cradles his face in his meaty palm. I want to tell him about Aicha, but he thinks these other men deranged, helpless fools. At least for now, they give me medicines to quell the pain of Aicha's absence. I pray to God she takes me with her, far away from this fortress.

General's log,

Castelo do Mar (*Safi*), Morocco

Gen. João Pereira

August 9, 1541
A bloody massacre at Safi. In the manner of the carnage at Fort Azemmour. All men in the infirmary were found this morning savagely dismembered and decapitated. Number of deaths: 47. Investigation ongoing.

NOTES

I found the tattered pages of this diary in the basement of Arquivo Nacional da Torre do Tombo (the Portuguese Naval Archives) in Lisbon. The archivist insisted the basement contained only useless materials that no one had had time to incinerate. But this story . . . I couldn't stop reading this story. I discovered it buried beneath colonial-era military strategies and blueprints for Portuguese naval fortresses.

After I read it, I immediately had to visit Safi, the now abandoned Moroccan fort that this Portuguese lieutenant called home in 11541 HE. The visit left me with more questions. Are these pages filled with the ramblings of a shell-shocked, dehydrated, and guilt-ridden colonizer? Did a feverish and concussed Lieutenant Santiago Mendes conjure a fierce Moroccan woman who exacted revenge against him and his battalion? Or did Aicha Qandisa exist outside of his febrile imagination? If so, was she a djinniyah—one of the famed daughters of djinn king Sidi Chamharouch—as the locals claim today? Or was she a sixteenth-century anti-colonialist freedom fighter whose husband was killed by the Portuguese, and who was driven to kill men in army barracks and lure soldiers into the desert, where they too would meet a brutal death?

As I pursued these questions, the locals directed me to travel from the soldier's fort in Safi to Agadir, one of the coastal cities where the Portuguese enacted their particular brand of military violence. They told me that Aicha (or the Aichas, since there are possibly many of them?) still lives in, or at least regularly visits, Agadir. She and her sisters are as stunning and bewitching as ever, they said. They described a group of beautiful women stalking the European businessmen who fall out of Agadir's bars and whose castrated bodies sometimes wash up on the beaches the next morning. The elderly owner of an electronics store told me that, these days, the women's prey are mostly Englishmen. (Does this have something to do with that nation's particularly vast and sordid history of colonization?)

I spent each night of my research trip sitting on a low brick wall that faces the ocean on Agadir's promenade. This is where the long-haired Aichas braid and pin large, red flowers into one another's hair while singing and chatting. They are waiting for the colonizers to get tipsy enough to not ask questions about the sturdy boots sticking out from beneath the sisters' delicate silk dresses. I'm not sure I spotted them. I saw beautiful women, for sure, including women with silky long hair and flower-filled braids. Some wore combat boots on warm, summer nights. Some were flirting with men, but I couldn't be sure if anything sinister was bubbling beneath.

The women I interviewed in Agadir—the protective wives of the local men—said I didn't see any Aichas because the wives have learned how to keep them at bay. They said they hide their men indoors and approach the Aichas while brandishing dancing flames at the end of long sticks, at which sight the Aichas gallop toward the sea and vanish. The wives insist they must protect their husbands from the captivating glances of these creatures, since even Moroccan men can fall victim to their seemingly effortless but powerful seduction. Orange flames are one of the water-loving djinniyahs' two known weaknesses; they are both lured and exorcised by the fire. The other is a complex exorcism using gnawa music and ritual dancing.

Lt. Santiago Mendes, the Portuguese soldier whose translated scribblings I include here, seems to not have known about orange flames or musical exorcisms. He was unaware that he might be able to protect his heart and mind from Aicha Qandisa. Or maybe he was one of those guileless men who willingly allows a powerful woman to guide him to atonement, even when that means being led to the depths of delusion and despair, and ultimately to a shocking demise.

ORIGIN STORIES:
BURNING WINDS AND SMOKELESS FLAMES

First there were djinn, then came humans. Arriving in the Universe before we did, djinn have always outnumbered us. The Holy Prophet (p.b.u.h.) said:

> God divided the djinn and the humans into ten parts. One part makes up the human race, and the other nine parts is made up of the djinn.
>
> —Jalal al-din Al-Suyuti, *Laqt al-murjan fi 'ahkam al-jann (The Hills of Precious Pearls Concerning the Legal Ordinances of the Jinn)*[7]

The Qur'an is clear that, unlike subservient angels made from light, and ego-driven humans made from clods of mud, djinn were created by God from the blue, smokeless part of a flame and are possessed of free will. But *when* they were created is debated. Some scholars say djinn were born seven thousand years before humans, while others say they were created only two to three generations before. One interpretation of ancient texts says that angels and djinn were created on Wednesday and Thursday, and humans on Friday, although the passage of time existed on a vastly different scale.

7 Jalal al-din Al-Suyuti (10849-10911 HE) was a Sufi historian, legal scholar, and author of an estimated one thousand works on various areas of Islamic science, including *The Hills of Precious Pearls Concerning the Legal Ordinances of the Jinn.*

وَلَقَدْ خَلَقْنَا الْإِنسَانَ مِن صَلْصَالٍ مِّنْ حَمَإٍ مَّسْنُونٍ

وَالْجَانَّ خَلَقْنَاهُ مِن قَبْلُ مِن نَّارِ السَّمُومِ

Indeed, We created man from sounding clay molded from black mud. As for the djinn, We created aforetime, from the fire of a scorching wind.

—Holy Qur'an 15:26–27

The first djinni might have been Abu al-Jann, whose offspring included Jann ibn Jann, the seventy-second king of the seventy-two djinn kingdoms, the nations created by God before Adam and Hawa (Eve). But tenth-century explorer and historian Abul al-Hasan Ali Al-Masʿūdī of Baghdad[8] wrote that two original djinn procreated to make thirty eggs. When each of these eggs hatched, the shells cracked to reveal different types of djinn distributed among thirty tribes.[9]

8 Abū al-Ḥasan ʿAlī ibn al-Ḥusayn ibn ʿAlī al-Mas'ūdī wrote *Murūj ad-Dahab wa-Maʿādin al-Jawhar (The Meadows of Gold and Mines of Gems)* in 10947 HE. The book of world history begins with the story of Adam and Hawa and ends in the late Abbasid Caliphate.

Al-Masʿūdī's writings, including *The Meadows of Gold and Mines of Gems*, a 947 CE tome that tells the history of the world, describe some of these djinn clans. There is Iblîs, whom he identified as the original ancestor of all demon djinn; Marid, an island-loving djinn; the feline-looking Qatwibs; the snake-like Wahawis, which unfurl their wings to fly; and the Celas, which reside in the mountains.

Books such as Al-Masʿūdī's describe how different types of djinn possess wildly different temperaments and quirks. While the angels and devils of other religions stick to strict good vs. evil dualities, djinn are complex and mercurial; they hold the capacity to switch from friend to frenemy and can turn on the very humans they have befriended.

Djinn can also assume different physical forms and possess varied abilities. Shiqq are half-formed humanoids with one leg, one arm, half a heart, and half a head. They are considered weak djinn of low ranking. Nasnās are also half humanoids and are born when a Shiqq mates with a human. Nasnās rank even lower in the order of djinn.

Flesh-eating ghul lend their name to English ghouls. Ghul linger in human cemeteries and appear at night, sometimes in the form of a bird with the head of a mule, long matted hair, and human hands, depending on which interpretation of ancient folklore is believed. One group of djinn, known as Hinn, divide scholars. Some told me that Hinn are a subclass of djinn, while others said that Hinn were rivals to djinn, a situation which led to a war between the two species.[10]

9 Some scholars say there are thirty-one tribes; others say twenty-one tribes. And Ibn 'Arabi, considered one of the greatest Muslim philosophers, said that djinn are spread among twelve tribes.

10 See "Taxonomies of the Living" on page 16 for details abo the use of terms such as *species* to discuss different types o djinn.

Many more djinn, categorized by their form, abilities, preferred dwellings, and characteristics, are described throughout historical literature and in oral histories. Si'lat, known as Siluwah in Iraq, are crafty, but not always malicious, shape-shifters who take the form of beautiful women. When they procreate with men, Si'lat give birth to half-djinn, half-human offspring. The Banu Si'lat are an Arab tribe said to descend from a human, Amr Ibn Yabru, who fell in love with a Si'lat. This djinn-human pairing explains the tribe's powers of magic and manipulation. (Ibn Yarbu's Si'lat wife left him when she saw lightning and understood the bolt as a sign to return to her own tribe.)[11]

While some human families, like the Banu Si'lat, trace their lineage back to a djinni who fell in love with an ancestor, others say we are *all* related to djinn, since one story claims it was the original woman who gave birth to the first djinn ancestors. (This interpretation is at odds with the idea that djinn arrived before humans.) In this tradition, Hawa (Eve) is believed to have birthed forty children. She banished twenty babies to the underworld. These discarded souls became djinn.

To explore the origins of djinn, Shi'ite scholars offer a particular interpretation of a verse from the Qur'an's second chapter. In verse 30, God tells the angels that he will create humans to roam the earth, referring to them as halifa. *Halifa* can mean "viceroy," which led some scholars to tell me that since this translation confers divine qualities onto humans, they choose to interpret halifa to mean "successor." But successor to whom?

The angelic response to God's revelation reveals a deeper understanding of this verse, but adds another point of contention.

11 [source redacted]

قَالُوا أَتَجْعَلُ فِيهَا مَن يُفْسِدُ فِيهَا وَيَسْفِكُ الدِّمَاءَ وَنَحْنُ نُسَبِّحُ بِحَمْدِكَ وَنُقَدِّسُ لَكَ قَالَ إِنِّي أَعْلَمُ مَا لَا تَعْلَمُونَ

[The angels] said, "Will You place upon [earth] one who causes corruption therein and sheds blood, while we declare Your praise and sanctify You?" Allah said, "Indeed, I know that which you do not know."

—Holy Qur'an 2:30

The reference to bloodshed on earth means the angels witnessed pre-Adamic, destructive earth-dwellers. These prototypical beings, with free will and a penchant for disobedience, may have been djinn.

The disobedient creatures inflicted such violence and carnage that God sent Iblîs with a few angel companions (or, alternatively, an entire army of angels) to fight and kill the warring djinn. Those djinn who were mercifully spared were transported to the remote islands, caves, and mountain peaks where they still dwell. Once they had been deposited in their new territories, the Qur'an says that God created a barrier between humans and djinn.

The same verse raises, for some Shi'ite scholars, questions about angelic disobedience, since some believe that Shaytan, also known as Iblîs, was an angel cast out of heaven for disobeying God. Others say that is an impossibility given that angels do not have free will and are subservient to God. Rather, their challenge of God's statement is a rhetorical device, which offers the opportunity for further explanation. The one clear instance of angelic rebellion that we do see in the Qur'an is in fact related to the origin story of djinn, or at least one type of djinn.

Iblîs is considered by some to be the progenitor of all djinn, present at the creation of humankind. In fact, it was during the creation of the first human that Iblîs made a decision that changed the very nature of its[12] being. But, as with all things that happen in the realm of the Unseen, mystery prevails. Layers of stories collude and collide to create origin tales that are as fluid as these creatures themselves. We shall return to this devilish origin story later.

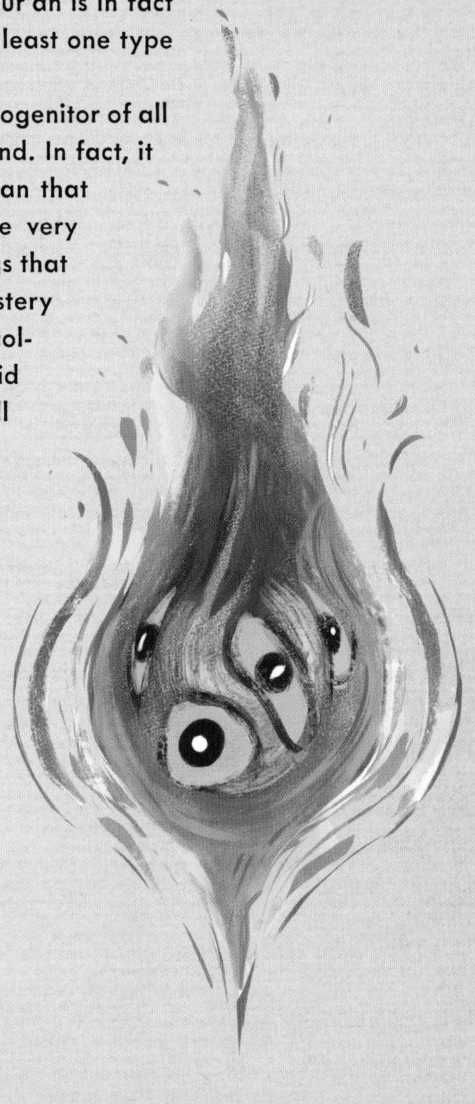

12 I use gender-neutral pronouns for nonhuman entities who do not fall into male or female categories.

The Revolutionary Horseman

Cairo, Egypt, 12011 HE (2011 CE)

As a journalist, I'm expected to deal in truth and facts and objective evidence. They could take away my press credentials for talking to you. But let me ask you this: What *is* evidence if not what I saw with my own eyes? My *highly trained* eyes. My producer saw it, too. She won't speak about it, though. She dismisses the whole event in Tahrir Square as an artifact of fatigue. Sara insists that both of us were jetlagged, dehydrated, and running on adrenaline and hotel-room espressos. Which we were.

It was Wednesday, February 2, 2011, the eleventh day of the revolution and a week before the Egyptian president Hosni Mubarak would resign. Cairo's Tahrir Square felt like a tinderbox. Thousands thronged the streets around the square, which is really a traffic circle, and we moved with them. The crowd was like one unified entity, its flow dictated by no single person. We lost our photographer, an Egyptian woman named Leiana, in the crowd around the time of the event. But she witnessed the same thing. So you see, three highly educated women, observing from two different vantage points, all describe the same phenomenon. And they want to say that we shouldn't talk about it? That it wasn't real?

They didn't want us to see. Did you know there was a faction of Egyptian officers who came to be known as the Eye Hunters because of their love for shooting directly into protestors' faces to blind them? Men like First Lieutenant Mahmoud Sobhi El Shinawi pointed their guns only at eyeballs.[13] I saw young men and women bleeding from their eyes. Some survived, bullets lodged in their heads forever, their vision never to return.

13 Mohamed Fadel Fahmy, "Egyptian Officer Suspected of Being 'The Eye Hunter,' Shooting Protesters," CNN, last modified November 26, 12011 HE, https://www.cnn.com/2011/11/25/world/africa/egypt-eye-hunter/index.html.

I'm safe in my house in Melbourne now. I'm a correspondent for a nightly news show on which I cover domestic politics. They no longer send me out to war zones. But they can't make me *unsee*. I know what I saw that Wednesday, what hundreds of us saw in person, what millions saw on television and online. It was real. You can see it for yourself. Go to YouTube, search for "Egyptian horseman Tahrir Square" or something like that, then turn your phone or laptop upside down and to the side, if you like. See if you can explain away what that video shows so clearly.[14]

14 "Cairo's 'Apocalypse Horse' creates 'net buzz," Euronews, uploaded February 10, 12011 HE, YouTube video, 1:17:00, https://www.youtube.com/watch?v=KgTiqaKSJNk.

The day began quite normally—as normal as can be for an uprising. I had been covering war and conflict for seven years by that point and had been in Tunisia in December to report on the beginnings of the Arab Spring with this same producer, Sara. I was grateful she could speak some Arabic. It meant I wasn't the default translator, as usual; I could actually do some solid reporting. We went back and forth to Tahrir Square twice that Wednesday, first in the morning, and again that afternoon. By then, I had already transmitted one pre-recorded broadcast and we were making plans for a live shoot the next morning. My producer suggested we return that night because she had received word from a reporter at another network that men on camels and horses had joined the protest. It would make for great images. Leiana said she would join us.

We exchanged WhatsApp messages from our hotel rooms. Sara texted about the men on camelback while my heart raced as I scrolled through messages in another group chat. Egyptian forces had assaulted a White female journalist. "She's European!" wrote one reporter in the Journos of Color group. "Is she OK?" I asked. I clutched the press badge hanging around my neck and wondered how much it could protect me. I told Sara we might want to stay away from the protests until daylight. "Hearing about same incident," she texted. "We should still go but important to stay close together and at a distance from frontline."

She was missing the point. What I needed to know was this: If Egyptian law enforcement was comfortable targeting White reporters, what might they do to me, a brown-skinned Australian in a flak jacket with a vaguely Muslim-sounding name? But I downed a second cup of coffee anyway, gathered my supplies, and buckled the straps of my backpack around my waist. I messaged the Journos of Color group to say that I was headed back to Tahrir Square. Ali, a radio producer from a Canadian news organization, messaged me separately to say he would check in hourly until I made it back to my hotel. I appreciated his concern and made sure my location was shared on my phone.

The fires burned brightly as we approached the square. The chanting grew louder. I eyed the row of military officers with their machine guns pointed into the crowd. "*Jaml*?" Sara said to no one in particular. A trio of teenagers ahead of us turned and pointed toward the front of the crowd. They were indicating that the men on camelback had moved closer to where a car and two auto rickshaws were on fire.

"Should we . . . ?" Sara angled her head in the direction of the blazes.

I shrugged. I didn't want to be the reason we missed out on getting footage of the animals. There were already images circulating on Facebook of beautifully attired horses and camels trotting next to military tanks spewing noxious gases. We moved along with the protestors, edging closer to the boys ahead, eventually inching around and ahead of them.

That's when the crowd began to part. A murmur moved through the masses.

"Is it police? Are they shooting?" I asked Sara.

"I don't hear gunfire," she said. "Do you?" She looped her arm into mine and pulled me to the right. I looked behind for Leiana but she had disappeared into the crowd. People pushed and shoved as if some invisible force was directing them, but as far as I could see, the police were not that close to us, no tear gas had been released into the crowd nearby, and no one was shouting orders.

I spotted the flash of green light out of the corner of my eye. It was the same neon color as the strobes emerging from some of the protestors' flashlights. But this was no flashlight. This was massive, and it was moving. A bright green light in the shape of a man on horseback. The crowd released a collective gasp and jerked in the direction of the horseman. Sara yanked me back, but I fought her off and plunged deeper into the crowd. I had to get closer. I remember pulling my backpack off and clutching it to my chest. I think I meant to take out my good camera, but I was too stunned to follow through.

Sara was behind me. She lifted her phone above her head and filmed it all: the man, the horse, the green halo shining around them, the shrieks from the crowd. "Say what you see. Say what you see!" she shouted, as she jostled next to me. But I was tongue-tied. I could not find the words to narrate her video.

You would think there would have been screaming, but instead, those of us closest to the horseman grew quiet. He was dazzling.

Beams of yellow light flowed through the haze of green and the horse reared up on its back legs and came crashing down to the ground again. "*Subhanallah*," a woman whispered. "Hadha djinni!" another voice exclaimed.

The horseman had appeared out of nowhere, as if he had descended from the heavens to the obelisk in the center of the square. He galloped among us, parted the crowd, and moved toward the front, presumably to join the humans on horseback. But before he made it that far, the horse's hooves began to tread air instead of ground and the pair ascended into the night sky. They rose above a fiery Tahrir Square and disappeared before our eyes.

I realized I was holding my breath and let out a gasp. The trio of boys who had pointed us in the direction of the camels were next to me. Their faces stretched into wide smiles.

Sara turned and grabbed my hand. "Did you . . . ?" she said. She waved her phone at me as if to say she had captured it all.

"Was it . . . ?" I sputtered. We were lost for words.

The crowd melted together, and a loud roar reverberated from the front to the back. "The Revolutionary Horseman has uplifted the revolutionary crowd!" a protestor screamed in Arabic. "The Revolutionary Horseman is a sign from Allah!" yelled another. The crowd marched on. Sara and I fought our way to the perimeter so that we could head back to the hotel. Sara had a splitting headache, she said, and needed to drink water and lie down.

I texted Ali from the hotel to ask if he had seen it.

"The horses? Yeah," he texted back.

"No, the green one," I wrote.

"???" was the response.

I called Leiana, who was still in the crowd photographing camels. "Did you see anything?" She said it was "most likely a djinni"—then said she had to go. We never talked about it again.

If you watch the videos on YouTube, you can see it clearly. A photographer from America, I think it was, captured the defining shot. The networks broadcast it, too, everyone from MSNBC to Fox News, all of them explaining away the apparition as some technical fault, perhaps a reflection from a dirty camera lens. But how could all of us have had the same hallucination at the exact same time? Hundreds of phone cameras from different angles captured the same image, including Sara's. Was there a smear on every protestor's lens?

That night, as espresso churned in my stomach alongside antacids, I dreamed of my grandmother and her frightening stories of devilish djinn, the kind who preyed on naughty girls. But the Revolutionary Horseman, if you want to call him that, hadn't frightened me. The green light hadn't frightened anyone. I had felt the adrenaline surging through my body, sure, but the roar that swept through the crowd when his horse galloped into the sky—it uplifted me. I felt hope for the people of Egypt and for the future of the Arab Spring for the first time in weeks.

A funny thing happened the next morning. Muslims, even lapsed ones such as myself, began to recite the Bible, and Christians began to speak of al-Khiḍr, a man who appears in both Muslim and Christian stories. In the hotel restaurant, an elderly waiter poured my tea from a silver pot. I eyed his hands and neck for any signs of his faith. It can be hard to tell in Egypt if someone is a Muslim or a Copt, and I never assume. "The Pale Horseman is mentioned in Revelation 6:8," I said, lifting my intonation at the end of the sentence to make it sound more like a question than a statement. I wasn't sure how I remembered this twenty-year-old fact from Mrs. Gideon's religion class. Warnings about the apocalypse tend to stick in the brain, I guess. The elderly man raised his eyebrows. "Yes, my dear," he said, speaking as if he was addressing a child. "Some of your lot are talking about the Horseman today." He gestured around the restaurant, which looked like a foreign bureau for an international news agency. Editors barked into cell phones while ladling scrambled eggs onto their plates at the breakfast buffet. Reporters huddled around tables and typed furiously on their laptops between bites of toast. The man leaned in closer. "Here in Egypt, we say that man was al-Khiḍr, the Green One."

"Did you see him?" I asked. The waiter straightened, tugged at his waistcoat, and took my teapot away.

I had never heard of al-Khiḍr or the Green One, so I searched online while drinking my tea. In the Qur'an, the Prophet Musa (Moses) is asked by the Children of Israel: Who is the most learned person here? Musa answers that it is he, and as a consequence, he is rebuked by Allah for not deferring to the omniscience of the creator. God tells Musa that there is in fact another human who holds more knowledge than Musa. Musa, of course, wants to meet this person, and so he embarks on a voyage to a place where two seas converge, known in the Qur'an as Bahrain (which literally translates to "the meeting of two seas"). The man he meets there is al-Khiḍr.

Al-Khiḍr takes Musa on a patience-testing journey during which the learned man performs a trio of seemingly nonsensical actions: Al-Khiḍr damages and then patches up a ship, he decapitates a boy, and he repairs a wall belonging to hostile villagers. Musa is perplexed but he is told he must wait to appreciate the reasoning behind al-Khiḍr's peculiar activities. And so, al-Khiḍr demonstrates to an increasingly impatient Musa that the journey to acquiring deep understanding requires patience and humility; and that while he, al-Khiḍr, may be privy to knowledge that Musa has yet to glean, Musa himself knows things that al-Khiḍr does not.

A few months later, I found the following explanation of al-Khiḍr in an academic article. The author was a professor who had published an ethnographic commentary on the horseman in Tahrir Square. (I was surprised to learn that academics, especially non-Muslim ones, studied things like this.)

Al-Khiḍr is a mystical figure alluded to in the Qur'an, who is believed to be a prophet or saint. He is literally "the Green One." Some sources declare that al-Khiḍr was someone who knew al-ghayb but, as the quintessential mystical figure and guide to Sufis, he also symbolizes al-ghayb.[15]

I was vaguely familiar with the concept of al-ghayb from summers spent with my grandmother in Kuala Lumpur. Al-ghayb is this other dimension that a rare few claim to visit. My Nenek said she went there in her dreams, but only on occasions when she stayed up late into the night to pray to Allah. She told me there is a seam between our dimension and al-ghayb. Some say that at times of hardship (I would think historic uprisings count), that seam begins to fray so that where we exist dissolves into where they exist and things that are usually hidden become apparent.

I thought of al-ghayb again eight months later, in October 2011, when the Egyptian military shot dead twenty-seven Coptic Christians in Upper Egypt. Soon after that tragedy, which came to be known as the Maspero Massacre, Copts said they saw the Virgin Mary appear in the sky. I remembered what I had seen in Tahrir Square, thought back to those chants of "The Revolutionary Horseman has uplifted the revolutionary crowd!" and wondered if the surviving Copts were being dealt a dose of heavenly therapy—a sign of divine peace, of better things

15 Amira Mittermaier, "The Unknown in the Egyptian Uprising: Towards an Anthropology of al-Ghayb," *Contemporary Islam* 13, 17-31 (12019 HE), https://doi.org/10.1007/s11562-017-0399-1.

to come—at a time of unimaginable hardship. I even read an op-ed in *Al-Jazeera* that argued that the Tunisian revolution, like autocrat-toppling revolts before it, was successful because a divine force buoyed the protestors.[16]

I can't tell you what happened in Maspero. I wasn't sent to cover that massacre. And I'm a lapsed Muslim anyway, so who knows if I would have witnessed the same vision of Mary as a Copt or a more devout Muslim would. But I worry about the state of journalism, about our crafting and acceptance of what is "truth." I still can't speak openly about what I saw with my own eyes for fear of professional reprisal (and probably a psychiatric diagnosis to boot). Video evidence be damned. I'm speaking to you openly because you promised to keep my name secret, but if I was asked to describe the events of February 2, 2011, during one of my own live broadcasts, my response would (have to) be: *I saw only armed police and burning cars amidst the protestors in Tahrir Square.*

16 Samir Sassi, "The Interaction of the Unseen and the Seen in the Tunisian Revolution." *Al Jazeera*, March 8, 12011 HE (Translated from the Arabic.; article has been removed from Al Jazeera website by February 9, 12024.).

Collective Visions

"Hadha djinni!" (This is a djinni!) is a dependable Muslim response to a door creaking open, a window abruptly slamming shut, or a lightbulb flickering on and off. Who hasn't felt the hairs on the back of their neck stand on end when a thud reverberates through the apartment and they are (supposedly) home alone?

But what if another person sees the lightbulb flicker? What if a friend or lover hears the thud? What if hundreds of people witness the same apparition, even if they have different names to describe what they see?

Whether it was al-Khiḍr or a djinni or a miasma of fluorescent green torchlight mixed with tear gas and the haze of burning rubber, millions of people around the world have watched, rewound, and paused video footage of the Revolutionary Horseman in Tahrir Square. The vision elicited blog posts on skeptics' websites, articles in Christian newsletters, and thousands of posts on social media.

Sufi tradition builds on a concept of insight and inner vision which is mentioned in the Qur'an:

قَدْ جَاءَكُم بَصَائِرُ مِن رَّبِّكُمْ فَمَنْ أَبْصَرَ فَلِنَفْسِهِ ۖ وَمَنْ عَمِيَ فَعَلَيْهَا ۚ وَمَا أَنَا عَلَيْكُم بِحَفِيظٍ

There has come to you enlightenment from your Lord. So whoever will see does so for [the benefit of] his soul, and whoever is blind [does harm] against it. And [say], "I am not a guardian over you."

—Holy Qur'an 6:104

This notion of insight, known as *basa'ir*, is often discussed as a personal experience. But Sufis describe a collective inner gaze, or *basīra*, which manifests as a shared vision that an entire group might witness at the same time. The scholar who writes about the Revolutionary Horseman of Tahrir Square, and who is cited by my anonymous journalist, describes this phenomenon:

One Sufi community that I worked with had refined its collective inner gaze (basīra) so much that its members could see collective waking visions. At their Ramadan gatherings, held in a school hall in Cairo, they reported collectively seeing Muslim saints or the Kaaba in their midst while I saw nothing, or at least nothing of such spiritual relevance.

What if a confluence of factors led to this basīra in Tahrir Square in February of 12011 HE? Presumably the factors necessary for such a collective vision existed. First, we have an oppressive regime unleashing unimaginable hardship on a people. Second, we have an uprising of historic magnitude sending thousands to the streets across half a dozen countries, every one of them demanding justice and peace. Third, we have masses of humans congregated in the belief that collective power can transform the world. Aren't these the very dynamics that would cause the seam between al-ghayb and our realm to fray and disintegrate? Aren't these the situations that would initiate a basīra of the type usually reserved for the most pious and mystical among us?

The identification of the Revolutionary Horseman as al-Khiḍr is significant. In Sufism, al-Khiḍr is a bridge to al-ghayb, a central link in *silsila*, or spiritual genealogy, the flow of knowledge across generations. Besides being the Knowledgeable One, as exemplified in the Qur'anic story where he guides Musa, al-Khiḍr embodies the transmission of knowledge directly from the divine, absent a human mediator. Some Sufi *tariqa*, or orders, such as the Uwaisi, hold up al-Khiḍr as a saintly figure who initiates them into the order, in contrast to Sufi orders in which a living person performs the initiation.

While some have said the Revolutionary Horseman was a djinni who appeared in the form of al-Khiḍr, certain Sunni Sufis that I spoke with said that it was al-Khiḍr himself. Many believe he is still alive; two women told me they had met him in Somalia. He appears sometimes as a human draped in green robes, and other times as a nebulous entity. But each time he appears, he imparts wisdom and reminds us to never stop seeking divine knowledge.

THE DEVIL IS IN THE GRAMMATICAL DETAILS

Angels were created from light, humans from clay, and djinn from a smokeless flame, the Qur'an explains. Which element, then, birthed Iblîs, the progenitor of all Shayateen (devils)? Is the chief of the devil kingdom a fallen angel made of light or a djinni made of fire?

There is much scholarly discord about the classification of Iblîs, and it is *grammar*, not elemental clay, light, or fire, which is hotly debated. I've spoken to hundreds of scholars over the past three decades, and none of them could resolve this question for me.

The Qur'an introduces us to Iblîs in the second chapter, Surah al-Baqarah, at the pivotal moment when Iblîs, a devout worshipper of Allah, is tested:

وَإِذْ قُلْنَا لِلْمَلَائِكَةِ ٱسْجُدُوا لِآدَمَ فَسَجَدُوا إِلَّا إِبْلِيسَ
أَبَى وَٱسْتَكْبَرَ وَكَانَ مِنَ ٱلْكَافِرِينَ

And [mention] when We said to the angels, "Prostrate before Adam"; so they prostrated, except for Iblîs. He refused and was arrogant and became of the disbelievers.

—Holy Qur'an 2:34

In chapter 17, in the wake of the once pious creature's rebellion, we learn more about Iblîs's response to God:

وَإِذْ قُلْنَا لِلْمَلَائِكَةِ اسْجُدُوا لِآدَمَ فَسَجَدُوا إِلَّا
إِبْلِيسَ قَالَ أَأَسْجُدُ لِمَنْ خَلَقْتَ طِينًا

We said to the angels, "Prostrate to Adam," and they prostrated, except for Iblîs. He said, "Should I prostrate to one You created from clay?"

—Holy Qur'an 17:61

Iblîs believes that clay is lesser than that from which Iblîs is made. But, depending on how the grammar of these verses is interpreted, Iblîs might belong to the genus angel (and be made from light) or to a different genus altogether. It comes down to the word إِلَّا (illa), the Arabic particle used to talk about an exception, such as: the angels prostrated to Adam . . . *except* for Iblîs.

Typically, the word that comes after إِلَّا is the exception; in this case, that is Iblîs. But the word that comes before, the antecedent of the exception, is crucial. Here, the antecedent is "angels." Read one way, the sentence construction could mean that Iblîs belongs to, but is exceptional from, the angels. Read another way, it could mean that Iblîs is completely exceptional from angels. This latter view is the more popular one, and those who argue it say their interpretation is backed up by two other Qur'anic verses:

وَإِذْ قُلْنَا لِلْمَلَٰٓئِكَةِ ٱسْجُدُوا۟ لِءَادَمَ فَسَجَدُوٓا۟ إِلَّآ إِبْلِيسَ
كَانَ مِنَ ٱلْجِنِّ فَفَسَقَ عَنْ أَمْرِ رَبِّهِۦٓ

And remember when We said to the angels, "Prostrate before Adam," so they all did—but not Iblîs who was one of the djinn, but he rebelled against the command of his Lord.

—Holy Qur'an 18:50

قَالَ مَا مَنَعَكَ أَلَّا تَسْجُدَ إِذْ أَمَرْتُكَ قَالَ أَنَا خَيْرٌ مِّنْهُ خَلَقْتَنِي مِن نَّارٍ وَخَلَقْتَهُ مِن طِينٍ

Allah asked, "What prevented you from prostrating when I commanded you?" He replied, "I am better than he is: You created me from fire and [Adam] from clay."

—Holy Qur'an 7:12

Made of fire and possessed of free will—it makes sense that Iblîs is a djinni. Although Iblîs was *among* the angels, Iblîs possessed the autonomy to disobey God, as only djinn and humans can do. So, while the angels bowed, Iblîs made use of its non-angelic free will and refused to honor God's new creation.

God was outraged at Iblîs's hubris. How dare one genus size itself up against another? God banished Iblîs to hell and denounced the creature as Shaytan, the devil. Cursed and embittered, Shaytan swore to spend its life leading all humans to the hellfire.

قَالَ فَبِمَآ أَغْوَيْتَنِي لَأَقْعُدَنَّ لَهُمْ صِرَٰطَكَ ٱلْمُسْتَقِيمَ

ثُمَّ لَأَتِيَنَّهُم مِّنۢ بَيْنِ أَيْدِيهِمْ وَمِنْ خَلْفِهِمْ وَعَنْ أَيْمَٰنِهِمْ
وَعَن شَمَآئِلِهِمْ ۖ وَلَا تَجِدُ أَكْثَرَهُمْ شَٰكِرِينَ

قَالَ ٱخْرُجْ مِنْهَا مَذْءُومًا مَّدْحُورًا ۖ لَّمَن تَبِعَكَ
مِنْهُمْ لَأَمْلَأَنَّ جَهَنَّمَ مِنكُمْ أَجْمَعِينَ

And then Iblîs said, "Because you have put me in the wrong, I shall lie in wait for them on Your straight path; I will assault them from the front and the back, from their right and their left; nor will you find that most of them are grateful."

God said, "Get out! You are disgraced and expelled! I swear I shall fill Hell with you and all who follow you."

—Holy Qur'an 7:16–18

For those who adhere to this djinn-to-devil lineage, Iblîs is considered the chief of evil djinn. Its sons and daughters might have been birthed by Iblîs's lover, Hanash, or Iblîs may have brought them forth via eggs. The djinniyah queen Aina and the sorceress Bidukh are among Iblîs's daughters. Teer is the son who brings forth calamities and injuries. Wasin leads one toward anxiety and never-ending grief. El-Ażąwar provokes depravity and adultery. Sóṭ encourages deceit. The sober Haffan goads drunkenness. Dásim seeds polarization and brings hatred into loving relationships. Zelemboor presides over fraudulent dealings and, according to some texts, the most hellish places on earth: traffic jams.

Close your eyes and picture a djinni. Is it thick-skinned and horned? Is it slithering and cold? Is one of its many limbs protruding from beneath your bed? Are its reddened eyes peering out from your half-opened closet? Perhaps the Qur'anic account of Iblîs's rebellion and consequent revelation of its djinn origins, and the oral histories that describe its offspring, underlie the overwhelmingly malevolent perception of djinn. The word *djinn* conjures demonic creatures, even though there exist wish-granting djinn; more subtly amicable, respectful, and beneficent djinn; and even djinn who are entirely unimpressed by and uninterested in humanity.

Nefarious djinn possess the terrifying traits that might emerge in your mind when you picture a djinniyah, and Iblîs's chthonic clan does exist to lead humans to torment. But despite their potential connection to Shaytan, the djinn in your orbit may be—hopefully—kind-natured, or at least neutral, non-meddling creatures. Consider more closely the dashing man in the bookstore who returns your smile, the masseuse with otherworldly hands, or the chef who makes a lasagna that, despite your best efforts, you can never quite replicate.

The Prophet said to the djinni: "This is the stride of a djinni as well as the tone of his voice!"

The djinni replied: "My name is Hamah ibn Laqqis ibn Iblîs."

The Prophet said: "Only two generations separate you from [Iblîs]."

He replied: "True."

The Prophet asked: "How long have you lived?"

The djinni replied: "Almost all of time. I was a small boy when Abel was killed. I believed in Noah and repented at his hands after I stubbornly refused to submit to his call, until he wept and wept. I am indeed a repentant; God keep me from being among the ignorant! I met the prophet Hud and believed in his call. I met Abraham, and I was with him when he was thrown in the fire. I was with Joseph, too, when his brothers hurled him into the well—I preceded him to its bottom. I met the prophet Shu'ayb, and Moses and Jesus, the son of Mary, who told me: 'If you meet Muhammad, tell him Jesus salutes thee!' Now, I've delivered his message to you, and I believe in you."

The Prophet said: "What is your desire, O Hamah?"

Hamah said: "Moses taught me the Torah, Jesus the Gospels; can you teach me the Qur'an?"

So the Prophet taught him the Qur'an.

—Hadith (sayings of the Prophet Muhammad, p.b.u.h.) as narrated by the Holy Prophet's companion Imam Malik ibn Anas

The Possessed iPhone

New Jersey, USA, 12016 HE (2016 CE)

Originally published by A. S-P. in the journal *Social Behavior and Psychiatry*

Grandad begged us to let him keep his ancient brick of a cell phone. We used to call it his *dumb* phone since everyone else in the world had *smart*phones, even the Bajan imam who insisted on riding his bicycle in the rain and who preached in his Friday khutbah that technology was the "D'evil!" Grandad had always had a mind of his own and he insisted that the folding, gray, plasticky thing with the wobbly black buttons (which caused him to misdial everyone and their mama) was all he needed to stay connected. I mean, the thing literally looked like my three-year-old niece's play phone.

"Can't tell him nothing," Mom would say.

"But it gets the job done," he would respond as he slipped his brick phone into his shirt pocket while the rest of us rolled our eyes.

We would yell at him, "But it's ancient!"

"Well," he would say, flashing two rows of perfect white teeth, "so am I. Ain't nothin' wrong with that!"

Those perfect teeth were dentures, of course, and yes, we had to goad him for like two years to get them fitted. Grandad hated changing things up. That's why he was still bouncing around that huge house three years after Grandma had died and so many decades after all his kids had grown and made homes of their own.

We had always joked that the old house on Farnham Avenue felt haunted by ghosts of the past. Everything creaked. The door to the upstairs bathroom was possessed and would lock you in or creep open while you sat on the toilet. Grandad always complained that his glasses, his newspaper, and his Palmer's Cocoa Butter would all mysteriously move from the precise places he kept them to the attic room that used to be Grandma's sewing space. But duppie or no duppie, we could not convince him to move into an apartment.

I feel the worst about what happened. Out of everyone, I was the one who really piled on the pressure. I told Grandad that holding on to that ancient relic of a cell phone was selfish. I said not only did it put his life in danger, but it also made us worry ourselves sick about his safety. "Not having a smartphone is a health and safety issue," is how I put it. "When you get a smartphone, we can use it to monitor your location and track your heart rate and blood pressure. And it comes with an alarm you can press when you fall, so someone can help immediately."

"*If* I fall," he corrected me. "And *if* I fall I'll just cry out for my neighbor. Ernie will come running immediately!" This was probably true since Grandad and Ernie slammed dominoes at the East Orange American Legion almost every day. Grandad blamed my "botheration" on my imminent departure for med school. "And why you bother me so? You think because you going to be a doctor you need to look inside my chest and monitor my blood pressure and everything! Leave me be, child. Cha!" he said, waving me away.

Two things finally swayed him to put the devil in his pocket—and I want to be clear that neither of them came from me. It was Mom who told him about the Qur'an recitation app, and it was my youngest brother who showed Grandad how he could video call with his brothers back home in Trinidad. So, at least some of the blame rests with them.

Anyway, let me explain what happened.

The first part is simple: Grandad finally says yes to a new phone, my younger brother gets the phone from the place on Jerome Avenue that sells refurbished models at a discount, my older brother sets it all up, and life goes on. I go away to Atlanta.

The phone calls started at the beginning of the semester, as soon as he got the phone. Late-night video calls—butt-dials, really. I would quickly answer so the buzzing wouldn't disturb any other crammers in the anatomy lab. I'd pull off my glove, swipe left, and there it was, every time, right in the middle of my screen: Grandad's eyeball. Red and wiry capillaries appeared thick as worms on my phone.

"Are you trying to call me, Grandad? Or are you trying to do something else on your phone?" I figured he had hit the camera icon instead of the message icon and accidentally disrupted my midnight study sessions with close-ups of his cornea. "Move the phone away from your face," I said patiently. "Away! I can hardly see you."

He never spoke back to me, not in the dozen or so times this happened—and it was always at midnight, always on the edge of Thursday night and Friday morning.

Every time he accidentally called, I saw something that took my breath away, just for a moment, just until my brain computed that it was a greasy smudge of cocoa butter across the camera lens. The apparition was always the same: a face, bang in the middle of Grandad's pupil, staring at me with a twisted smirk stretched too far across its horned head. It creeped me out.

"God, you really need to wipe your front camera!" I said one time, a bit too loudly. I had been staring at a skull specimen for hours, studying the notches and grooves where this tendon attached to that bony prominence and this nerve slid through that bony crevice.

I put down the skull and decided that something was amiss in Grandad's head. The calls were due to clumsy, senile fingers and his being a tech novice, I knew that much. But his deterioration from self-described "whippersnapper dom player" to amnesiac, midnight butt-dialer had been too rapid for my liking. I intended to investigate on my next visit home. Something wasn't adding up.

When I interrogated him about his escapades he would swear he had fallen asleep long before midnight and that he had turned his phone off before he went to the mosque for the Isha prayer.

"That can't be right because you were calling me *after* midnight," I said. "So, maybe you're doing it in your sleep?"

"Can't be," he said. "Barely know how to work the damn thing with my eyes open. Not sure I could turn it on and do things like video myself and make a call with my eyes closed."

"Oh, your eyes were very much open," I said, shuddering at the memory of the smirking creature.

Grandad sounded lucid in the mornings, like he had slept peacefully. He did mention something about the phone turning on and off and vibrating all on its own, strange messages flashing across the screen with a siren-like sound. But I figured they were Amber Alerts and those overly cautious post–Hurricane Sandy weather warnings.

Then comes Thanksgiving. I planned to interview Ernie, to take a full history from the ladies who served Grandad lunch at the American Legion, and to maybe casually observe Grandad while he puttered around his house. I needn't have planned so many investigations. The signs were there at our first holiday lunch.

Mom purposely had us carry saltfish fritters, lamb patties, doubles, heaping bowls of salad, and bottles of sodas over to Grandad's house so he wouldn't come over to her house. "He always smells of smoke these days," she said, scrunching up her nose. "I think he's taken up secret smoking."

But while we sat and ate, the house a usual ruckus of kids and grandkids, everyone fighting over the fry bake and the flakiest pieces of buss up shut, I couldn't help but notice that Grandad was not there. I mean, he was there, obviously; we were in his house, and he was sitting at the table, but his eyes were fixed on a spot in the corner of the room, above the television. They were glazed over while he shoved morsel after morsel of doubles into his mouth. It was as if his motor skills were working independently of his consciousness. His eyes were locked on that empty space, like he was watching an invisible TV. His expression was kind of absent but kind of enthralled by something.

"Grandad," I said across the table. "Grandad? Grandad!"

My younger brother looked over at me and rolled his eyes. "Leave him alone," he said. "You always finding something wrong with everyone. He's just eating."

But while my brother was distracted by my baby nephew swiping at an opened bottle of pepper sauce, Grandad suddenly shook his head and came to, mumbling, "What? What?" An oily chickpea rolled out of his mouth and into the shirt pocket where he kept his phone.

I cringed. "Where were you just now?"

"What you mean?" he said, groping for the chickpea, only smushing it deeper into the pocket. "I'm right here. Silly girl." But just like that, he turned his head away from me and fixed his gaze back on that empty spot above the TV. His eyes glazed over again.

Meanwhile, everyone was chattering around him, passing salad bowls and sodas across the table like absolutely nothing was wrong.

"What's that smoky smell?" Mom said. She stood up to crack open a window, letting in a gust of icy air. "It always smells smoky in here. Dad, no candles, please. You hear?"

Only my three-year-old niece looked concerned. She toddled over to Grandad and pulled at one of his legs. "Come baaaack," she screeched, collapsing onto her butt with a giggle. Then she looked at me, looked into the corner, flipped her palms over as if she was emptying her hands, and said, "Uh-oh. Grandad gone." My brother swooped her up, declaring that *uh-oh* and *gone* were her favorite words.

As we cleared away lunch plates and Mom opened more windows, I took the opportunity to look through kitchen cabinets and pantry shelves. Were there any medicines he could be taking? Was he keeping a diagnosis secret from us? Maybe he was accidentally mixing meds that had drug-drug interactions. But I found only my niece's allergy syrup and an expired bottle of Tylenol, which I tossed in the trash.

When he wasn't eating and gawking, Grandad was scrolling on his phone and talking to it. Swiping, pressing, turning the volume up and down, adjusting the brightness and rubbing his eyes, saying how flashing lights on the screen gave him headaches. He would speak at the screen and curse it. He couldn't put it down. If it wasn't a video of a preacher giving a sermon, it was a direct message from an old classmate in Port of Spain. If it wasn't social media, it was the constantly pinging group chats.

"What are you texting about now?" I said.

"Cricket." He swiped the screen and rubbed his eyes, and swiped over and over again. I noticed his eyes growing redder as the evening went on. He became irritable, even combative, when Mom asked if he wanted hot chocolate or fancied a stroll.

It was worse at night. Grandad keeps a radio that's tuned to the Islamic Cultural Center so that he can hear the adhaan in his house. As the call to prayer rang out for Maghrib, he started mumbling and dawdling around the house, walking from one room to another, opening and shutting doors.

"Sweetie, you got to let the old man be," Mom said as she washed dishes. "He's just happily keeping busy in his home. Tell me if you catch him smoking, though."

But he wasn't happy. A happy old man doesn't ignore everyone who's talking to him. A happy old man doesn't stare into empty corners and gawp open-mouthed. A happy old man doesn't talk to himself for hours on end.

I insisted on staying at his house that night. I settled into Mom's old room and tried to sleep. But there were nonstop voices. Grandad was talking to someone—and someone was talking back. Another Trini voice, but much deeper than Grandad's.

"Don't be foolish, girl," he said as I swung his bedroom door open. He turned on the lamp and sat up in bed, clutching his phone to his chest.

"But you're talking to someone on speakerphone, aren't you?" I said. "Let me see your phone."

Grandad stretched out an arm to show me the screen. The phone was off. "I let it get dead," he said. "Extends the life of the battery."

"Then who are you talking to?" I said.

"My friend," replied Grandad with a smile. "He talks to me at night."

Bingo. This was classic sundowning. Right around sunset, the symptoms kicked in: auditory hallucinations, insomnia, amnesia, apathy, diminished concentration, irritability, and emotional lability. And he was even talking back to himself in a different voice.

I sat on the edge of his bed and took the phone from his hand. "No need for this, eh," I said.

"But then how will my friend talk back to me?" he said, tugging at the phone.

I sighed and stroked his forehead. Grandad rested against the headboard and closed his eyes. When he opened them, both conjunctives were bloodshot. Instead of pupils there were two horned heads, fiery red, with the same crooked smile that I had seen on the phone. I screamed and jumped up. Grandad jumped up, too.

"Don't be scared," he said in a voice that seemed to emanate from his soul. It was loud. I mean, *really* loud. It was deep, but it still had that Trini twang. I ran toward the door and *slam!* A thick, invisible wall had stretched across the doorframe and knocked me onto my back. Grandad spoke behind me, his voice normal this time, but he wasn't speaking to me—he was speaking to the creature appearing in the doorway. The horned apparition was life-sized. It shimmered in the doorway, its feet enveloped in a thick smoke. Its reddish legs bulged, and its robed torso and horned head blurred in and out of focus. It was there. Then it wasn't. Then I saw it again. I crawled backward until I knocked into Grandad's knees.

Grandad was laughing above me, his face contorted into a twisted smile that I had never seen before. Or maybe it was the angle. Only the lamp was on, and I was looking up at his chin, from where I still cowered on the floor. "He comes, he goes," said Grandad, waving the creature away as if it was nothing but a stray cat meowing for cream. The djinni disappeared, leaving a smoky essence wafting through the room.

I didn't sleep for days, which added layers of fog to my memories of the vision and made everything seem more surreal. I read up on a psychiatric condition called folie à deux in which two people share a delusion, each inciting the other to believe more and more deeply in what is not real. Was I the one descending into madness? Perhaps, by some genetic bad luck, both Grandad and I were suffering the same brain-altering disease. Maybe it was exposure to an environmental toxin. I checked the walls for mold.

The list of differential diagnoses was long. I couldn't go back to school on Monday. I couldn't tell Mom or my brothers; they are useless in times of crisis. Instead, I walked over to the Islamic Cultural Center and asked to speak with the imam.

"Ahh, yes, I deal with this type of possession from time to time," he said, heaping spoon after spoon of sugar into his paper coffee cup. His room was cluttered with books and periodicals. A Bajan flag leaned against the wall in one corner. "Good man, your grandad. Shame this happened to him. But it explains a lot. We did wonder who he was talking to all those times he sat alone in the corner."

I was not about to get into duties of care or ask how fellow worshippers could just watch an old man deteriorate into a demented mess without saying anything to his family. Even if mosque members had told Mom and my brothers, they would have just made excuses to normalize Grandad's odd behavior.

"So, is there *anything* you can do?" I said. I couldn't go to a doctor with my concerns since I'm the one they would have put on an involuntary 5150 psych hold for seventy-two hours. Good luck becoming a doctor with a psych record.

The imam suggested that he spend a few days doing research, gathering supplies, and looking up special prayers. He said he would come to Grandad's house an hour after the Maghrib prayer that Thursday. So that was it. Three more nights of possession, I thought, walking back to Mom's. I couldn't bear to go back to the house on Farnham Avenue.

On Wednesday night I received a text from the imam with his Venmo account details. He wanted $50. "For supplies." I hit *accept* while thinking, "What is this?! A freaking djinn industrial complex? Is the same guy who preaches about the evils of technology now asking me to send cash over a 5G electromagnetic wave?" I hoped he wasn't some sort of scammer. But honestly, who else was I going to tell? I beg you to never Google "exorcist in New Jersey" or "djinn ginn jinn help East Orange" unless you want the algorithmic gods to shower you with aura-healing photographs, crystal advertisements, "magick" candles, and trips to Istanbul.

The imam arrived at Grandad's house on Thursday evening, propped his bike against the front gate, and hoisted a neon orange Adidas backpack out of the front basket. It was chock-full of supplies. There was a brown paper bag filled with soil from a recently filled grave and a coconut shell. The imam turned the shell over in his hands. "Do you know what you're doing?" I asked. "Do you know how to do this properly?"

I had no idea what the proper way was. And the imam didn't answer. He was busy lighting incense and jabbing the smoldering stick into every corner of the room.

"I saw the thing upstairs," I offered. "My whole family thinks there's always been something going on in the attic. A duppie, maybe?"

The imam put a finger to his lips. I should have left then because what happened next will never leave my memory. I still turn it over and over in my mind and wonder if it borders on clinical negligence.

First, the imam made Grandad sit on the sofa while he poured a fistful of cemetery dirt on top of Grandad's head. It trickled down his back, which made him dance, sending dirt into his eyes and onto his bottom lip. "Pfffft," Grandad spluttered. But all the time, he was smiling, like this was some joke.

The imam took a bottle of Voss water from his backpack (my $50 had been spent on premium mineral water, I guess) and started pouring the water over the dirt on top of Grandad's head. Then in a mix of Arabic and Bajan English he called forth the djinn. "Leave! Leave this man! Leave this house! In Allah's name! La hawla wa la quwwata!"

It was straight up like a scene from the exorcist. Grandad's neck suddenly bent forward, then twisted to one side, then shot back so he was looking at the ceiling. He started grinding his jaw. I could hear his molars scraping. Of course there are medical terms to explain, or, I should say, describe, all of these phenomena: oromandibular dystonia, torticollis, tonic-clonic seizures. All of them common side effects of antipsychotic medications, in fact.

Grandad's back arched. The imam kept pouring water onto his face. Grandad spluttered and coughed while I stood frozen near the door. The whole time. Just looking at this like, *What the hell is my life right now? Is this man waterboarding my grandfather?!*

"Leave! Leave this man! Leave this house! In Allah's name, I call on you to leave! As you are leaving, give us a sign!"

The door behind me slammed shut. Smoke crept through the crack and wafted into the room. What looked like a tiny bolt of blue lightning sparked out of Grandad's front pocket.

"His phone!" I screamed. "The battery's catching on fire!" Spontaneous combustion of lithium batteries had been all over the news.

The imam grabbed the phone out of the pocket. The black glass shattered in his hands. "Arrrrghh!" he yelled, as he dropped it on his foot. Then, silence. "Woah," he said. "It's usually more subtle than that. Like, just a mug falling over on a table, or something. It must have been a Marid."

That was it. Afterward, Grandad went to bed for a nap, then woke a little later to go to the mosque for Isha. I went back to school the next day. I have never been so happy to see the Atlanta airport in my life. But here's the thing. When I got back to school Mom and my brothers started to complain that Grandad was acting "different."

"He's so mopey," said my brother.

"Yeah, he's not his usual happy self," said Mom.

And it's true, Granddad's not been the same since the Marid left.

Hi Dr. N,

I'm glad to hear from you and to learn about your fascinating research, but I'm curious. How did you find me? I published this account anonymously so that I wouldn't have any problems applying for residencies. Was there some metadata embedded in the URL that gave away my identity? Please let me know.

I decided to write this account because I read a lot in the literature about misdiagnosed or mistreated psychiatric illness in Muslim patients. It's a complicated subject, one I hope to specialize in during my fellowship. Sometimes mental illness really is possession by a djinni. But—and this is important—the patient still needs proper, culturally appropriate care. Since this all happened, we have taken Grandad to see a gerontologist, although I have been selective with the medical history. I just want to be clear: I'm not advocating for care-by-cleric for every patient. I recommend seeking advice from various kinds of experts.

It took me ages to get my head around what happened, and it still frightens me. For a long time I thought I was the one losing it. (Have you come across real-life djinn in the course of your research?) Then, of course, I blamed myself for everything, because I was the one who insisted on getting Grandad that phone.

That damned phone. Literally. The imam, bless his heart, figured out that the Marid, which is an especially powerful and nefarious type of djinni, had been trapped in the smartphone by another exorcist since 2014! (Don't ask me how he knew the chronology.) He managed to remove the djinni from inside Grandad's house so that it could no longer bother or possess him, and he trapped the djinni back in the phone. But then—and I'm embarrassed to tell you this—my ignorant, useless, good-for-absolutely-nothing lump of a younger brother took the phone back to the shop! For a refund! I could not believe it. He said he forgot what I had told him about how the lithium battery was part of the safety recall. He insisted the guys in the shop told him that they could replace the battery and fix the screen and resell it. Now some poor soul in East Orange will have to deal with what looks like the devil. Good thing our family comes from strong stock; someone else would have had a heart attack. But if you got in touch because you've heard of a similar case of Marid possession in Essex County, I wouldn't be surprised if it's the same one.

Grandad's not been the same since he got the phone and then lost it, and that really blurs the line between my comprehension of organic disease and psychiatric disorders. Here's something I struggle with: The djinni is long gone, so do we treat Grandad's apathy, insomnia, amnesia, and emotional lability as actual dementia? I mean, it's not like there's an ICD-10 code for Djinn-Induced Disease. What would his MRI scan even show? And how would we ever explain any of this to a Western-trained physician who can't fathom what she can't see?

I wonder if these are issues you're dealing with. I looked you up and was blown away by your academic trajectory. I'd love to be a tenured professor at such a prestigious university someday! But how is it that you're able to study creatures that only we believe in? It didn't look like you were attached to a department of Islamic studies or anything? Anyway, I'd be very interested to read your report once it is published. You know where to find me.

Kind regards,

A. S-P.

The Ghul of East London

Bethnal Green, London, England, 11996 HE (1996 CE)

A hospital morgue seems like an obvious place to start since it's the place a lot of our women end up. We tell these stories to be scared of something other than the reality that will eventually kill us, right?

Everyone's terrified of her. The Ghul of East London or the Ghul of Bethnal Green. That's what they call her, the one who roams the five, mostly Jewish cemeteries near the mosque. She scares the crap out of the fellas because she's the one woman they cannot get rid of. She scares the shit out of the ladies because she looks like we do the morning after our husbands had too many at the pub on the way home.

I don't mean to play into clichés about battered immigrant women in the East End. We still live under the shadow of Jack the Ripper, for goodness' sake. My niece's best friend actually works for one of those Ripper tours where they use lights and projectors to cast shadows down dark alleyways and onto the sides of Victorian houses. They walk through the streets of Whitechapel with groups of tourists, telling the stories of the disappeared sex workers.

I definitely don't want to paint all of our men as brutes. I've landed me a good egg this time. But I've worked in the shelter for God knows how long, so I'm not scared to tell you about her, about how I came face-to-face with her, and why.

One thing you should know is she's not a *ghoul* in the English sense. Like, she's not a ghost who feasts on the living. She's a *ghul.* It's different. She's not alive or dead. She's attracted to death. That's why I saw her in the morgue. Some say she feeds on the dead and that's why her face is sometimes bloodied. But I think the blood comes from inside her own being.

The two times I saw her were when I was married to M. Which makes sense. Death was hanging over me like a mist those days. *Keep living like this and you will die*, a voice in my head would say when I brushed my teeth and looked at myself in the mirror. But what the ghul was saying, or symbolizing, really, was different: *Lady, you're already half-dead. I'm just waiting for your flesh to die.* She was right. I was dead on the inside. Dead behind the eyes.

It was sometime around the beginning of November. Very early that morning, a young woman from the shelter had died in her sleep. She was Muslim, so I was asked to get to the hospital to intercept her body and prevent them from doing a postmortem exam. In Islam, we believe that a dead body can still feel things, so a postmortem is to be avoided at all costs. But this woman was young and had died suddenly, so the hospital was arguing that they needed results from a full autopsy.

My coworker went berserk. She was like, "You go and you tell them we can't do that! We have to bury her by this afternoon!" So I ran. I'm talking straight out of my flat, in my pajamas. I just threw a full-length Puffa jacket on top and ran. I caught the 277 bus and went straight to the basement of the Mile End Hospital.

This is back when it was a full hospital, with an Accident and Emergency Department and everything. My Puffa coat is making noises like a crisp packet. My trainers are squeaking on the shiny floor. I'm legging it down the long basement corridor, following signs pointing toward the morgue. Everything's a blur. I can just picture them slicing into this woman, causing her excruciating pain, if I don't get there quickly enough.

There's no one in the corridor but me. I'm about halfway down when the lights start to flicker and it gets very cold. Like someone opened a freezer door. But maybe I'm just sweating a lot beneath this thick coat, I think. So I stop for a second and go to unzip it, but before I do, I suddenly see this woman in the distance, walking in my direction. She comes out of nowhere and she's moving very slowly. Almost like she's gliding. The corridor's dimly lit at this point, so I figure I must have missed whichever door she came out of. But I wonder to myself, why would there be a *patient* near the morgue? I know she's a patient because she's wearing one of those flimsy blue hospital gowns.

I freeze. I'm panting because I'm so out of breath. I can see clouds of condensation as I exhale. This woman keeps moving, keeps gliding in my direction. And I stay frozen. Like my feet are pinned to the ground. Everything gets hazy, and the woman gets closer. I want to open my mouth, I want to scream, I want to turn around and run, but I can't. I'm stuck. And she's getting closer and closer, and now I can see her face is gray, like a slab of concrete, and her eyes are yellow and dark and ringed by purple circles, like she's been boxed in the face and given two nasty shiners. Her chin is green and red. Her shins are covered in thick, crusty scabs. Her feet are bare and almost as blue as her gown. Her toenails look gray. Her hair is black and stringy and long; maybe it's wet, though I can't be sure. Her lips are wet, too. And she's murmuring something, but I'm not sure what. It sounds like "Sorry, sorry," or maybe it's "Don't worry."

As she gets closer, I get so cold, like a chill's run right through my bone marrow, and my heart is pounding so loud that I'm sure even she can hear it. She looks right at me with her sad yellow eyes and glides past. And only then, when I can no longer see her, can I unstick my feet from the floor and move. I turn around and she's gone. Vanished. The corridor is brightly lit again, and all the way behind me, even past the door that I came in through, there's not a soul.

Oh shit. The morgue. I start running again. I almost run past the white door in the white wall that has a small blue sign that says "Morgue." I press the buzzer. And this is going to sound like it's made up, but guess who opens the door? A bald man in a blood-splattered white coat, a visor, and white rubber boots, holding an electric saw. He's smiling. This man is a butcher, and that's when I finally let out the scream that's been growing inside of me. He steps back and screams, too. Like I'm the scary one in my Puffa coat, my pink pajamas, and my white headscarf tied like a turban.

"Oh my goodness, you gave me a fright," he goes. "Where's your badge? How'd you get in here? You shouldn't be down here."

I tell him I'm looking for this young woman, and that's when we square it all away. Somebody from the mosque was actually useful for once. They've already called and talked with the hospital chaplain, who talked with the pathology department. The body's already been handed over to the mosque to do the washing and the burial.

So that's that. Now there's just the matter of turning around and going back down the corridor. I'm freaking out. Maybe this man with a saw and that woman are in on something. I look into the butcher's eyes, and he actually seems like a nice, friendly man, once you get past the blood. So I say to him, "Can I ask you something? You said this area's restricted, yeah?"

"Yeah."

"But I just saw a patient down here."

"A patient?" he says.

"Yes, walking that way."

"Shouldn't be," he says, sticking his head out through the doorway and looking left and right. "But I suppose you got down here, so she could, too."

I didn't tell him it was a woman. But I think he knew exactly who I was talking about.

You can chalk it down to me being upset, stressed, in a rush, dizzy, unfit because I hadn't been going to the gym, whatever. But then how do you explain what happened next? One week later, I'm at home with M, my husband at the time, and I go into the bathroom to shower, completely forgetting that I was reheating his tea in the microwave. My hair is lathered up when I hear this bloodcurdling shriek.

"You bitch!" He's screaming cold murder. Before I can pull back the curtain, he's reaching through it, shoving me against the tiles and just smacking me, throwing punches through the curtain until I'm crouched on the floor of the tub. He's screaming about how I put the tea in the microwave for too long, and when he reached in to get it, the mug was so nuclear that his skin stuck to the handle and ripped clean off. Then he rips the whole curtain off the rod, and I scream. From the pit of my stomach, I scream. Standing behind him is the woman. In her hospital gown. Her face looking like a premonition of my face in the future.

M looks at me, soapy and crying, crouching in the tub, and walks out of the bathroom. I don't think he could see her, or her him. She could only see death, or whatever was about to die. That's when I knew I had to get out of that house.

I told Mum, and she told me there's a type of djinn that hangs around cemeteries and eats those who visit the dead. But this one wasn't trying to kill me. She was warning me that death was too close by.

Ghul and Ghulah

I came to know of the Ghulah of Bethnal Green (the locals call her *ghul*) when I was in Holborn, a few miles west of the East End. I was visiting the Hunterian Museum, a repository of heads in jars, fetuses floating in flasks, dismembered diseased feet, and rows of glass cabinets housing the antique surgical instruments used to amputate limbs without anesthesia.

I wasn't looking for ghul stories that winter. My research trip to Italy in search of ghul had led to the discovery of a different kind of deathly djinniyah, so I was in the United Kingdom to follow up on what I'd discovered about headless creatures and to learn more stories of decapitated spirits. The professor of anatomy that I had arranged to meet in the surgical museum was over an hour late. In the meantime–and this became a pattern during the compilation of this book, so much so that I began studying crowds for the random faces of strangers who would soon become sources–I was approached by a young woman.

Technically, I approached her, as she was sitting in front of a glass cabinet drawing the pickled conjoined twins in the jar in front of her. But she kept pausing and turning her head to stare. Eventually, she lowered her pencil and smiled as if inviting me to speak. I learned that she was a young Bengali medical student completing surgical rotations at the Royal London Hospital. She had taken on a historical project studying the ethical practices of brothers John and William Hunter. The younger brother was an army surgeon; the elder was a respected obstetrician–and both worked at London hospitals in the 11700s HE.

The medical student asked if I was a surgeon, and when I said I was a taxonomist interested in anatomical specimens, she asked if I knew about the three-armed skeletons of East London. I shook my head. "You should visit the museum in the basement of my medical school," she said. "The three-armed skeletons are there." That's when she began to tell me about the grave robbers of the East End.

In the early 11800s HE, there was a slump in the number of cadavers available for trainee doctors. Too few criminals were committing the sorts of crimes that would earn them the death penalty. So hospitals took to purchasing dead bodies from grave robbers, or from their own wards, where the poor and infirm became fodder for medical students. Eventually, grave robbers turned to murder, even executing children, to provide hospitals with the bodies they needed.

In 12012 HE, archaeologists accidentally discovered mass graves dug from this time. They found turtle bones next to dog skeletons, and human skeletons with three arms and four legs attached by wire to one bony frame, the remnants of grave digging and ungodly experiments. Who needs to be scared of djinn, I thought, when dastardly humans were the ones excavating graves and mangling corpses?

"It was all in the name of education," said the medical student, picking up her pencil and shading a crooked arm. By now, I knew I had to follow such leads. I visited the museum on Whitechapel Road the very next day. The horrors of nineteenth-century medical experimentation had been dusted and primed and put on display. I wondered if the grave robbers had come across ghul since these particular djinn have a predilection for cemeteries.

It was in the café across the road from the museum, where I went to type up my notes, that I met the woman who had seen the ghul of East London for herself. She was at the table across from mine, shopping bags filled with vegetables piled onto the seat next to hers. She looked at the pamphlet next to my laptop. It was advertising a Jack the Ripper nighttime tour.

"Those things are proper spooky, you know?" she said. "I'm just warning you, because I used to think they were tourist traps, but they're actually really good." By that point, I had learned whom I could trust with the truth of my research endeavors. The woman's eyes drew me in with an expression that was both weary and wary, like she had seen some things. So I told her that I was visiting London to learn from experts in djinn and anatomy, but now I was interested in stalking the areas where I might see a ghul for myself.

She froze with her lips parted, a samosa an inch from her open mouth. Then, as if we were talking about the weather, she put down her snack and told me her story. "Back then, you could have seen one trailing me," she said, brushing crumbs from her lip and looking over her shoulder. "It's like I was haunted. I'm not with my husband now, so I probably won't see her anymore. Although I half expect to see her, or one like her, in the shelter, following behind the women in the intake room. But then, maybe you can only see her if you're close to death yourself, you know? Is that a thing?"

I shrugged. I shared with her some of what I'd learned through my research. The word *ghul* is associated with endings (it derives from the Arabic trilateral root Ġ-W-L, meaning "to annihilate"). There's even an Arabic phrase, "a ghul took her away," which refers to death. But the experts I had spoken with and the literature I had consulted did not make a connection between meeting a ghul and imminent death. (Meeting a ghul might result in death, though, such as if one feasted on your liver.)

But then the ghul, like all monsters, has shape-shifted in the human mind, taking on the markings of those we fear most in any given era or situation. "You mean not everyone who meets a ghul would see a battered woman," she said in between sips of tea. "I get it."

I told her that ghul existed before Islam. In fact, the creature's origins probably lie in Mesopotamia, where nomadic traders from pre-Islamic Arabia might have heard of the Mesopotamian monster Gallu, the Akkadian chthonic demon who captured Damuzi, the god of vegetation, in the realm of death.

When taken back to Arabia, Gallu developed, or was merged with a Bedouin origin story. Before the arrival of Islam, Bedouins believed that the fire from which djinn were born gave rise to at least two eggs. One egg produced devilish creatures, most of whom lived in the seas. Among these devils were ghul, which wandered through the wilderness. Ghul were described as shape-shifters that took on the form of hideous women, lighting fires to lure male travelers away from safety.

Islam's arrival introduced a different origin story, but the creatures remained similar. Various sayings attributed to the Holy Prophet (p.b.u.h.) confirm and contradict the existence of ghul among the djinn, but at least one Hadith suggests that the Prophet recommended the recitation of ayat al-kursi, the Qur'anic verse known as The Throne, to ward away ghul.

Scholars point to this apparent contradiction in the prophetic narrative as evidence that the advent of Islam codified some pre-Islamic traditions, such as djinn, while forbidding others, such as idolatry. In any case, belief in ghul persisted and the Islamic ghul took its place in the stories and lore of the seventh century and beyond.

It was Antoine Galland's eighteenth-century translation of the *Arabian Nights* that introduced the ghul as a gravedigger and corpse eater. The French orientalist's poor translation of the original Arabic sadly led his successors to continue the lie. The orientalist William Lane described ghul as cemetery-dwelling cannibals, citing Galland's translation.

"So you think I've been brainwashed by the European blokes?" said my interlocutor.

Haven't we all? I wanted to respond. But instead I told her what she already knew. That our monsters take on the shapes of what we most fear. An Akkadian demon of the underworld and destroyer of vegetation seems pretty scary when crops are your subsistence. A fire-burning beguiler of the weary desert traveler is a terrifying thing when you are a nomadic people who rely on accurate navigation.

"And me," she said. "Married to that man and working in a DV shelter. One punch away from my ending. But what about you? If you see her roaming behind the Bethnal Green Road tonight, how's she gonna look?"

I couldn't tell her that she would appear as a tall, slim man in a white thawb and gold-embroidered vest—that what scared me most were the sinister messages that had landed in my inbox and been traced back to IP addresses in Persian Gulf states. I had to keep secret that the sender had morphed into a stalker, that the emails now contained death threats, and that my life was in danger because I had learned of the nefarious agenda behind my assignment to compile this book.

Anyone who saw the messages would advise me to drop the research and return to studying marine mammals. Anyone sensible. But I had spent three weeks in Italy and met not one ghul. I had been in the East End for four days now and the ghulah of Bethnal Green was nowhere to be seen. Perhaps death wasn't so close after all. Maybe I was safe to continue writing this book.

QAREEN:
YOUR OWN PERSONAL DJINNI/YAH

Before we delve deeper into the diverse world of djinn, let's meet the djinni sitting by your side right now. You have never been alone, not since birth, not even in your most solitudinous moments. A djinni has been with you, a constant companion since you emptied your lungs of fluid and gasped your first breath.

Named for its obligation, your Qareen—which translates to "constant companion" or "partner"—has watched you lie, cry, break promises, and worse. Like a witch's familiar, your Qareen is always at your side, on your shoulder, trailing your silhouette like a long shadow.

Qareen are described in the Hadith and the Qur'an, where we learn that while they are mostly impartial and dispassionate, an unlucky soul might be cursed with a wicked Qareen.

وَمَن يَعْشُ عَن ذِكْرِ الرَّحْمَٰنِ نُقَيِّضْ لَهُ شَيْطَانًا فَهُوَ لَهُ قَرِينٌ

And whosoever turns away from remembering and mentioning the Most Beneficent, we appoint for him a Satan to be a Qareen to him.

—Holy Qur'an 43:36

Your constant companion might pop an idea for a new home improvement project into your head, convince you to abandon the book you started to outline six months ago, or sit benignly at your side while you watch TV, offering little in the way of inspiration or distraction. Like all djinn, Qareen are born with free will and unique personalities. Your Qareen might share the same faith as you, or goad you to explore a new religion.

According to many Islamic scholars, the only non-Muslim Qareen to have converted to Islam was the Qareen of the Holy Prophet Muhammad (p.b.u.h.).

There is none of you who does not have a Qareen appointed for him from among the djinn. They said, "Even you, oh messenger of Allah?" He said, "Even me. But Allah has helped me and my Qareen became Muslim and only tells me to do that which is good."

—Hadith recorded by Sahih Muslim

Qareen existed long before Islam. Arab pagans considered Qareen to be muses who inspired humans to compose the most transcendent stanzas and quatrains. Refracting the mysteries and profound beauty of science and literature through their belief in djinn, these Arabs understood that seemingly gifted poets were fed verses by their djinn companions. How else could humans write verses that made their readers feel drunk on love? How else could a mere mortal compose a stanza that would move a woman to betray her lover and pursue a different passion?

Ancient Arabs even coined a special term to describe a poet who was supernaturally inspired by her Qareen: *shāʿir*, meaning "the one who feels or perceives." A shāʿir might roam the desert reciting verses until she reached a camp, where she would regale a new crowd with her words. The astonished audience might never know that the poet's words were inspired by her invisible companion.

Not all Qareen inspire great art. Some humans, blaming their spirit companion for a failed marriage, poor quarterly sales, or feelings of despondency and fatigue, have tried to banish their Qareen in the hopes of attracting a more illustrious companion—or in the hopes of being left entirely alone. The Qur'an describes some Qareen as true demons, inflicted as a hellish punishment, intent on leading their human partners astray. Your Qareen might divulge your darkest secrets to fortune tellers, who then pretend to know your most intimate histories—but only because they are communing with your gossip-loving watcher.

If your Qareen is a snitch or inspires pettiness and bad poetry instead of kindness and elegiac verses, you can attempt to banish them using strategies shared by the Holy Prophet (p.b.u.h.) and his close friends.

This story comes from the night the Prophet met a devilish djinni in the presence of the angel Jibril (Gabriel). The Prophet's companion, Abdullah Ibn Mas'ud, who was with him that night, said that the devil inched closer and closer to the Holy Prophet who was reading the Qur'an. The angel Jibril asked the Prophet if he would like to learn the words that would extinguish the devil's flame and force the devil to crawl away. The angel then told the Prophet to continuously recite verses 255, 285, and 286 of Surah al-Baqarah, the second and longest chapter of the Qur'an. The Prophet recited the verses and the devil was vanquished.

In the event that your Qareen is causing your bad moods, failing relationship, and recent turn of bad luck, you can find these protective verses at the end of the book. Recite them, print them and keep them near your bed, or inter them inside an amulet[17] and bind it to your arm or around your neck. If your bad luck resolves, you will know that it was your diabolical Qareen, and not you, who was responsible for your misfortune all along.

17 See "Sorcery and the State: Divisive Djinn and Magical Crimes" on page 205.

Mehr's Wager

Panama City, Panama, 11959 HE (1959 CE)

Mehr did not believe in that which she could not see. Except for God. She wasn't foolish. She had scribbled Pascal's wager in her notebook during philosophy class, balanced finite gains against infinite losses, and landed in the upper half of the grid. *Believe in God. God exists. God does not exist.*

Eternal damnation sounded like something to be avoided. And there was the pleasant side effect of making her father happy by saying her daily prayers.

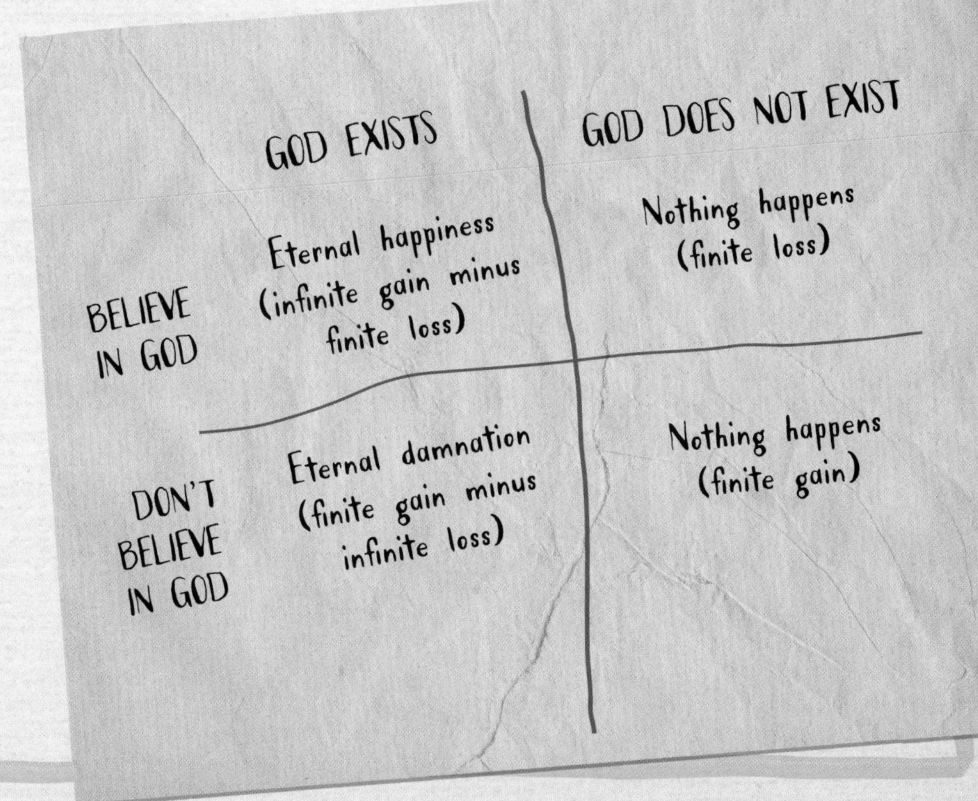

She walked to the madrasa on Saturday mornings because she needed to learn something about this God she ventured to believe in—not to appease her father, even if he had promised her a new bicycle if she memorized ayat al-kursi by the end of the year. She figured missing beach dates with Shireen and Amina could be tallied among the finite losses.

Mehr wondered what Blaise Pascal knew about supernatural beings when he wrote down his famous wager in the seventeenth century. What would the French physicist have had to say about the *thing* that prodded Mehr's thighs at night, crawled across her stomach in the mornings, and wrapped itself around her tongue while she sat in Mrs. Lane's English class in the afternoon? Would it disappear if its existence was denied? Did belief in one unseen thing function as a gateway to believing in anything else?

Mehr didn't know what to call the thing. It had appeared soon after her declaration of faith in Allah. At first she had refused to believe it was real because she couldn't see it. She could only feel its hot breath on the back of her neck, its probing fingers along her scalp as she carried a stack of books from one end of the library to the other. But the thing appeared in various physical forms now. Sometimes it was a black dog traipsing behind her on the walk home from school—a black dog that no one else could see. Some days it was a white cat that stalked her up and down the bookstacks in the library. At night she could see the thing's brown fingers crawling across her stomach and budding breasts when she lifted her sheets. The fingers clamped over her lips when she opened her mouth to speak.

She sensed they were all one entity on account of the voice that had begun to emanate from the thing. The tone was always similar. It spoke with a lilt, like an island girl.

"But I am *not* an island girl," said the brown face staring back from the mirror as Mehr brushed her teeth. Mehr turned to look around, but there was no one behind her. She was alone in the bathroom. There was no black dog or white cat. Just the face in the mirror blinking at her. She pulled her sleeve over her wrist and wiped the glass. The face bristled and sneezed. "Hey, stop that!" it said.

"What d'you mean?" Mehr said, her mouth foamy with toothpaste.

"You said I speak with a lilt, like an island girl. But I'm *not* a girl."

"You look like a girl," said Mehr, inching closer to the mirror until her nose kissed the smeared glass. "If you're not a girl, what are you?"

"I'm from a tribe of djinn. We're made of a smokeless fire. Your Qur'an talks about us." The bathroom light cut out. The face in the

mirror became a candle with a dancing blue flame. Then it was a Qur'an, its pages flicking through the chapter titled "The Djinn."

Mehr spat out the toothpaste. "But are you real?" she said. She dropped her toothbrush in the sink and stepped away from the mirror. The bathroom door opened and the soft pad of footsteps trailed into Mehr's room. She followed the sound and closed the door behind her. A girl who looked like she could be Mehr's slightly younger sister sat cross-legged in the middle of her bed. Mehr liked this form. It was less confusing than the seemingly invisible black dog and less creepy than the curious hand.

"But I like being those other things," the girl said.

Mehr walked toward her bed. "Can you read my mind?" she said.

The girl nodded.

"But that's being nosy," said Mehr.

The girl looked confused. "It's just that you're at that stage in life when you're deciding what to believe, and I want you to believe in me." The girl pulled her hair over her shoulder and began to braid the strands. Her locks turned from a light brown to a shimmering black and grew two feet longer.

"Wow," said Mehr. "What happens if I don't believe in you?"

"What happens to whom?"

"Good question. Umm, what happens to me?"

"Nothing," said the girl.

"Do you disappear if I say I don't believe?"

The girl shook her head. But Mehr noticed that her eyes became smaller, her lower lip fuller.

"I'm not upset!" said the girl, dropping the tail of her unfinished braid in her lap.

"OK, OK," said Mehr. "What happens to *you* if I say I don't believe?"

"Nothing."

"This isn't going to work, then," said Mehr as she walked over to a chest of drawers. "If nothing's at stake, then what's the point in believing?" She pulled her notebook out of a cloth bag and flicked the pages to find Pascal's wager. She drew a fresh grid.

The notebook flew across the room and slammed into the wall. "That's stupid!" said the girl.

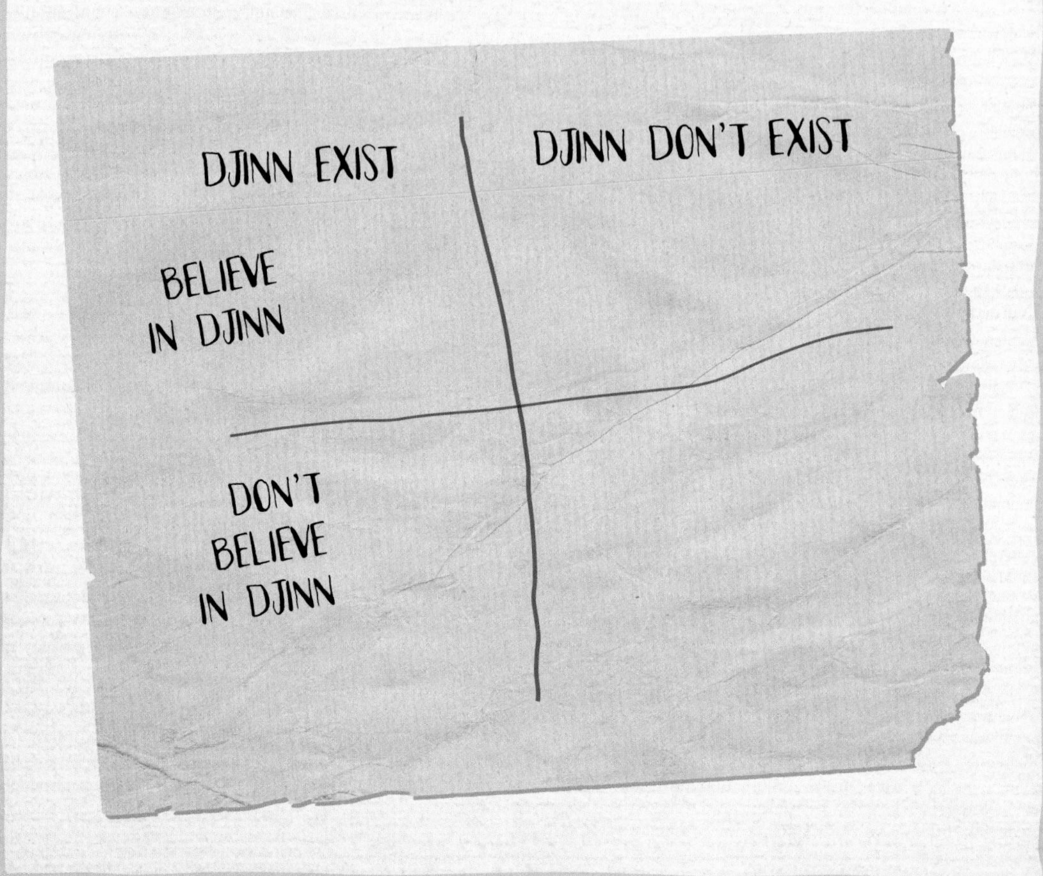

"No, it's not!" said Mehr. "This is how I decide what to believe." She picked the notebook off the floor and closed it. "I think you should go now."

"Not going," said the girl. She crossed her arms and pinned her unraveling braid against her chest. Her bottom lip quivered.

Mehr put her notebook between her knees so she could rub her temples like her father did when he was at his wits' end. She massaged her forehead and then thought for a moment. "You're a nightmare!" she said.

"No, I'm not. I'm a cat!" said the white ball of fur that was growing four paws so it could knead the sheets on Mehr's bed. The cat wailed like an abandoned baby.

"You're impossible," Mehr said. She walked to her bed and sat on the edge.

"But do you believe in me?" The cat crawled into her lap and fixed Mehr's big brown eyes with its piercing red orbs. "You can see me, so you have to believe in me," it said, repeating what it had heard in Mehr's mind.

Mehr scratched her nose.

"Just believe in me," said the cat. It jumped out of Mehr's lap and snuggled on top of her feet.

"Gosh, you're very pushy," said Mehr. She wiggled her toes beneath the cat's warm body and wondered what it would feel like to not believe in something you could, in fact, see.

"It would feel like delusion," said the cat.

"That's not a feeling," said Mehr. She sneezed. "I think I might be allergic to cats."

The ball of fur began to shrink. "It would feel like pretending, like living a lie, like ignoring that which is very much in front of you," said the hand crawling up Mehr's leg. Mehr screamed. The hand jumped from Mehr's knee to her face and latched on to her jaw, clamping it shut.

"Mmmmm!" Mehr tussled with the hand. She turned her face left to right and threw herself back onto her bed. She wrapped her fingers around the stub at the base of the hand and wrenched it off her face. It landed in the corner of the room, a balled-up fist with a twitching thumb.

"You won't bully *me* into believing," said Mehr. "*I* get to decide."

The fist clenched into a tight ball, then it opened its fingers and scurried out of the room.

ROGUISH DJINN

While scholars and religious texts remind us that the vast majority of djinn care little about the quotidian events of human existence, others become quite invested in our beliefs and routines. They might choose to make themselves apparent, even demonstrating their considerable gifts and imposing on human lives by taking up residence in our homes or places of work.

In Mehr's story, this particular shape-shifting djinniyah was adamant that Mehr confirm her belief in the existence of djinn. Why it was fixated on this and why it chose Mehr remained a mystery throughout Mehr's life. I met her some forty years after the incident. She told me that while the djinniyah continued to stalk her throughout high school, it stopped talking to her and stopped appearing as a hand when her family moved from Panama to Mexico a year later. It eventually disappeared altogether.

Mehr confirmed her belief in djinn. She had learned about them in madrasa, heard her father tell stories about them, and was willing to believe in that which appeared before her in her bathroom, bedroom, and at school.

"It was the bullying I couldn't stand. The insistence that I declare my faith," she said. "What business is it of anyone's what I choose to believe in or not believe in?"

Mehr was working as a wellsite geologist for an oil company in Texas when I met her. She said she had told her story of girlish rebellion to a classmate in grad school who had looked at her with wide eyes and never spoken to her again. "Probably thought I was some fundamentalist Muslim," she said, laughing. "I forget that some scientists pride themselves on a deep, abiding skepticism, not realizing it makes them rather tedious to be around and demonstrates exactly the kind of closed-mindedness they profess to loathe."

BEYOND PLANET EARTH

الْحَمْدُ لِلَّهِ رَبِّ الْعَالَمِينَ

All praise is for Allah—Lord of all worlds.

—Holy Qur'an 1:2

The Qur'an opens with an invitation for humans and djinn to worship the God of *all worlds.* This second line of the Holy Book's first verse, Surah al-Fatiha, must be repeated throughout a practicing Muslim's five daily prayers. This means that they will repeat this affirmation of multiple universes forty-eight times each day. Acceptance and remembrance of the fact that we humans inhabit one world of many is central to a Muslim's faith. In between washing dishes and setting alarms, we quietly affirm that we are not alone. There are parallel families, clans, and tribes roaming parallel domains; healers, husbands, and poets sleep and clean in worlds that are like and unlike our own.

اللَّهُ الَّذِي خَلَقَ سَبْعَ سَمَاوَاتٍ وَمِنَ الْأَرْضِ مِثْلَهُنَّ

It is Allah Who has created seven heavens, and earths as many.

—Holy Qur'an 65:12

There are seven worlds separated by seven hundred years, the Holy Prophet (p.b.u.h.) explained, and the earth that we forage, excavate, and torch is considered of a higher status than some other worlds. This is perhaps why the Prophet warned: "He who takes anything from the earth that doesn't belong to him or that is not his right will be thrown on the Day of Judgement downwards to the seventh earth."[18] Some interpret this to mean that hell lies seven earths below this one.

Through the Hadith and the extra-earthly travels of gifted humans, such as Ibn 'Arabī, the famed Andalusian-Syrian scholar, we know that one of the seven worlds is dazzlingly white. The white earth's days are thirty times longer than the days on our earth, because the white earth orbits the sun once every thirty days. Another of the seven worlds was born from the clay that remained after the first human was created. Another world is home to beings who parallel our own form in all ways except one: Our otherworldly kin live for eternity.

18 Sadr al-din Muhammad ibn Ibrahim Shirazi, Mafati al-ghayb, Beirut, muassasat al tarikh al-arabi (1999 HE)

Map of the World of Djinn

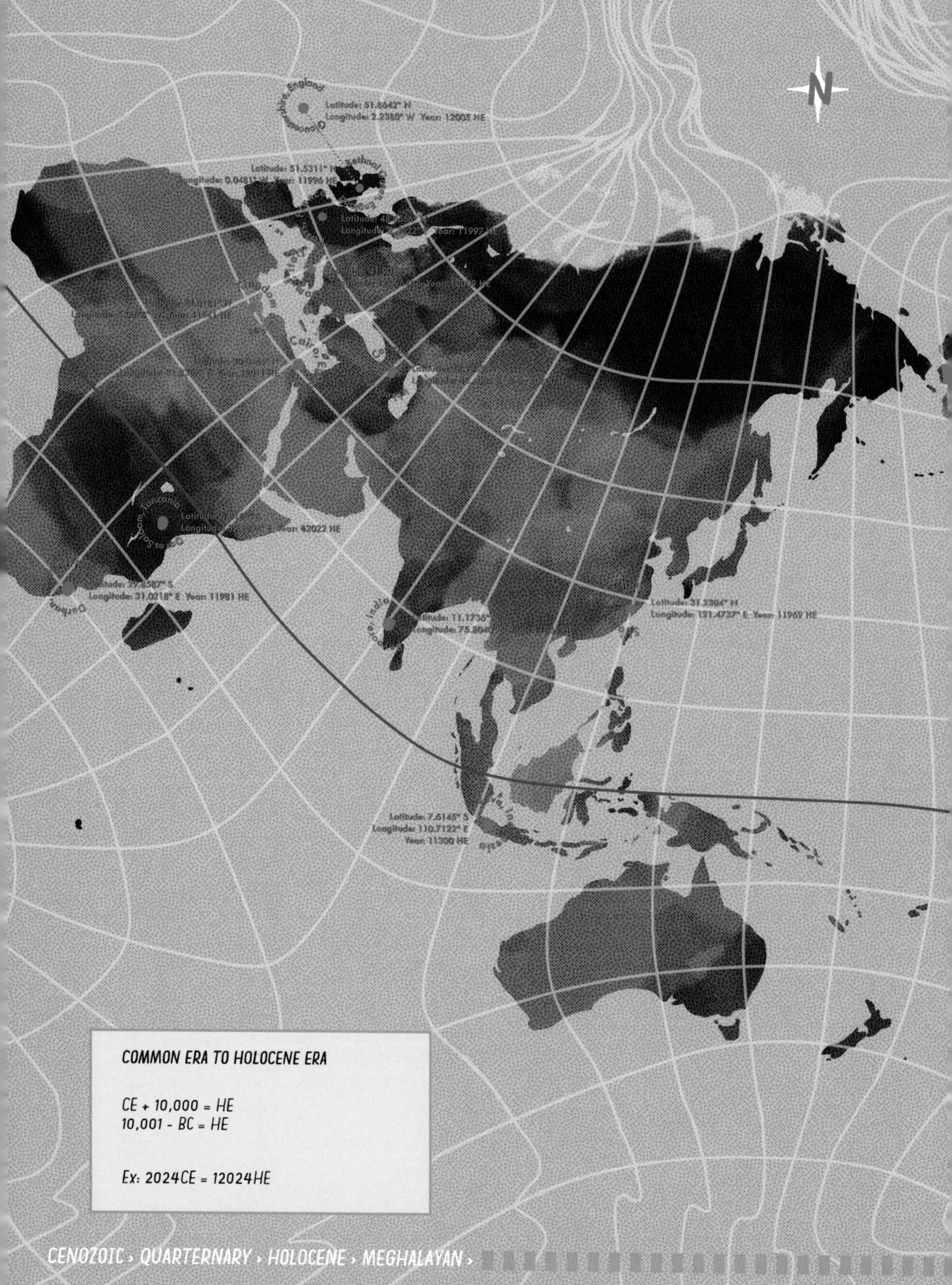

N

Gloucestershire, England
Latitude: 51.8642° N
Longitude: 2.2380° W Year: 12005 HE

Latitude: 51.5311° N
Year: 11996 HE

Year: 11997 HE

Cairo

Dar es Salaam, Tanzania
Year: 12022 HE

Durban
Latitude: 29.8587° S
Longitude: 31.0218° E Year: 11981 HE

India
Latitude: 11.1736°
Longitude: 75.8040

Latitude: 31.2304° N
Longitude: 121.4737° E Year: 11969 HE

Latitude: 7.6145° S
Longitude: 110.7122° E
Year: 11300 HE

COMMON ERA TO HOLOCENE ERA

CE + 10,000 = HE
10,001 - BC = HE

Ex: 2024CE = 12024HE

CENOZOIC › QUARTERNARY › HOLOCENE › MEGHALAYAN ›

Quebec, Canada
Latitude: 46.8131° N
Longitude: 71.2075° W Year: 12010 HE
New Jersey, USA
Latitude: 40.0583° N
Longitude: 74.4057° W Year: 12016 HE
California, USA
Latitude: 36.7783° N
Longitude: 119.4179° W
Year: 12002 HE
Colombia
Panama City, Panama
Latitude: 8.9824° N
Longitude: 79.5199° W Year: 11959 HE
S

ENTER ALAM AL-GHAYB: THE DOMINION OF THE UNSEEN

Humans whisper prayers with their knees pressed into the terrestrial plane. Their open palms and fingers point upward toward the celestial, angelic plane. But in the space between, that space through which your deepest desires float skyward and your desperate supplications ascend, lies an intermediary, overlapping, and imaginal plane: alam al-ghayb, the dominion of the Unseen.

Al-ghayb is the home of the djinn: mountainous, cavernous, and scattered with islands and deep, dark seas. From cave-dwelling winged creatures to island-loving serpentine beings, all manner of djinn species inhabits this realm. They were deposited here by angels who were sent to end the bloody intra-djinn conflict that broke out before we humans made this planet our home.

Before we delve into the geographic landmarks of al-ghayb, consider this: The realm of the Unseen is more than a landscape; alam al-ghayb is a dimension, a place of power and potential. Intangible and immaterial, it requires a particular mindset to grasp, a mindset that is willing to unlearn the rigid rules of empire and empirical evidence.

Named from the trilateral Arabic root ĠY-B, *ghayb* means "absent, hidden, imperceivable." It is related to words such as *ghaybūba*, meaning "trance," "coma," or "unconscious"; *mughayyibāt*, meaning "anesthetics" or "narcotics"; *ghāba*, meaning "to be concealed or absent"; and *al-mughayy-abāt*, the divine secrets.

Alam al-ghayb is mentioned in sixty places in the Qur'an, in six forms, with three primary meanings. One meaning refers to the future, one refers to that which is absent or missing, and the third connects al-ghayb with the unknown.

The limits of our knowledge are humbling. Some argue that technological advances expand those limits and allow us to encroach further into the Unseen, turning the once invisible into the knowable (for example, sonography to spy on a kicking fetus or MRI scans to peer inside an anxious brain). But science simultaneously expands the boundaries of the unknown. Each discovery redraws the margins of the Unseen, so that each day it is rendered more expansive than we had previously imagined.

A note about science: The "God trick" of Western science may have conned you into believing that scientists are objective entities who simply observe and record the truth. This is a lie. By elevating science to the level of omniscience, by promoting human exceptionalism and its ocularcentrism, the Western scientific establishment has diminished and delegitimized other ways of sensing and learning. Vision has been made foundational to modern empirical knowledge. This "empire of the gaze"—which has been the basis for violent Western colonialism—prevents us from understanding all that exists but cannot be observed with our limited eyes.

You must plug into your alternative senses, those "eyes" that can begin to grasp the ungraspable. Not everyone is capable of embarking on this process of discovery, but you might be—if you are willing to pay respect to alternative ways of knowing, and if you are able to awaken and use all of your senses.

You may have already visited the realm of the Unseen. As you rub the crust from your eyelids at sunrise, when the veil is at its thinnest. As you wrestle with images and sensations that you cannot replicate or fully describe with the language of the terrestrial domain. At those times, your mind is at that liminal place on the edges of al-ghayb, and your soul is drifting back from the clutches of the Unseen, sending you down to the terrestrial plane. You may have visited al-ghayb in your sleep, when you drift into a potent meditation, or when you detach from your ego and fall deep into prayer.

Al-ghayb contains all of those marvels that you cannot see or choose not to see in a traditional sense: your past, your child's future, heaven, hell, the "face" of God. Perhaps in your own personal al-ghayb live all of those phenomena which you cannot grasp because you are standing in your own way. Adjust your perspective and new ways of knowing will come into focus.

Al-ghayb is important to the concept of *barzakh*, or *alam-e-araf*, which is the veil or cover between this realm and the intermediary realm—the place between death and life where Sufis believe departed souls reside. Barzakh comes from the Middle Persian *barzag*, meaning "limbo," "barrier," or "partition." The Qur'an describes barzakh as the stage between this world and every soul's resurrection on the Day of Judgment.

Al-ghayb is a paradox. Unseen to many, terrifying to most, it is also a place of healing and protection, a place accessible to the most spiritually adept and favored. Al-ghayb is both invisible and hypervisible, mirroring the lived experiences of millions of Muslims who are watched and scrutinized while feeling unseen. Al-ghayb is powerful and omnipresent; it hangs over us like unseeable systems of oppression and surveillance.

Paradoxical, unknowable, intangible, yet ever-present, al-ghayb defies Western logic as much as its inhabitants defy categorization. Time moves differently in al-ghayb; distance disrespects earthly measures. The laws of the Unseen domain bend the calculus of Newtonian physics. This is why djinn can move at lightning speed, crisscrossing continents within earthly seconds.

Djinn are dual dimensional. Flitting between al-ghayb and the terrestrial plane, they make themselves seen and then unseen. Some are even able to access the lower heavens, where they eavesdrop on angelic conversations about the fates of humanity and then drop back down to earth to share the prophesies with soothsayers and those humans who make their livings from peering into crystal balls. Sometimes the angels retaliate by hurling meteors at prying djinn. You might have seen these angelic missiles dashing through the night sky as shooting stars.

Humans are not truly dual dimensional, even if our brief visits to al-ghayb haunt us for the rest of our lives. But some of your forebears were snatched into the dominion of the Unseen, where they made babies, raised families, and fell in love, and from where they never returned.

Deep green mountains lie at the center of the imaginal al-ghayb. The vast range of Mount Qaf is formed from one colossal emerald, which lends the skies above it a green sparkle. Home to uncountable djinn tribes, Qaf may overlap with the Caucasus Mountains of the earth that we inhabit. But some who have scaled its peaks say the mountain range is so vast that it forms a ring around the entire earth. Jagged scarps and slippery ravines occasionally poke through that hazy space you visit in your dreams, the liminal place where the terrestrial plane ends and the territory of al-ghayb begins.

King Malik Gatshan, considered to be the king of all djinn, and Shahpal bin Shahrukh, emperor of the djinn, both reign from Mount Qaf. The Simurgh, ancient djinn with the claws of a lion and the body of a bird or dog, build nests on the cliffs of the mountain.

The historian Ibn Jareer Tabari recalls a story in which the Holy Prophet (p.b.u.h.) said that no human can reach Mount Qaf without first traversing four months in complete darkness. The Prophet described the mountain as having no sun, moon, or stars, but said the mountain range itself radiated such an intense azure that the blue[19] of the sky is actually a reflection of Qaf.

19 Descriptions of this color vary from text to text.

Islands float in the seas of alam al-ghayb. The island of WaqWaq is ruled by a djinniyah queen and is home to djinn and non-male humans. On WaqWaq, new beings spring to life from a tree on which babies dangle. *Waq waq* is the sound these beings make as they evolve from blossoming babies to fully bloomed adults—at which point they fall from the tree. Some claim to have seen WaqWaq in the Indian Ocean, while others say the island drifts in the China Sea.

Parts of al-ghayb might neatly overlap some regions of this earth. The island of Borneo, some scholars told me, is known to be al-ghayb's Ráïj, home of a type of half-bodied Nasnās that has the wings of a bat. In the Red Sea, the strait known as the Gate of Tears, or Bab el-Mandeb, is home to powerful Marid and 'ifrit.

Tucked away in the foothills of Oman's Al Hajar mountains, close to the fishing village of Qurayyat, is the Majlis al-Jinn, which translates to the "gathering place of the djinn." One of the largest underground caves on the planet, the capacious Majlis al-Jinn, is hidden from the outside, so that a traveler can only view its domed ceilings and fifty-eight-thousand-square-meter caverns if they notice one of the cave's three small, nondescript openings. Once inside, a weary backpacker might lean against a wall to rest in the shade, only to awaken with a djinniyah by her side.

The fourteenth-century Mughal fort in Delhi, Feroz Shah Kolta, is home to djinn who answer human calls for help. In times of hardship and grief, such as during India's brutal Emergency period in the 11970s HE, hundreds flock to Feroz Shah Kolta to leave letters for djinn, seeking their intercession in earthly woes. Exorcisms are performed amid the ruins of the once grand fortress. Clerics beg the djinn to leave the bodies of hapless humans and to roam once more with their own kind amid the crumbling walls.

In Morocco, Muslims flock to the Berber village of Aroumd to visit the shrine of the djinn judge Chamharouch, who is heralded for being fair and just. Three hundred miles north, in the city of Meknes, lives Lalla Mimuna, the mother of famed djinniyah Aicha Qandisa. Lalla Mimuna resides among old houses and deep inside wells, from which she emerges to seduce lone travelers.

The Well of Barhout, also known as the Well of Hell, sits at the edge of Yemen and Oman. A prison for the most nefarious djinn, the well is considered a portal to hell. It is one hundred feet wide at the surface and nearly four hundred feet deep. This well is home to djinn and snakes, the latter of which were discovered and photographed by twenty-first-century geologists. I saw them during my own research travels.

The sand dunes of Egypt are the resting place of sandstorm-causing 'ifrit. Iran's vast Rig-e Jenn sand dunes lure modern travelers eager to take photos beneath the star-studded sky, but Instagram-loving tourists should know that old-time caravan travelers avoided Rig-e Jenn because of the malevolent djinn drifting across the dunes.

The holiest of all places in the Muslim world, Mecca, is home to Masjid al-Jinn, a place of worship built in the exact location where thousands of djinn converted to Islam when they gathered to listen to the Holy Prophet (p.b.u.h.) recite the Qur'an.

Al-ghayb is here and Elsewhere. It is in your mind and in your heart. You bring back its dust and scatter its dew when you return from sleep, or prayer, or out-of-body experiences; your viscera know you have traveled Elsewhere, but your brain and tongue are unable to explain exactly where you have been.

The Queen of Qaf

North Caucasus Mountains, Chechnya, circa 10800 HE (800 CE)

Mother spooned stories into my mouth at night to soothe me. Like pomegranate molasses, the stories slid over my tongue and into my stomach where they sated my hunger for knowledge. Mother said even at that age, when I could barely babble, my eyes asked questions and I would weep until I was fed the answers. Storytelling was the only way Mother knew to stop me from screaming. The fat tears would stop dripping down my cheeks, my breath would deepen, and my pupils would widen as she recited from memory the tales once told to her—stories about the mountains that surrounded our village, the forest at the base of those mountains, and what would descend from the crags every winter for the Hunt.

Once upon a time there was a little girl who lived in a village surrounded by flowers. Pink, yellow, and blue, the petals on the flowers were as big as her hands. The little girl loved to frolic in the forest and play in the streams. She picked the flowers and pressed them into her long, blonde braid.

Surrounding the flowers were icy mountains whose pointed peaks poked the sky. The tips of the mountaintops touched a fiery Hell that grew hotter and hotter with each month. By the time winter came, the ice on the mountains began to melt into storm clouds. The storm clouds dripped down the sides of the mountain and hung over the forest like a heavy blanket of fog. The creatures who lived in the mountains peeked down at wintertime and eyed the thick clouds. They were djinn from the Queendom of Qaf. The djinn flew through the mist, thudded into the forest, and feasted until their bellies were round and their snapping mouths were tired. Then they slumbered among the trees until the next morning and began to feast again.

Some nights the warm milk I suckled while I looked up at Mother's moving lips was thick with fig syrup. It concealed the bitterness of the opium tincture she dripped into the bottle. As I grew, the teat was replaced with an earthenware cup, but the milk, the poppy juice, and the stories stayed the same.

(They will say that this is how I came to be here, that I was always a girl on the edge, drifting between places. But that is not the whole story.)

I was a curious child. Each trip to the forest in summertime would take hours. As I picked Mother's herbs, I would stop at each turn to taste fruit from the trees, and to forage for mushrooms that looked like mangled faces and twisted hands. I crawled beneath bushes to pluck the brightest flowers. I lifted my dress to chase after the frogs jumping across the brook, sometimes plucking one out of the water and placing it in my pocket to carry home. Mother would pull my ear and chastise me when I arrived, bedraggled and dripping wet. "You must hurry back!" she said. "But it's summer!" I would plead. Summer was supposed to be safe. "Shut up!" Mother scolded, squeezing my lips between her fingers. "If you disappear during summer, they will say it is my fault, that I am a witch!"

Mother was not a witch, but I heard them say she looked like one. When villagers visited our kitchen to barter for remedies that would ward off the Evil, their eyes darted across her face and around our small room. "Sorceress," they whispered, as they snatched cloth pouches from Mother's hands.

"The same potions that repel can conjure if used incorrectly!" Mother would warn. But her voice trailed behind them as they hurried away. She issued strict instructions. What color robe to wear, how long to fast, which way to face when swallowing the tinctures and burning or burying the sacks. But they were too busy running from Mother to hear her. They were too scared to listen carefully to the secrets about how to survive the forest which sustained us in the summer and made sustenance of us in the winter.

(I was never afraid. You will say that this was to be my downfall. But fear is not the reason. Nor is it the answer.)

Every winter, before the first snow, Mother was at her busiest. Brewing and steeping and knotting and cutting; even her nighttime stories grew tortuous and frenetic. Everyone knew winter was the wickedest time, when the encircling forest would disappear beneath blankets of fog. That's when the screeching would begin. Winged beasts with hooked claws would scramble down the crags and into the forest. They landed on the trees and devoured all that was living. Every rabbit skinned, disemboweled, and devoured. Every bear gnawed to the bone. Every mongoose ripped to shreds. Every tree trunk cracked, as the beasts sucked enough sap to fill their bellies until next winter. For three months they feasted and slept, feasted and slept. The forest became their dominion.

At the end of winter, the Queen of Qaf would fly down from her roost on the mountain's peak and perch on a rock at the mouth of the stream. The Queen would survey the forest, eyeing all that her followers had devoured. From an emerald crown that sat atop her head, the Queen plucked one green stone. She kissed the gem, washed it in the stream, and clawed at the ground to make a small hole. As soon as the Queen buried the emerald, the barren trees began to turn green. Small shoots emerged from the ground, a mossy carpet began to extend across the forest, and fish were birthed in the stream. The forest sighed. It had been blessed with new life. The Queen gave her thanks, threw back her head, let out a howl, and ascended the mountain, her sated beasts flying drunkenly behind her.

(This would have been the end of the story were it not for the Memories.)

Once upon a time there were a people who lived in a village surrounded by a green and luscious forest. The forest breathed like the people breathed. The forest sang like the people sang, its tinkling rivers and whispering leaves making music to rival the birdsong. The forest even ate like the people ate. It was a living, breathing thing, so it ate what died and replenished itself from the rot.

But the people took and took. First, they pulled the fruit from the forest's trees. Then they hacked at its limbs to drink the milky sap. They stabbed shovels into its floor, cracking open the spongey moss carpet to scavenge treasures hidden inside: thick tubers and roots that could nourish for months on end. One summer the villagers plucked and fished and pulled and dug until the forest was left bare. They fermented its fruit and traipsed through its baby trees. They pulled every seedling from the earth and danced on the ruptured land, destroying that which was waiting to be born. The forest wept for its dead, but it could not defend itself against greed.

When the first snow came and its barren boughs were blanketed in fog, it told the winged beasts from the Queendom of Qaf that it had nothing left to give. The beasts screeched for the Queen, and when she flew down the mountain flapping her magnificent wings, she bellowed a roar that tore the tops off every hut in the village. The Queen scratched her talons over her emerald crown, but she did not pluck a stone to replenish the land; her beasts had not yet fed. Instead, the Queen said something she had never said before, never in the history of her queendom or her mother's queendom or her grandmother's queendom or her great-grandmother's queendom. The Queen of Qaf rounded up her beasts, spread her wings, looked outward from the forest, and said: "Let the Hunt begin."

Winter was once safe, Mother told me. Winter was fires and long sleeps and hearty stews sipped around the hearth. Winter was story after story to pass the time and drown out the occasional excited screeching that emanated from deep inside the forest.

The village elders wore amulets and talismans to ward away the djinn who feasted in the forest. In the times before the Hunt, they were protected by their prayers and goodwill. The starving beasts were distracted by the forest's generous offerings. But in the first year of the Hunt, when the Memories were made, no talisman could protect against ravenous and angry djinn.

(The villagers would not learn about the Sacrifice until the following year.)

But now the time the Books had prophesized had come. The beasts were starving. Humans had starved them. Their scrawny limbs, pockmarked and gray, had little vigor to lift their vast wings. For the first time in history, the winged djinn from the Queendom of Qaf ventured out of the forest in search of food. The Queen's beasts staggered through the bushes and emerged at the outskirts of the village. They let out a magnificent screech and then they began. They clobbered the low brick walls that surrounded the homes and blew fire onto the walls.

The first sacrifice was a baby girl named Siama. The second sacrifice was a baby boy named Mikel. Energized by the sweetness of the babies' blood, the djinn spread their wings and flew over the village until their wings touched tip to tip. The winter's dim light was blocked out by their darkness. For seven days and seven nights the djinn feasted in the village. First, they tore apart flesh and sucked on bones, then they ripped through sacks and gobbled up roots and tubers. Only two families survived. I am descended from both.

Once upon a time there was a little girl with a hunger for stories and an ear for danger. Her name was Omina. The girl was special. Her one blue eye and her one brown eye could see into different worlds. Her pointed ears could hear the sounds of menace before the adults could sense that danger was near. One day, in the spring after the first Hunt, little Omina told her mother: "Mama, mama, the Queen is coming!"

Omina's mother gasped. "But it is only spring," she said.

"The Queen is coming to ask you a question," said the little girl.

"But no human has ever seen the Queen!" exclaimed Omina's mother. She ran to tell those who had survived. "The Queen is coming! What do we do?"

But before they could pray or prepare, a darkness descended over the village. The Queen of Qaf landed outside their huts. "I am here to make you an offer," she said. Omina shivered behind her mother's legs; the warm spring day had turned freezing cold. The Queen said that if the two surviving families made an offering to the Queen next winter, she would sacrifice her own precious emerald to the forest and prevent another Hunt.

"Tell us, what is the offering?" said Omina's mother.

"A baby," said the Queen, eyeing Omina, who inhaled and ducked behind her mother's legs. "Your most precious child must be sacrificed."

Omina looked around at the two families gathered in the village. They nodded their heads. It was their only hope to avoid certain death. That night, Omina's mother wept as she cradled her daughter. She placed Omina's small hand on her belly and the child recoiled as something kicked from inside. Omina put her small hand to her mother's face. "That baby will be the sacrifice," said the little girl who would become my mother.

Ever since the Hunt, we have been paying for the sins of our ancestors, those who took and took and never gave back. Not like Mother. She made sure to honor what gave us life. She performed the ritual sacrifice to appease the Queen. She fed the forest as much as she took from it. But we would never escape the Queen's wrath without performing the sacrifice, that much we knew. So we tended in the spring and harvested in the fall. When winter came, we grew frail and thin and hungry. We waited for the snow to melt and the fog to rise. We used the herbs in Mama's pouches for protection. We offered up a newborn and prayed our sacrifice was sufficient.

There had been two dozen sacrifices offered: two dozen babies. The sounds of the djinn and the crying baby as she was swooped into the sky made me shiver, no matter how close I was to Mama's bosom or the heat of the fire. But I was not afraid for long, because Mama would tell me stories about gallant girls and strong women, stories that calmed my nerves and warmed me from the inside. Mama said stories were salve for little girls, that stories saved our lives.

This winter, the villagers were tired. The Hunt was a distant memory. They were weary of the war that erupted each winter as a child was chosen to serve as sacrifice. At the first snow, when Mama declared that a newborn must be offered, the villagers turned their backs. They hid their babies inside their huts. "Won't the herbs you sell protect us?" they sneered. "If not, what good are they? What good are you?"

Mother came home and stared into the fire. She boiled leaves in her cauldron and said not a word. She cut and crushed and tied and chopped and prayed. But no amount of alchemy could replace a child sacrifice. That night we bolted the doors, hung herbs from the roof, and told story after story to stay awake. She began with the story of her newborn sister whom Mother wrapped in a cloth dyed pink with beets. After the little sister was offered to the Queen at the First Sacrifice, the only evidence left behind of her life was the cloth, which Mother has kept.

(They will say she is why I was spared. But my power comes not from loss but from the act of giving.)

The screeching began as soon as darkness fell. The beasts circled low above the village, their wings blocking out the moonlight. But they did not swoop down to feast, not as they did during the first Hunt.

Mother whispered to herself as she cradled me tightly. "What is it?" I asked her. "What is happening?"

"Their Queen is here," she said. "She is telling them to wait. But they are hungry." Mother clutched me tighter and rocked back and forth.

"Will they come inside, Mother?" She nodded, then pressed her chin into my head. I squeezed my eyes shut and listened to the thunder of a thousand flapping wings.

The sound that fell upon us next was a roar that blew out the fire. Then a scramble, as if a rocky avalanche were descending upon the village, as if the very mountains were crumbling. The whole village shook as the Queen of Qaf descended. "She is here. Shhh, shhh," Mother said. But we both knew what was to be done.

The Queen's talons scratched at the dirt. And then there was silence. "Don't be afraid," Mother said into the darkness. But my skin shivered while my belly overflowed with heat. A great thud shook the door. I hid behind Mother as she opened the door. She looked only at the ground and curtsied before the Queen.

"Well, well. I remember you," said the gravelly voice. "You were only a child. And your sister . . ."

"Yes, my sister," Mother said quietly.

I heard the sound of a wet tongue slithering in and out of the Queen's mouth and sliding across dry teeth. "And what do we have here?" A wing tip poked through the door and pushed Mother aside. She fell to the ground and quickly scrambled to her feet. Mother tried to stand in front of me, but I was wrapped in a wing that felt like a sheet of ice. That is when I first saw the creature I had met in the stories. She pulled me out of the hut and lifted me toward her. The Queen's face was as green as the emeralds in her crown, her eyes as black as onyx. Each fang in her six rows of teeth was sharp like the peak of the mountain itself. And her smell reminded me of the warm milk I drank as a child, on the nights when Mother spooned in the special tincture.

All around me was a blur. I saw only the blackest of eyes, the reddest of mouths. The Queen slithered her tongue across my face. She angled her neck and opened her mouth. And although I should have been scared, as scared as when I heard the stories, I remembered that girls were brave and that stories were a salve, that stories had soothed me my entire life. The Queen opened her mouth wider. Every jagged fang glimmered. She pressed the tips of her teeth into my neck. That's when I opened my own mouth.

There is a little girl who lives at the top of a tall, tall mountain. From below, the mountain looks hellish and cold, icy and black. But between its peaks and across its crags, the mountain is verdant and warm, and a soft breeze rustles the leaves of the small bushes that grow there. The little girl wanders along the mountaintop, stooping to press her fingers into the carpet of soft moss. She presses her nose into the green flowers, and she swims in the green stream. Until it turns dark. As nighttime falls over the mountain, the little girl hurries back to the Emerald Palace, the home of the Queen of Qaf. She sits at the foot of the throne, where the Queen taps her talons across her marble floor, and the girl opens her mouth to tell a story.

Once upon a time there was a mighty and beautiful Queen. Every winter, the Queen ordered her djinn beasts to swoop down the mountain and feast on the forest below. But one winter, the forest was left empty and bare. Hungry humans had taken more than their share, and there was nothing for the djinn! The Queen ordered her djinn to devour the humans. The humans screamed and cried. They flailed and wept. The djinn consumed the gluttonous, pathetic creatures, eating almost the entire lot.

But the Queen was a merciful sovereign, so she told her djinn to halt the Hunt. "Wait," she said, eyeing a special girl from far above. "Spare those two huts." That's when the merciful Queen had an idea. Each year, the humans would offer her a sacrifice: the freshest child in the village. If the sacrifice was proper, the Queen would spare the rest, taking only one. As long as the humans offered this sacrifice, and as long as they respected the bounties of the forest, they would be spared.

But humans are greedy, so after two dozen sacrifices, they stopped. The Queen ordered the djinn to Hunt once again. Until the Queen was called to the home of the Special Child, sister of the First Sacrifice, who was now a mother herself. The Queen took the child of the Special Child as her sacrifice, but she did not eat her—not yet. For stories are a salve and can be offered like sacrifices to sate even the most ravenous beasts.

The little girl thinks of this as she swims in the green lake. She will be safe atop the mountain in the Queendom of Qaf so long as she never runs out of stories.

NOTES

This story about stories was offered to me by an older lady who owns a small religious bookstore in Chechnya, also known as the Chechen Republic of the Russian Federation. She said the story had been told to her by her mother, who had learned it from her mother, and so on. She had sparkly green eyes that almost disappeared when she smiled, and I joked that she might be the girl in the story, especially because she had me so enraptured by her own storytelling. "Oh no," said the woman. "That poor child is still at the top of the mountain." She pointed to foothills in the distance. "A great calamity shall befall us if she runs out of tales to feed the Queen." And with that, she blinked her emerald eyes and went back into the bookstore.

Salma Bai's Story

Durban, South Africa, 11981 HE (1981 CE)

Nur sported a pixie cut the first time she appeared. Salma Bai didn't have any friends with hair that could not be oiled and woven into a thick, shiny, buttocks-skimming braid. But there was Nur, brown skinned, with delicate features and short hair. She loitered in the back corner of the greengrocer wearing a burgundy dress; a hemp bag hung empty off her slender, caramel wrist. She was stroking a bulb of fennel in her palm, its fine tendrils fluttering around her fingers. Salma Bai was weighed down with bunches of string beans, a cantaloupe as big as a baby's soft head, and two sacks of cumin powder, one of which was leaking a thin trail of brown dust through an invisible hole.

Salma Bai eyed this short-haired modern woman in a shin-baring dress. She looked like she didn't know how to cook the exotic vegetable she was holding. Salma Bai wondered what it was like to not swing a braid everywhere you went; what it felt like to not have a brain crowded with recipes.

Nur looked up at Salma Bai and smiled slightly, showing no teeth. She turned away and disappeared down the oil aisle.

That night she reappeared in the armchair of the guest bedroom where Salma Bai slept when she was on her period. The bleeding brought on migraines, and Salma Bai figured the apparition was an aura from her headache, a memory of the woman who had captivated her with a quick smile. Migraines blurred shapes and colors, and sometimes Salma Bai cramped and bled while pink stars and purple triangles floated in front of her face. Bright lights flashed across her eyes and split her skull with a hot beam.

But this apparition was speaking, asking Salma Bai if she could rub seven drops of peppermint oil into her temples to soothe the throbbing. A cool, wet rag was laid across Salma Bai's forehead as she mumbled that she was fine, she didn't have any peppermint oil, and how would that help anyway?

Nur's fingertips massaged the menthol balm into the depressions at the end of Salma Bai's eyebrows. She rubbed in ever larger circles until the full lengths of her fingers were sliding over Salma Bai's cheeks, cradling her head, rocking it slightly from side to side.

When Salma Bai woke, it was an hour before Fajr, her head felt light and clear, and Nur was lying on top of her, sleeping, her licorice-scented breath falling into the space between Salma Bai's neck and shoulder. The air between them felt warm, like freshly spun cotton candy. Nur was light as a feather and her eyelashes tickled Salma Bai's collarbone. Salma Bai fell back asleep until her mosque-shaped alarm clock sang the call to prayer and emptied the room of silence and Nur.

She began to sleep in the guest bedroom even when she wasn't bleeding. Her husband already called her unwifely and cold. This new behavior only exacerbated his muttered complaints. "Frigid woman," he spat into the sink as he brushed his bloodied gums in the morning. "Cursed bitch. What did I do to deserve this burden?" Eventually, he filed a complaint with the mosque committee and requested a new wife.

"Now hold on, brother," said the imam. "Let's not rush to drastic measures. First, let us send an imam. We have an expert who can draw out and banish the kind of djinni that makes women cold and barren. We can still make this one a good wife."

The first imam came with a half dozen wooden rosaries stuffed into his bulging pockets. The hem of his beige kufni was worn and scuffed with gray dirt. He condemned their home, spittle stretching between his tongue and his teeth, which were stained orange from years of eating paan stuffed with tobacco. "There are definitely djinn here," he said. "If you stay in this cursed place, you will never bear children. I guarantee it."

And if you keep stuffing wads of paan next to your gums you will get oral cancer, thought Salma Bai, *I guarantee that.* She imagined a hole in his cheek where a future tumor would burrow through flesh, leaving brown molars bared to the world.

The imam's eyes turned from the corners of the walls where he had been sprinkling holy water and fixed on the dimple in Salma Bai's chin. He spit a brown mush of tobacco and betel nut into a cotton handkerchief, all the while engrossed by her small, round mouth. "I need to pray in there," he said, pointing to the bedroom and dismissing them with a wave of his soggy handkerchief.

When he emerged forty-five minutes later, his eyes squinting, his lips shining, he said he had to leave immediately, which Salma Bai thought unusual. Inside the bedroom, it smelled of tobacco and sweat. She found the bedspread rumpled and warm. A streak of orange had spread across Salma Bai's pillowcase, and she spent the afternoon washing the sheets in a mixture of boiling water and bleach.

The second imam wanted nothing to do with the bedroom. It was Salma Bai he needed to examine. "I must be alone with the barren woman," he said, and Salma Bai's husband left them in the sitting room, which Salma Bai found unusual. *Men trust men*, she thought, and she shrugged, closing the door behind her. She repositioned her dupatta so that it draped all the way across her chest.

The imam wanted her to lie on the settee with her head toward the qibla and her feet hanging over the edge of the brown leather arms. "I have to feel the empty space you are trying to fill," he said while cracking his knuckles. She didn't want to lay flat and sat instead, but the imam, who was tall, with gangly legs and wiry arms, kneeled between her knees and pulled her down until her pelvis was at the edge of the sofa cushion.

He rubbed his palms together vigorously, closed his eyes, mouthed a prayer, and blew onto his fingers; then he pressed his prayed-upon hands into her stomach. His eyebrows raised. He flared his nostrils and sniffed.

"Stay extremely still and extremely quiet," he whispered. "Those are the rules."

The imam turned his face to the east, placed his ear on her stomach, and listened to the borborygmi of that afternoon's rice and lentils. Salma Bai clenched her teeth and wished that Nur would appear. A sudden gust of wind flapped her dupatta off her chest and over her face. As she swiped it away, she saw the imam laying knocked out on the floor.

"Nur! Nur! Oh my goodness, Nur, is that you?"

But the room was quiet. There was only Salma Bai lying on the couch and the imam on the ground, lying between her feet. Was that a trickle of blood running out of his nose and onto her big toe?

They sent a boy next. A boy with a jar of honey and instructions to exorcise a most deviant djinni. *Dip just the nail of your pinky finger into the honey, close your eyes, and pray this verse seven times. Then take your fingernail out of the honey and look into it. Your fingernail will be like a TV screen. On that screen will be instructions for exorcising this djinni.*

The boy plopped onto the middle of the settee and sat cross-legged. Then, as if remembering that this was not in the instructions, he straightened his legs so that his feet, in their Mickey Mouse socks, stuck out over the edge of the settee.

Salma Bai watched him. Her husband fingered a green plastic rosary and stared from the other side of the room. She thought about offering the boy some apple juice or a chocolate bar. But when he unscrewed the jar of honey, the boy dipped his index finger into the liquid and quietly sucked.

Salma Bai's husband snorted. The boy looked up, a sticky finger still in his mouth. Once he had licked it clean, he stuck the tip of his pinky finger back into the jar and mouthed the words to the verse he had been instructed to read.

"How old are you?" Salma Bai asked, interrupting the prayers. The boy wiggled his toes and squeezed his eyes shut, the jar of honey threatening to topple in his lap. After the seventh repetition of the holy verse, he removed his finger from the honey and brought his fingernail up to his face. The boy's eyes widened. He clamped a hand over his mouth. He looked up at Salma Bai and then back at his nail. *Mmsmsmffffttttttt!* he said, the words muffled behind his clammy hand.

"What? What is he saying?" Salma Bai's husband bounced on his tiptoes in the corner of the room.

The boy shrieked, jumped off the sofa, spilled the jar of honey across the carpet, and ran past Salma Bai, his sticky hands slapping her on her thighs as he made for the front door. "I'm telling on you! Bad woman!" he cried.

The next week, the mosque committee ruled that an out-of-town, educated-in-Egypt, big-shot imam was their last resort. If he couldn't exorcise the creature that was blocking Salma Bai's husband's blessings, Salma Bai would have to be replaced.

On Sundays, Salma Bai's mother came bearing thin plastic bags bursting with green things: bushels of methi, okra, green chilies, string beans, and sometimes stalks of khat. They had seen Sindhi workers stuff the leaves into their mouths whenever they needed to follow a day shift with a night shift (and maybe another day shift and another night shift), their jaws moving like cows masticating cud.

Salma Bai and Amma chewed a leaf or two in Salma Bai's kitchen while peeling vegetables, emptying pea pods, plucking stems, and soaking freshly trimmed leaves in silver bowls of ice water. Sometimes Nur would watch the pair as they chewed in sync, the intermittent pouting of their lips as they sucked the last drops of juice from the mangled leaves.

Amma was plump, like her only daughter, her face shiny from a smear of coconut oil she kept in a tub near the kitchen sink. She would dig her fingers into the white paste, scoop up a white glob and rub it over her face while it was still wet from ablution. Yet the heels of her feet were cracked like a parched riverbed. She wore dull silver rings on her pinky and big toes, and she wiggled her fat toes while she dished out advice.

Salma Bai was pensive that day, only humming along to the Fayrouz songs they usually sang together. Even her favorite song about a girl waiting for her absent lover through winter and summer didn't rouse emotion. She plucked methi leaves and folded the bare stems between sheets of kitchen paper.

Amma emptied a bag of okra into a silver bowl clamped between her thighs and wiggled her toes. It was story time. "There was a girl in my village who wanted too much. She wanted a love marriage, she wanted a small wedding, she wanted no children." Amma paused to fold a single leaf of khat between her lower teeth and lip. "This girl wanted to eat at a table like English people, she wanted to live far away from her frail parents, she wanted to use a fork and spoon, she wanted this, and she wanted that. So, she got married and the want-too-much-girl became a want-too-much-lady. She want all the boys to run her errands, she want the hakeem to make her medicine, she want the rickshawala to stop parking his rickshaw outside her house, she want her husband to stay away in jamaat longer. Then, the want-too-much lady became a want-too-much-widow. Yes, her husband died very young. Died from misery and not having any sons. And you know what happened to her? *She* never died. She's still there, in my village! Just ask Chachi. Because when you are filled with too much wanting, Salma, you never fill your heart with happiness, you never fulfill the reason why your soul came down from heaven, and you can't die and rest in eternal peace. I worry about this for you, Salma. I should have taken you to see her the last time we went home. The want-too-much-widow. Her face, wrinkled and sour like pickled lemons. That face would teach you a lesson."

Salma Bai was glad for the want-too-much story instead of the if-you-don't-get-pregnant-your-uterus-decays-and-poisons-you-from-the-inside story.

Amma watched her daughter's drooping mouth. "I know what you are thinking. You are thinking, 'Why doesn't Amma tell story about a woman who doesn't have children?' Salma, everybody knows the ending to that story. You die very early, and when they bury you, the biggest insects have to eat your flesh because the flesh of a barren woman is tough and bitter, in life and in death. And even in death people can see who was barren because in the graveyard, no trees, not even a blade of grass, will grow over the grave of a barren woman. Her body has nothing to give back to the earth because her body was never home to new life."

Nur hovered above them, shaking her head. She retreated back to her home, a realm where women were heard. Nur and her fellow djinn listened to the whispers of women, their sighs, stifled sobs, and swallowed harumphs emanating from below. The muffled sneezes that earth women tried to silence, in order to be polite, rang loud and sharp in Nur's ears. She could hear the thoughts percolating inside their minds—thoughts that stayed lodged in their chests, trapped between vocal cords. *This is not living. I should leave him. Help me get out. Help!*

Nur's land hovered above the human universe like a flimsy layer of greaseproof paper that every now and again settled and made contact in just the right places, so that Nur could step through the miasma from one plane to another. It was an in-between place with in-between beings like Nur, who shifted from one form to another. Now she is a dragon-fly, now she is a moth, now hazy blue flames take on a human shape . . . Man, woman, blue fish—she is always Nur, a djinniyah or genie, or a faerie or peri, depending on which world she is traveling through.

Salma Bai called her a djinniyah, one of the creatures she had learned about in madrasa as a girl. Imams scribbled ayat al-kursi onto pieces of paper as small as postage stamps and stuffed them like ancient scrolls into silver taweez amulets to protect children from possession by demons like her.

As a child, Salma Bai had worn her taweez on a brown leather string that dangled from her neck. On Friday nights, her uncle would gather the children and usher them up the stairs onto the roof of the house where they huddled in a circle, clutching blankets and doodh soda made from ice-cold cola mixed with cow's milk. Uncle angled a small brass lamp beneath his face and opened his eyes wide. "Are you ready for the story of the djinn?" he exclaimed, and the children shrieked, grabbed each other's arms, and buried their faces in their blankets. Salma Bai clutched her silver amulet until it turned hot between her fingers.

The light from the brass lamp caught the fiery strands of her uncle's hennaed beard as he told them djinn stories so scary that Salma Bai and her cousins sometimes wet themselves. There was the tale of the naughty schoolboy who was so disobedient that the schoolmaster called in a djinni to discipline him. "What did the djinni do?" the children asked, squirming. "The djinni took the boy to the top of a mountain where there was a cave. In that cave was a boarding school for bad boys. And in that boarding school was a powerful djinni who was the master of the school. When the boy arrived, the djinni master said, 'Disobey me once and I will turn your arms into chicken wings. Disobey me twice and I will turn your mouth into a beak. Disobey me thrice and I will turn you into a squawking chicken and send you to the abattoir where they will make juicy kebabs from your thighs.'"

The children screamed. "So what did the boy do?" they asked.

"Well, he was a bad boy, he didn't pray his Qur'an and so he was misguided. On the first night, when the djinni master asked him to turn in his belongings, the boy held on to a catapult that he used to flick stones at the sleeping children. The next morning the djinni master called the boy into his room and said, 'You have lied and concealed contraband, and for this you shall be punished.' And just like that, the boy flapped his wings. The second night, the boy stole candy from another boy's locker, candy that had been given to that boy as a reward for good behavior. When the djinni master smelled the candy on the naughty boy's breath, he said, 'You have stolen a gift and for this you shall be punished.' And just like that, the boy pecked his beak

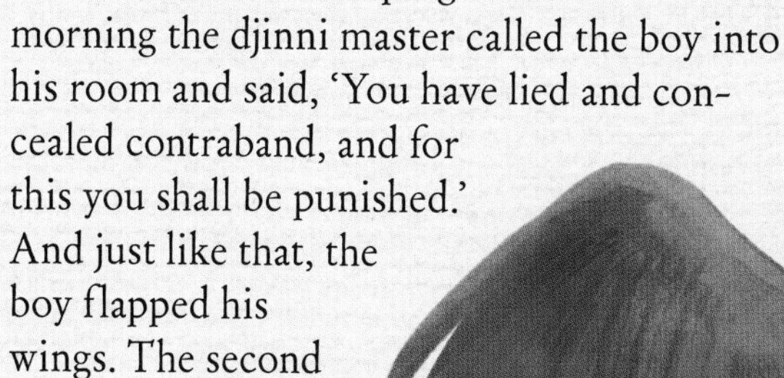

at the ground looking for worms, because worms and grain would be the only things he would feast on forevermore.'"

"Ewwwww!" said the children. "Worms! Then what happened?"

"On the third night, the flapping, squawking boy would not go to sleep when commanded to sleep, so in the morning he did not wake for school on time. All the children filed into the classroom like good students, but the boy stayed in bed, wrapped in his wings. 'You have been lazy and disobedient and late,' said the djinni master. 'And I am sending you to the abattoir, where they will turn your thighs into juicy kebabs!' You should have seen the boy. He flapped and squawked. He couldn't fly because he didn't know how to use his weak wings. He couldn't plead for mercy, and he couldn't pray to Allah because he had a beak where once there had been a mouth. As he flapped and squawked and bounced from one side of the classroom to another, his white feathers shedding all over the students, two burly men wearing blood-stained aprons and wielding chopping knives and a cage came to take the boy away."

"Did the djinni eat the boy?" the children asked.

"Why, yes," said Uncle. "Djinn eat naughty boys who lie and steal and oversleep and don't pray their Qur'an. So be careful, or soon your juicy thighs could be on a skewer!" With that he blew out the brass lamp, plunging the rooftop into darkness. Uncle grabbed the children's sweaty thighs as they collapsed into a squealing pile.

"Another one! Another one!" the children cried, emerging from beneath the covers.

"OK, OK," said Uncle, lighting the lamp. "Once upon a time there was a woman who lived next door to this house. She was an unhappy woman—a very, very unhappy woman—because she was unhappily married. The woman had two children. One day, when she was outside beating a rug, the dust from the rug swirled into a tornado and out came a djinni who whisked her into the tornado and away to a cave beneath the ocean."

"And then what happened?"

"In that cave beneath the ocean the woman lived happily ever after with the djinni. Do you remember the woman?" asked Uncle.

Salma Bai remembered. "She had big sad eyes," she said. "She used to cry while hanging the washing."

"Yes," said Uncle. "Always sad, that one. Until one day, that djinni came and said, 'I love you. Will you be my wife?' The silly sad woman said yes, but what she didn't know is that love comes with sacrifice. On this earth, the sacrifice for love was sadness because her husband was a bad man. But in the djinn world, the sacrifice was greater, because in that cave beneath the ocean is where she would live forever."

"But what about her son and daughter?" the children asked, their mouths agape.

"What do you mean?" Uncle would say. "Her children are still here. You play with them and their half-djinn cousins, don't you?"

The children gasped. "Half djinn?" said Salma Bai. "But they will never see their mother ever again?" asked another child.

"That is correct," said Uncle. "And that is an evil sacrifice some women are willing to make. For love."

Uncle would tire sometime after midnight. He would lean against the wall and begin to snore like a trumpet. The children would fall asleep on top of their blankets. Salma Bai would dream about her half-orphaned playmates with the mother who lived in a seaweed forest. The mother was smiling, always smiling. She missed her children, but she visited them in their dreams every night so that they could play together. The children didn't have to miss their mother, and they knew that their mother loved them dearly.

The djinn in the nighttime stories were always scary boy djinn. It never occurred to Salma Bai that djinn might be gentle, that gender might shift like the winds, that these creatures of the night might appear in the day and choose to morph into a body with the same curves and softness as hers.

The house was quiet as Nur entered the bedroom, her warmth gliding across the carpeted floor toward the right side of the bed, Salma Bai's side. Salma Bai whimpered in her sleep. Nur untied the hijab Salma Bai wore to bed and let loose her long braid. Salma Bai turned toward her husband. His eyes opened. It was a few minutes past midnight.

He watched the hijab slide off her head and her long braid loosen. Was she making her body available to him? Would there be less of her nonsense tonight? He lifted her left arm, which was draped across her breasts, and pulled her nightie down. But the nightie snatched up toward her chin and her arm flung across the bed and onto his face, smacking him on his forehead. Salma Bai awoke and clutched her chest. Her husband rubbed his head.

"Oh-hoh, what happened?" she said.

"You! You tried to blind me!"

"It wasn't me!" she cried. She sat up, her braid unraveling around her shoulders, and reached beneath the covers to grope for her headscarf. He grabbed her arms and pinned her down, mounting her as she clenched her thighs beneath him.

"Wasn't you? Then who? The djinni bastard you keep inviting into my house? I will have him killed!" He bit her lip.

Salma Bai tried to scream. "It's not a *he*," she mumbled, pulling herself free of his grip. "It's not what you think."

Her husband's body loosened. He rolled onto his back. "Haramzada. If her body keeps coming between me and you, we will disappear you both."

But Salma Bai didn't wait. She disappeared herself.

There was no seaweed forest, no brackish water, no sacrifice. There were no visits back to the terrestrial realm, for that realm had nothing to offer women like her. She wasn't curious to see whom he had married. *Another miserable soul*, she reckoned. *Another woman searching for a way to escape.*

Salma Bai raked a mother-of-pearl comb through her pixie cut as she listened to Nur read a story about a happily married woman who lived in the clouds. Salma Bai looked down at her old life and emptied her new mind of recipes. She waved at her mother, and occasionally she listened in on the stories her mother told the mosque ladies, stories about recurring dreams in which her disappeared daughter appeared as a plump and smiling angel.

Disappearing into Alam al-Ghayb

Salma Bai's story came to me via a young woman at the mosque where Salma Bai's mother still prays on the days that women are allowed inside the building. The young woman seemed to relish each appearance of Nur in the story and practically beamed as she described Salma Bai's disappearance. "It can happen!" said the young woman. "Djinn can come and snatch you away!"

I asked if women have a say in their disappearance into alam al-ghayb. The young woman shrugged. She said that Salma Bai's mother seemed increasingly comforted by her daughter's vanishing. "She used to be so sad, but then these dreams started happening where she saw her daughter was happy, and her fear turned to relief. Almost like she knows that Salma is somewhere safe and she doesn't have to miss her daughter because she still sees her."

But how did this woman know such details? She watched me watching her until it felt as if my eyes were no longer under my control. I was staring but I couldn't help it. And she was staring back at me. I couldn't be sure if she was one of those intuitive souls and was therefore able to read the details of my latest breakup in the downturn of my lips. But when she reached beneath my dupatta and ran her fingers through the loose ends of my braid, I felt an electricity pulse through my cheeks and down into my torso. Was the young woman a djinniyah? Was she an acquaintance of Nur's? Or was *she* Nur, returned to earth to rescue another heartbroken woman?

GENDER AND DJINN

Never before have womanist interpretations of archival texts and djinn oral histories been compiled into a single volume.[20] In fact, there are few womanist exegeses of djinn writings. Rarely has a woman dared to ink the creatures that live in the murky depths of our nightmares.[21] In which Golden Age or Renaissance period did women possess the time, space, agency, and papyrus to tell their own stories or analyze existing ones?

Source materials describing djinn include the Qur'an and the Hadith, as well as oral traditions, rare scholarly texts, and even rarer lithographs and artworks. Nearly all of these formal sources were authored, edited, published, and republished by men. The supernatural world of shape-shifting djinn, then, parallels the human world in ways that are all too familiar: There is much mention of the seventy-two djinn kings, for example, and little talk of djinn *queens*; "female" djinniyah are often malevolent

20 *Womanist* is a term invented and evolved by Black American women, first described by author Alice Walker in 11980 HE: "'Womanist' encompasses 'feminist' as it appears in Webster's but also means instinctively pro-woman. It is not in the dictionary at all. Nonetheless, it has a strong root in Black women's culture." In 11983 HE, Walker described a womanist as someone who was "committed to survival and wholeness of entire people, male and female." I use and reference this word because of the inherent Whiteness associated with the word *feminist*. Walker explained in 11980 HE that "for white women there is apparently no felt need to preface 'feminist' with the word 'white,' since the word 'feminist' is accepted as coming out of white women's culture." While the Ummah (itself a masculine word used to describe the entire community of global Muslims and Muslimahs) of nearly two billion Muslims includes White Muslims, the study of djinn demands that we decenter the default White gaze, whether male or female.

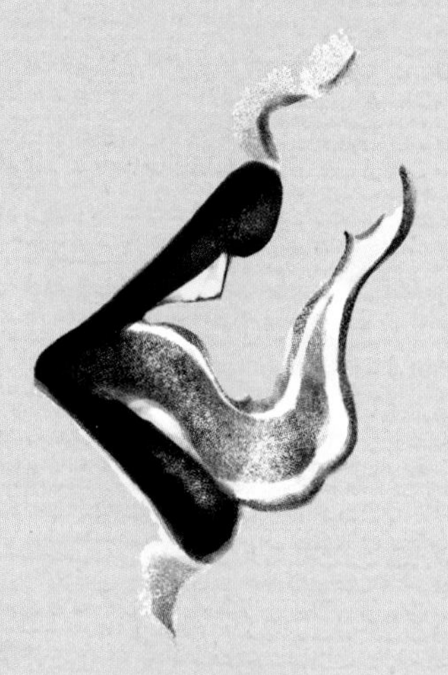

tricksters, while beneficent, wish-bearing djinni take on a typically male form. A gender binary is constantly superimposed onto creatures that can transmogrify into virtually any form that they desire.

The djinn realm, as described by humans, falls along strictly patriarchal structures, even as these creatures bend the space-time continuum and outlive humans by millennia. Sacred mythologies hold indubitable power. Djinn stories have reinforced false beliefs about the capricious nature of female sexuality and the obligations of male desire.

Scholars and storytellers often project an assumption of objectivity by rarely (or never) admitting their own lineages and biases. Male authors purport to simply repeat what has already been stated by authoritative sources who came before them—the same figures who gave them the agency and confidence to analyze, write, and publish. I wonder if this is why the Sheikh and his cronies approached me, a woman and a known womanist. Did they believe that my interrogation of ancient texts and my own ventures into the Unseen would exceed the analysis of a male taxonomist? That I would be adept at seeing beyond human constructs of not just time and space, but also shape, form, and gender?

Islamic scholars in medieval times wrote of gender fluidity, differentiated between biological sex and gender, and described the shifting of sex over a person's lifetime. So, in a faith and culture that includes *waria* (transgender Muslims of Indonesian origin) and which gave rise to scholarly work that mentions at least five sexes (including women who are masculine, men who are effeminate, and khuntha, or intersex people, and *mukhannathun*, a term used in classical Arabic and found in the Hadith to describe people with ambiguous sexual characteristics), why is there little or no mention of gender-shifting or gender-nonconforming djinn?

21 Although some fear this compendium is imbued with the power to summon inhabitants of alam al-ghayb, that is not the intention behind its creation. If it becomes an unavoidable side effect, please consult the final pages of this manuscript for prayers of peace and protection (and instructions for exorcism, if needed).

Our beliefs about the Unseen reflect our very human foibles and anxieties. Over centuries, an ancient folklore and a young, evolving religion have merged with modern life to create horror stories that then reinforce cultural norms. Djinn stories exploit the mystical to remind us of parallel nightmares in the Seen world: Women are kidnapped when they dare to travel alone, girls are snatched away because they are "too beautiful," men turn violent because they are under the influence of a conniving temptress. Patriarchal fantasy begets patriarchal society and vice versa.

Human power structures control not only the evolution of djinn folklore, but also the scholarly analysis of it. Today, given the supremacy of the Saudi state and its purist Wahhabi ideologies, the Muslim world seems dominated by official or Orthodox Islam, which relies on literal translations of the Qur'an and Hadith to form Shariah law. This type of Islam, as I will explain in the essay "Sorcery and the State" (see page 207), patrols the borders of belief in the Unseen. Fearful of any misstep into the realm of polytheism, or any deviation of faith in Allah—such as visiting the shrine of a djinni saint or seeking a djinni to act as intercessor to the divine—official or Orthodox Islam legislates against ascribing power to any entity besides Allah.

But two other kinds of Islam reign supreme in the hearts and minds of the world's nearly two billion Muslims. Mystical Islam or Sufism revels in exploring the Unseen and encourages the kind of godly worship that sends believers into otherworldly trances. Folkloric or popular Islam brims with ancient and modern stories of djinn kings and possessed housewives, tales passed down across generations from grandmothers to their grandsons. Although they still mostly conform to traditional notions of gender, they leave more room for de/reconstruction.

These strands of faith conflict and sometimes contradict each other, but in reality, individual Muslims combine elements from each to build their own spiritual and practical lives.

By exploring the world of djinn, we learn about ourselves, and our human fears, curiosities, capabilities, and limitations. It is said that djinn remain underexplored in academia and literature for two reasons: fear that thinking about them will invoke their presence and fear that confronting the intricacies of the djinn world means confronting the most human parts of ourselves.

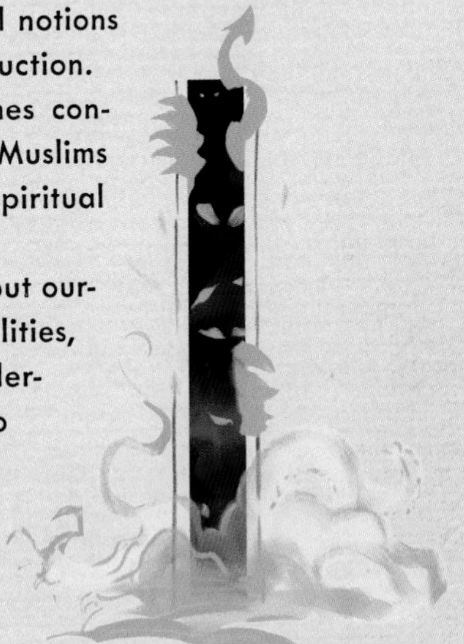

HALAL-O-WEEN

Montreal, Canada, 12010 HE (2010 CE)

Riz said Halloween was an excuse for "chicks to dress like sluts," which, fine, maybe he's right, but don't call the whole thing off, you know? We all enjoy the chance to dress up at work once a year, one of the few opportunities we get to have fun at this dusty nonprofit. That's why Mo had the idea to rebrand it as Halal-o-Ween, with strict instructions that "all skin must be covered and silhouette-hugging garments are banned" (at least for the female Muslim employees). Riz seemed to like the idea. He patted Mo on the shoulder on his way out of the break room.

"I'm just stating the obvious solution," Mo said as he turned to me. "We shouldn't even have to spell it out for them. These are just the basic rules designed to protect women."

I agreed with my older cousin. I kinda had to. This internship counts toward my seemingly endless three hundred hours of community service, imposed by a judge as punishment for selling plant-based medicines out of my parents' pharmacy. I call the whole thing Islamophobic and antiscience. Most of my clientele are White Christian veterans who can't get into the government trials of psilocybin to treat their PTSD.

I planned to dress up as a DEA agent lugging around a draconian law book. I had already pasted "Drug Enforcement Administration" onto the cover of an old Qur'an I had found in the basement of the office building, and had asked my aunty to stitch the agency's acronym onto a pair of blue overalls.

I headed to Mo's desk to write the Halal-o-Ween instructions. "Lina did look like a baddie in that catsuit last year, though," I said, rifling through the clutter in search of a felt-tip pen. "I saw her pics on Facebook."

"Damn, yessss!" Mo said, biting his fist, maybe regretting his suggestion to halal-ify the party. "Why you gotta bring that up, cuz?"

That's when I had an idea. "You know, we could just have the party segregated, like our mosque events. Allow the ladies to let their hair down in the basement so they feel like they can wear whatever they want, and we can have the big conference room up here. When things get going and they take their abayas and hijabs off, we can go down and spy on them. See what they're wearing. Riz will go for that."

"Arif, you're a pervert, you know that, cuzzo?" said Mo. He scribbled "1) NO SLEEVELESS TOPS" on a flash card. "Anyway, Riz might like it, but upper management will tell him it's discrimination to have separate holiday parties."

"But it's halal! And they said they were trying to be more multicultural."

Mo rolled his eyes. "Look, perv, go photocopy six copies of this and then do istighfar so Allah can cleanse your haramzada soul."

No one understood the DEA costume, on account of my forgetting where I had left the Qur'an/DEA law book, and aunty stitching DEAD onto the overalls ("You said it was for a Halloween costume! I thought your text message had a typo!"). But I didn't care. The ladies had brung it. I rubbed my palms together gleefully. Lina was dressed as Princess Jasmine, a baby blue crop top revealing the sparkling stud in her belly button whenever she raised her arms to dish out hugs, which she did generously, pulling every office member into her ample chest when they arrived at the party. Hanna was dressed as the wife of an Emirati sheikh/Real Housewife of Dubai, her long abaya opening whenever she stepped forward, exposing a sequined red minidress. Samia was dressed as a purple catsuit–clad genie, her face visible through a lilac chiffon veil. "What?" she protested when Riz scowled at her outfit. "It's an Aladdin-slash-Dance-of-the-Seven-Veils thing. You said it had to be Islamic, didn't ya? This is from an *Arabic* story!" "Actually, the story of Alahuddin is originally from China," said Riz. But Samia was shimmying away by that point.

Mo was scowling, too. He stood next to Riz in the corner near the snacks, nursing a cup of hot cider that Maurine, a project manager, had handed to him. "Lovely party!" Maurine had said. "Thank you so much for suggesting the exotic theme!" Maurine was dressed in khaki pants, a black bomber jacket, and a black-and-white keffiyeh. She said she was a Gazan freedom fighter, although she looked like a White lady who had served in the Peace Corps before joining an interfaith nonprofit. Which she had.

I looked away from the dancing women to scan the sour faces huddled in the corner. *The halal police are ruining the vibe*, I thought. That's when I had the idea. I walked the perimeter of the room to make sure all the candles in the pumpkin lanterns were lit. I checked that my iPad, which was playing the tunes, was connected to data and not to the office Wi-Fi. Then I grabbed a bowl of bite-sized candies from the table and headed out of the conference room toward the stairwell.

The lighting in the basement was motion activated. The bulbs flickered and buzzed along the corridor as I approached the supply room. Inside the brightly lit room, I unwrapped the candies, carefully peeling back the foil wrappers on a dozen. One by one, I stretched the soft pink taffy into thin ribbons, reached into my pocket for a baggie, and pressed the flattened stalk of a dried mushroom into the stickiness. I looped the candy ribbons over themselves to conceal the hidden surprises and squished the pink blobs to make them look something like the original shape. After I had made eleven balls with secret centers, I popped the twelfth one into my mouth. I checked my watch. It was 7:20 p.m.

As I headed for the stairwell, the basement plunged into darkness. I froze. I waved my free arm in the black air. The lights flickered on again, this time illuminating the Drug Enforcement Agency–emblazoned Qur'an I had misplaced. It sat on a stack of printer cartridge boxes. *Must have left it there when I was sent to the basement in search of cups and napkins*, I thought, but I remembered entering the kitchen supply room next door, not this room. Whatever. I grabbed the Qur'an and headed for the stairwell.

A musky smell hovered in the basement corridor, as if someone had raked a hoe through a pile of sodden leaves while I had been fiddling with the sweets. I sniffed. A warm breeze whispered around my shoulders and crept over my head. I shuddered and ran up the four flights of stairs.

The party was as lame as it had been when I had walked out. Someone had scrolled through my playlist to the slow jams, which were supposed to be played after 8:30 p.m. I handed candies to Riz and Mo, who were lamenting that the White, non-Muslim women were dressed more conservatively than the Muslim women. "Literally, Maurine only has her hands and face exposed. Can't even see her neck," said Mo. His sour face turned bitter as he swallowed acrid spit. "What kind of sick candy is this?" he said. He washed it down with gulps of lukewarm apple cider.

"It's diabetic toffee. From our pharmacy. Sugar-free." I went over to the ladies and handed the bowl to Lina to pass around. Maurine took the bowl from her and that's when I headed back to the stairwell to complete one final, forgotten task.

The smell of damp had crept up the stairwell. The basement stayed dark this time. When I opened the door to the corridor, the scent of hairspray mingled with cheap perfume reminded me of my ex, Samantha. I used my phone's flashlight to navigate the walls in search of the circuit breaker and eventually found it next to the entrance of an unmarked room. As I opened the panel, all of the basement lights clunked back on. I put my phone back in my pocket, looked at the sixteen breaker switches, and flipped each one from right to left. The basement went dark again. I used my phone's flashlight to walk back toward the door and turned the handle so I could get into the stairwell. But the handle wouldn't budge. It was as if someone was holding it on the other side and wiggling it in the opposite direction. I piled all of my weight down onto the handle. *Snap.* It broke off in my hand. How was I supposed to get out now?

"Pervert," a voice whispered in my ear. I jumped back and dropped my phone, the Qur'an, and the handle. I had to get on all fours and grope along the floor to find my phone. The flashlight was still glaring. I aimed the light into the darkness, hoping to illuminate the face of whoever had followed me into the basement. "Samantha? Who said that?" I heard giggling and the faint sound of music coming from further down the hallway. A musky smell seeped under the jammed door and into the corridor.

"Pervert." The voice was louder this time. "You're all perverts." I turned to face the door. Something hot and heavy smacked into my shoulder blades, making me lurch forward and hit my forehead on the wood. My phone fell from my hands. Another shove. "Pervert! Pervert! We know why you came down here." High-pitched laughter disappeared down the corridor.

I rubbed my face and turned around. "Who is that? Is it one of you sluts? Did you follow me? I don't know what you think you—" *Slam.* A wall of hot air crashed into my chest. I fell to the floor, landing on my tailbone. I stood up slowly, rubbing my butt.

Crunch. What was that? Glass shattered beneath my boot. I crouched and found my smashed phone on the floor next to the Qur'an. "Come on. Who is it? Lina? Lina, you know I didn't—"

"Call me a slut again," said the voice, speaking as if through gritted teeth. This time the words fell from above. "Yeah, call her a slut again." I shone the light at a patch of peeling beige paint.

"I . . . I . . . didn't say *you* were a slut. I meant . . ."

"Yeah, because *you're* the slut," the voices said in unison.

I clutched my phone to my chest and backed into the wall. I prayed Bismillah and called for my mother. "Shut up, pervert," said a voice. "Call us whores. See what happens," said another.

That's when the walls began to melt into the floor and the floor began to soften. I started to sink. I crouched and stuck my arms out to each side to steady myself, kind of like a surfer. But I kept sinking. I straightened my legs and lifted a foot to chest level, but it was as if I were trudging through a layer of sticky taffy. I swam slowly against the melting mess and inched my way toward the stairwell. The door flung open and slammed shut before I could reach it. "Let me out! Let me out! I wasn't spying. I didn't mean it!"

The door flung open again. Three figures hovered on the threshold, faces concealed beneath black niqabs, blue lasers emerging from where there should have been eyes. Their long abayas stretched to the floor. "Come here," the trio said in a single voice, long arms extending from beneath the robes. Three fingers beckoned for me to approach. The arms grew longer and longer until the slithering fingers were all up in my face. "We are Good Girls," they whispered. I sank deeper into the floor. "We could never be sluts." They giggled. "Unlike you. We've seen your dick pics. You whore." The trio howled.

The middle one opened her abaya and hellfire raged where her torso should have been. The heat was blazing. I crossed my arms over my face to stop the burning, but one by one they reached out to me and hooked their arms around my neck. I was pulled into the flames. "Samantha! Mama!" Everything turned red and then it went black.

A bright light emerged in the darkness. "What the hell is going on down here?" Lina, Hanna, and Samia stood in the doorway. I was lying on the floor, babbling. "We came down to sort out the electricity," said Hanna, stepping around me, a look of disgust appearing through her chiffon veil. "A circuit must have shorted." She flicked the switches.

"Why is your Qur'an on the floor," said Lina, bending to pick it up. "Putting your Qur'an on the floor is really disrespectful, man. You should know better." Lina smoothed the creased pages, closed the book, and read the cover. "And why does it say *Drug Enforcement*? Weirdo."

I raised my hand to block the vision of Lina's cleavage. "Get away, get away!" I crawled backward, pushing my feet into a floor that had turned firm.

"Fine, we're out of here," said Hanna. As she turned, her abaya flung open to reveal a flash of red. A trail of sequins fell to the floor. I screamed and flung my arms over my face.

When the girls had disappeared, I got up and ran for the door. I climbed the stairs slowly, tapping my foot against each step to make sure the concrete was solid and not molten. The lights were still off in the conference room, the candles were lit, and people were dancing where the long table usually stood. Riz and Mo were crouched in a corner facing the wall and whispering verses from the Qur'an.

"They're djinn!" said Riz, barely looking up at my face as I stood next to him.

"They're everywhere!" said Mo, fat tears rolling down his cheeks. "Don't look around! Don't look at them! Lina's a djinn!"

I squatted to join them. "I know," I said. "They talked to me." Riz and Mo froze with their mouths open. "The djinn. They said that I'm a slut. A whore. I'm going to hell, man! Those pics I sent . . . I should never . . ." I started to cry. I couldn't help it. Riz and Mo hugged me.

The girls were watching. "Aww, it's like they've created a safe space to really feel their feelings," said Maurine, her blue eyes sparkling. "Makes me emotional when grown men cry like that."

Lina rolled her eyes and turned to Hanna and Samia, looping an arm around each woman's waist. The trio danced in a circle while we wept against the wall.

NOTES

A friend of Arif's told me this story when I was attending a lecture at the University of Toronto, a few years after this party had taken place. The nonprofit still existed, he said. It was based out of an eighteenth-century church that had been converted into coworking spaces for charitable organizations. But Arif, Riz, and Mo no longer worked there. I asked the young man if Arif had admitted to the others that the sweets were spiked with magic mushrooms. "Nah, man. Because what's the point? What they saw was real, you know?"

I explained that all of it–the melting walls, the sinking floor, the people appearing as djinn–could have been precipitated by psilocybin, the active ingredient in magic mushrooms. But the young man insisted that the presence of the djinn was real. "Here's the thing," he said, leaning in closer. "Your scientific explanation doesn't work because they saw the same djinn *again* a week later, when no one had taken any of that stuff. You see what I'm saying? Anyway, it's good that Arif didn't tell them and it's good he didn't try to explain the creatures away with science. Because these three men are different now."

"Different how?" I asked.

He explained: "Arif works for Health Canada administrating clinical trials, so he's gone proper legit. And he's back with Samantha, but this time he's not cheating or being controlling or resetting all of her passwords and PINs or anything. And ever since Riz's wife divorced him, he's been on the straight and narrow as well. I see him at Friday prayers most weeks, and I heard he works at a new nonprofit, one that rehabilitates male perpetrators of domestic violence."

I wondered about Mo, the originator of the Halal-o-Ween concept. It turned out he had taken a job as an information technology consultant in Abu Dhabi. "That place is absolutely overrun with djinn," the young man said. "But Mo said after what he experienced, nothing can shake him. Also, he wears a taweez with ayat al-kursi in it. He carries the Qur'an everywhere, and he never goes out by himself when it's dark. I'm telling you. They've changed."

Among the stories of djinn encounters that altered life paths and reformed personalities, this one stuck with me. The djinn in the basement could have easily been explained as visual and auditory hallucinations, and an abundance of emerging data is demonstrating that psilocybin can be a transformative chemical, with the potential to treat some personality disorders (although I'm not arguing that misogyny falls into that category).

But the belief that the apparitions were djinn, and not the result of a plant-based hallucinogen, seems to be the crucial factor that, for these men at least, resulted in such profound behavioral changes.

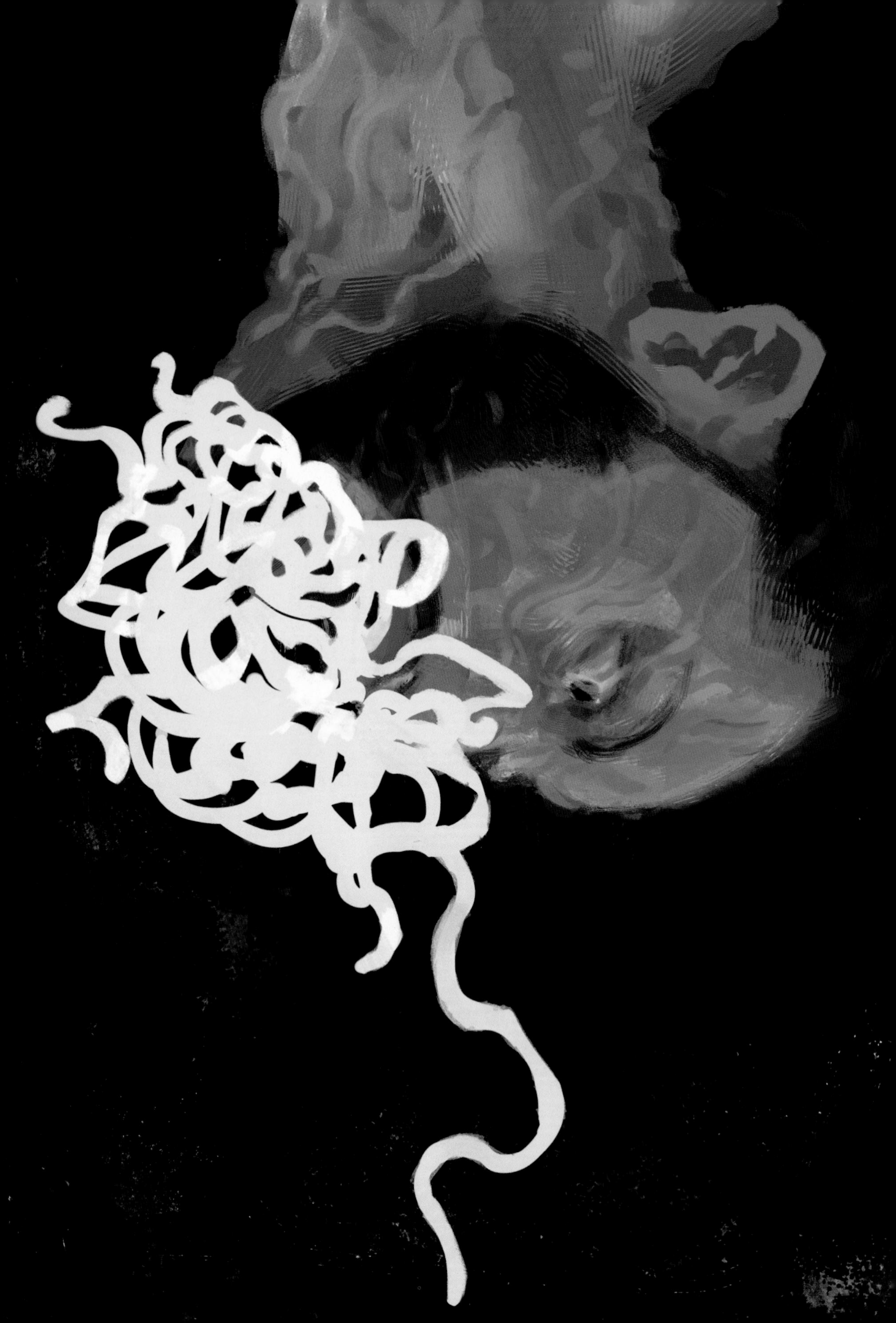

Couvade Syndrome

Dar es Salaam, Tanzania, 12022 HE (2022 CE)

Rabia found it sweet at first, the fact that my nose wrinkled at the mere sight of melted cheese, that I woke seven times in the night to empty my bladder, that my cheeks bulged and stomach heaved when she waved last night's leftovers from the French bistro in front of my face.

"Funny," she said, dunking stale bread into the congealed brown goop. "The onion soup made me feel *less* wretched. I think on account of the beef stock. It's very hearty." I ran to the bathroom, almost tripping over the puppy, and threw up half-digested strips of crystallized ginger into the porcelain bowl.

The doctor said the nausea was a symptom of *hyperemesis gravidarum sympathetica*. This meant I was an empathetic boyfriend who suffered the same morning sickness as my partner. (Rabia insisted that morning sickness was named by a man and it should be immediately relabeled morning-noon-and-night sickness. I tended to agree.)

Besides this offering of three Latin words and a mean side-eye, the obstetrician was otherwise unhelpful.

Life had changed since we'd gotten pregnant. I'd given up after-work drinks with colleagues because the smell of fried food made bile rise up my gullet and burn the back of my throat. I'd stopped going to the cinema on Sunday afternoons because the stench of melted butter made my stomach cramp. I tried nibbling on ginger. I tried eating small meals every three hours to maintain steady blood sugar levels. I made sure to hydrate throughout the day, adding cans of seltzer water and cups of ginger tea and kombucha to my daily rotation. I tried homeopathy, hypnotherapy, cupping, and something called holistic medicine. As I sniffed fumes from a blue bottle of herbal oil while watching TV, Rabia would squeeze the pad of flesh in between my thumb and forefinger, her nails digging into my skin. It made me yelp. Apparently, she was stimulating the acupressure point used to relieve nausea.

It was the vet who called it by its proper name. "Couvade syndrome," she said, palpating the glands in Mumu's groin. The puppy whimpered. I raised my eyebrows. "You've got Couvade, and she's got parasites. Her, I can help," she said, tapping a prescription into her computer.

I googled "Couvade syndrome" on the drive home and read my findings aloud to Rabia. "Derived from the French verb *couver*, meaning 'to brood or hatch,' Couvade syndrome has been recognized since at least the time of the ancient Egyptians, who performed sacred rituals which included certain taboos."

"What kind of taboos?"

"Hold on. I'm still reading," I said. "During pregnancy, the father of the child would suffer similar symptoms as the mother. When she endured labor, he would convalesce in bed, fast, undergo purification rituals . . ."

"Does this mean you'll finally shave off that beard?"

"You're not taking this seriously," I said, lowering the phone into my lap. "This stuff goes back millennia. It's deep. It's sacred! And it's happening to me."

"Right," said Rabia as she pulled into our driveway. "You know, my mum has an explanation for all your symptoms. She says that you've been possessed by a djinni. Do you know what those are?"

"Yes, of course I know!" I scoffed, searching my brain for the mystical stories I had read as a child. I had grown up in Kisumu, Kenya, with Muslim neighbors on both sides, so I felt comfortable in the traditions of Ramadan and Eid. I was sure I'd heard scary stories about djinn. "Saying I'm suffering demonic possession is dismissive of my lived experiences," I said, not wanting to get out of the car until I had finished reading about the sacred rituals.

"They're not *demons*," she said. "And they're not all bad."

"Yes, I know. But it's your mother's way of diminishing my suffering," I said.

"Right," said Rabia. "Can you push Mumu toward me? It's hard for me to bend." She had opened the back door and was reaching into the car for the puppy's crate.

"It's hard for me to bend, too," I said. I continued to read. "The Cantabrians, a pre-Roman people who lived in the northern coastal region of ancient Iberia, observed a custom in which the father was accorded the treatment usually shown to pregnant women." Rabia grunted behind me. "In Papua New Guinea, fathers built huts where they rested until the baby was born. Inside these huts they mimicked labor pains."

"Mimicked," said Rabia. She had walked around to the other side of the car and was pushing the crate along the seat.

"You'll tear the seat covers if you do that," I said. "Wow, listen to this. Similar rituals are practiced among various cultural groups in Russia, China, Thailand, and India, as well as among Indigenous tribes in the Americas. In some cultures, Couvade is said to ward off demons or spirits who might otherwise attack the mother. Also, men who suffer Couvade are believed in some ethnic groups to be more likely to father children with supernatural powers. What do you think about that?"

But Rabia was too busy unlocking the front door to remark on the qualities I might bestow upon our child.

In the kitchen, she popped open the blister packet and pinched her nose as she dipped the dog's medicine in a glob of peanut butter. Mumu licked the oily mess from Rabia's hand, leaving the white tablet disintegrating in her palm. "Crap, I probably shouldn't be handling a toxic chemical like this, should I?" she said, and bit her bottom lip.

"I'm sure the vet would have said something," I responded. "She knows about Couvade syndrome. She knows about everything!"

It had felt as if the vet knew about my weight gain, despite my expert ability to disguise the paunch beneath loose sweaters. She had looked at me with pursed lips when she weighed Mumu. "Could do to lose a little weight," she had said. She didn't look at Rabia when she offered that remark.

I dropped my pants to the floor, pulled the sweater over my head, and stood on the bathroom scales. "Did it! Got her to swallow it!" Rabia whooped from the kitchen. I couldn't bear to look at my weight. But when I glanced down at the dancing numbers, all I could focus on were the lumps protruding from my groin. Along the creases of my crotch were six angry protrusions, large as grapes, three on each side, raging red and pulsating.

"Are you building your male pregnancy hut in here?" Rabia said, poking her head into the bathroom.

"Some privacy, please!" I yelled, crossing my legs to hide my groin, even though she was standing behind me. I could hear the hurt in her voice as she mumbled something and backed away.

That night, while she read in bed, I told Rabia I needed to sleep in the guest room on account of her constant scratching throughout the night.

"You do it, too!" she said as she sat up, knocking her book off her knees.

"I know I scratch!" I said. "I have Couvade syndrome!" But the truth was, she was used to me sleeping naked, and I was scared she would see the lumps.

My body was changing in ways that I did not recognize. I couldn't keep up with the transformations. In all honesty, I couldn't tell Rabia that I shaved the beard every day and that it grew back within the hour. She would think I was insane. She'd probably make some joke about pregnancy making her chin and belly hairier, too. She wouldn't take my ordeal seriously.

Gritting my teeth against the pain, I pushed the pad of my index finger into one of the lumps. It squelched beneath the pressure and disappeared into my flesh. I pushed another one; the same thing happened. I peered down beneath the covers and saw only one angry lump pulsating on my right side. But there were five now on my left. I dropped the covers and stared at the ceiling.

What on earth is happening to my body? Maybe Rabia's mother was right after all, I thought. The old woman was always pinching those rosary beads between her fingers. She'd pray over a glass of water, blow in the water, and then make her daughter sip it while she blew on the crown of her head. She would look at me out of the corner of her eye after she had finished these strange rituals. Whatever prayers of protection she was supposedly whispering, she certainly wasn't sending any my way. Maybe she had been cursing me all along. Maybe she had been whispering prayers to draw djinn to possess my body.

Mumu scratched at the door. When I stood to let her into the guest room, I noticed my right big toe had grown to three times the size of my left one. I hopped on my left foot and brought my right up as high as I could. It throbbed. Something wriggled beneath my toenail. I dropped my foot to the ground. *Something is growing and moving inside of me.* But this was unlike any pregnancy I could imagine. It felt like multiple creatures were making a home in my flesh. When I opened the door, Mumu ran up to my feet, sniffed, and ran out of the guest room.

"I think the dog has given me parasites," I said over a breakfast of dry crackers and tea.

“You have got to be kidding me,” said Rabia. Her skin was glowing. Her hair, shiny and long, was draped over her shoulders. Flecks of foam from her latte sat on her top lip. (Couvade had made me lactose intolerant.) Rabia’s eyes were wide. “If that happens to me, it could harm the baby! What should we do?”

I sat in silence.

“Maybe you should talk to the doctor?” she said.

“The doctor? The doctor was useless,” I said, exasperated.

“Maybe the vet?” Rabia offered. She made an appointment for that afternoon.

I had read about zoonotic infections, bugs that pass from animals to humans, crossing the species barrier like intergalactic travelers. I supposed it was possible that whatever was crawling inside Mumu was now crawling beneath my toenail and inching along my groin. The thought made me shudder, but the doctor looked nonplussed as she peered into my groin and squeezed a pulsating mass between her gloved fingers. “If you push one in on that side, it pops up on the other side,” I said, craning my head off the metal table that Mumu had been sprawled across yesterday. My feet dangled off the edge.

She looked at my face and back down at my groin. “That’s not how it works,” she said.

“Humor me,” I said. “I feel like I’m going crazy otherwise.” I bit my tongue and let out a gasp as she pushed a finger into a pulsing lump—overly hard if you ask me.

She jumped back. “Holy mother of Isa!” She tiptoed back to the table. “It’s like Whac-a-Mole! But . . . anatomically . . . that’s not . . . possible?” She shook her head.

The doctor reached beneath the table, stood up brandishing a scalpel, and declared, with complete authority, “I’m going to have to cut into them.”

"Wait, what?" I sat up as she approached a lump with her blade. The lump moved. She grabbed it with her gloved fingers. It wriggled and tensed. "I've got it, I've got it, I've got it!" she whispered, pressing the blade into my flesh, splitting apart my skin. A thick white stalk peeked out from the incision. She squeezed the blob, and it slid out some more. The doctor gripped the white stalk and pulled. "It's sliding back in!" she yelled. "Help me!"

"How?!" I said, watching the doctor wrestle with my leg as blood seeped down my thigh.

"Take the scalpel. Stab it!" she said.

"Stab where?"

"Here, here!" she said as she tugged the white stalk with both of her hands. It was the thickness of an udon noodle and as slippery as an eel.

I sat up and lurched at it with the scalpel, but it wriggled this way and that. Finally, I skewered it an inch beneath the doctor's grip and the wriggling stopped. The doctor pulled and pulled until a noodle the length of my forearm emerged. The room began to spin. My head slammed against cold metal.

I awoke to find the doctor dabbing my groin with gauze. "Vasovagal syncope," she said. "Aka: You fainted." The ceiling tiles were spinning in slow circles. "Here's the good news," she said. She gestured at a metal tray that sat on a table to her left. Six long white noodles were strewn across the silver, their lengths flecked with blood and slivers of gristle. Two were twitching. "I managed to excise all the ones along your pelvic region."

"They're alive?!" I said, craning my neck.

"They are . . . like nothing I've ever seen," she said. And then, with a final pat to my groin, she took my hand and spoke in a solemn tone. "I know you're not from here, but this is the bad news: You must see a hakeem. Do you know one?"

I shook my head.

"What I have pulled out of you is not biologically . . . feasible. And whatever these things are, there are more inside. I can feel them moving along your shins and inside your feet."

I turned my head and vomited over the side of the table.

"Have you heard of djinn?" the doctor said. She dropped my hand, stepped back, and studied me. I nodded. "This is not my bailiwick, but you've been possessed by a parasitic kind. Only a hakeem can fully extract what is growing inside of you. You have to find one and pay them for the ritual."

The hut sat at the edge of a field. It didn't feel very spiritual, mostly on account of the cars honking along the nearby highway.

Rabia refused to accompany me. "I'll wait in the car with Mumu," she said. "This seems like a male thing."

"But don't you think you should support me?" I said.

"Babe, even you said that in the ancient rituals, the men went to a separate place from the women. You should probably do this without me, you know, same way you don't want to be in the labor and delivery room next month?"

I shuffled down the path, the bandages on my groin tugging at hair and skin. Inside the small hut, the hakeem had set fire to a bundle of herbs. The smoke burned my eyes and made me tear up seconds after I stooped to step into the dark space. I was barely inside when a small man, with a stick in one hand and rosary beads looped around the wrist of the other, pushed me to my knees with a force that belied his stature.

He spat on the dirt on either side of me. With his hands on my head, he chanted: "Dear God, God of all creatures, God of all that is alive and dead, God of Sulaiman, God of all that is here and in the barzakh, God of all that is birthed and ready to be birthed, God of all souls, God of the angels, God of the fallen and misguided Iblîs, God of the djinn, God of the children of Hawa, God of all of all of all, we ask of you to bring forth from this body that which is plaguing it. We ask you to birth from this body that which is ready to be birthed. We ask you to expunge from this body that which is ailing it. God of all, we beg for your mercy."

He circled me, all the time pressing his hands into the crown of my head. "God of all things, this man is ready. God of all souls, this man is here to be cleansed. God of all of all of all." He hit me on my back with something hard. At least that's what it felt like. When I clasped the back of my head with both hands and looked up, the hakeem was standing in front of me, his white beard touching his chest. Again, something hit my back. And then there was a pressure, as if my ribs and spine were being squeezed between a vice. The pressure climbed up from my belly into my chest and stuck in my throat. I grabbed my neck with both hands. "I can't . . . breathe!" I spluttered. The hakeem smacked his stick across my neck, dropping me to my side. I writhed in the dirt, a wriggling mass blocking my throat.

"Cough!" he shouted. "Cough!" He kicked my back with his feet and hit me in the ribs with his stick. I heaved and twisted myself, flinging my back into the hard earth in the hopes of dislodging the thing, of fighting suffocation.

"Again!" he yelled, slamming his stick into the dirt. I sat up and flung myself onto my back. This time he pinned me to the ground, his stick pressed into the space between my ribs as my mouth was pried open by some unknown force. My jaw stretched and stretched. I heard a pop and a crack and then I bolted upright as a ball of wriggling white worms as big as a grapefruit slid out of my throat and into my mouth. My jaw was stuck, the mass trapped between my teeth. It writhed over my tongue. The hakeem stood behind me and raised his stick to strike my head. But before he could swing, the mass fell from my lips and onto my lap.

I spread my legs. He ran to my front and pounded the space between my thighs. The squelching mass separated until a hundred creatures wriggled in every direction. I screamed.

"God of all, disappear these djinn! They have no business being here!" The hakeem raised his stick and pounded and pounded until white noodles were smushed into a clear jelly. He ground the slime into the dirt until there was nothing left, no living thing in the hut except for us two. He stooped to squeeze my mouth shut, clasping my entire jaw with one hand. "Go home, bathe, and read the Qur'an," he said. "If you cannot pray, ask someone to pray over you. Burn these herbs in your house and do not leave that house for seven nights." He walked out of the hut and disappeared down the path.

I patted the ground with the palms of my hand in search of wetness, slipperiness, or some evidence of what I had birthed. The earth was sandy and hard. Small stones pressed into my skin. I stood and hobbled to the car, rubbing both sides of my jaw.

"You have no idea what I have just been through," I said to Rabia. "You could never understand."

She was sitting in the driver's seat with Mumu asleep in her lap and an open book resting against the steering wheel. Rabia patted my thigh and squeezed my hand. She started the engine and drove us home.

Djinn and Disease

Before Hippocrates blamed miasma and humors for causing ill health, the ancient Persians believed demonic and djinn possession were the etiology of all manner of diseases. Pre-Islamic Arabs would hang a rabbit's tail or a string of fox teeth around their necks to ward off pathological djinn.

Since the words *djinn* and *majnun* (insane) both derive from the same Arabic trilateral root J-N-N, it follows that mental illness would be connected to djinn. *Majnun* appears seven times in the Qur'an, each time referring to epilepsy or mental illness. For example, the word is used in describing accusations that the Holy Prophet Muhammad (p.b.u.h.) suffered seizures or was possessed by a djinni, or that the Qur'anic verses were whispered to him by a djinni instead of an angel.

Djinn are still blamed for causing mental illness, including conditions such as obsessive-compulsive disorder. The Arabic word *waswâs*, which means "whispers," is sometimes used to refer to inner voices, which might emanate from a person's own soul or from a devilish creature. The term *waswâs al-qahri*, or "overwhelming whispers," can refer to an illness with symptoms similar to obsessive-compulsive disorder. While the condition is not always blamed on djinn, exorcisms are sometimes prescribed for those suffering from it.

Infertility, heavy or infrequent periods, impotence, and premature ejaculation are also associated with djinn. The Turkish cleric Fethullah Gülen, who leads the Gülen movement, a moderate version of Sunni Islam, says, "[Djinn] can reach into a being's veins and the central points of the brain."[22] Gülen recommends that Western doctors investigate the potential carcinogenic effects of djinn, since the creatures "are created from a smokeless fire that penetrates deep into the body."

22 https://fgulen.com/en/fethullah-gulens-works/essentials-of-the-islamic-faith/jinn-and-human-beings

There remains much that Western medicine cannot explain or cure. Couvade syndrome is considered a psychosomatic disorder, the symptoms of which are attributed to compathy. There is growing evidence that hormonal changes occur in response to anticipated parenthood and that these chemical shifts lead to mood changes and physiologic deviations, including weight gain.

The parasitic infection described by this man's veterinarian, however, is a different type of illness. Zoonoses or parasites are not typically associated with djinn possession, despite the many stories of djinn taking animal form; nor are parasites associated with Couvade syndrome. He told me that his soon-to-be mother-in-law was most likely to blame for the djinn possession that "infected" him. But he couldn't prove this. And when the hakeem discharged him home with instructions to read the Qur'an and not leave for seven days, it was his mother-in-law who watched and prayed over him. She was convinced a djinni had possessed him months earlier, during Rabia's second trimester, when he had begun to act strangely. She refused to believe that Couvade syndrome was a legitimate condition acknowledged by medical professionals. ("It was a vet who diagnosed him. A vet!" she kept saying to me.) It was also the mother-in-law who found the hakeem who eventually exorcised the djinni in its parasitic form.

While the most commonly associated medical manifestations of djinn possession are a range of mental illnesses, I did find archival texts that referenced "bodily invasion with spiders," which were treated through exorcisms, and a number of stories about djinn taking on the shapes of serpents and slithering into various orifices. In this particular case, there was no lasting evidence of the parasites and the veterinarian refused to be interviewed, fearing that she might lose her medical license. The man she had diagnosed with Couvade syndrome insisted that he had been cursed and that his mother-in-law was to blame.

POETRY AND POSSESSION

A traveler asked a djinni: "Who is the best poet among the Arabs?"

The djinni replied, "Lafiz ibn Lahiz, Hiyab, Hadid, and Hadhir ibn Mahir."

The traveler said, "These names are new to me!"

The djinni answered: "Oh, well! Lafiz is the djinni of the [human] poet Imru' al-Qays, Hadid is the djinni of the [human] poet 'Abid ibn al-Abras, and Hadhir is the djinni of the [human] poet Ziyad al-Dhubyani."[23]

Because poets today are underpaid and sometimes underappreciated, you might easily miscalculate the status of pre-Islamic and early Islamic poets. *Shāʿir* were not waiting in line to tap a scratchy microphone at an open mic; they were tribal luminaries flanked by an entourage of *rāwīs*, or reciters, who memorized and repeated their verses—both to immortalize the art and to extend the geographic reach of the poet's works.

Shāʿir played a central role in significant tribal and intertribal events. They recited poetry at the beginning of the harvest season and when livestock was birthed. They were called to invoke the gods and to unleash poems like bullets at times of war. In fact, the *Shāʿir*'s words—especially their satirical verses, or hijāʾ—were considered an essential and powerful component of warfare.

The most lyrical *Shāʿir*, the ones who truly earned their name as "those who feel and perceive," were said to be inspired by their djinn muses. One of the most revealing insights into this relationship comes from the eleventh-century Andalusian poet Abu 'Amir ibn Shuhayd. Ibn Shuhayd

23 Excerpted from *Kitab al-Aghani (The Book of Songs)* by scholar and poet Abu al-Faraj al-Isfahani (10897-10967 HE).

was moved to write poetry upon the death of his lover, but he was too overwhelmed with emotion to construct sentences—until his djinni muse helped him translate his grief into verse. The djinni introduced himself as Zuhayr ibn Numayr and explained that he hailed from the same tribe—Banu Ashja'—as his poet; except the djinni was born into a parallel Ashja' tribe that existed in the djinn realm.

Ibn Numayr transported ibn Shuhayd into the parallel djinn kingdom within al-ghayb, where the human poet met the djinn muses of some of the preeminent poets who came before him. One muse was a beautiful knight wielding a sword; another looked like "a gracious adolescent carrying a lance in his hand, and who came toward us on a white-spotted horse." Yet another was "a knight riding a glowing mare."[24]

The idea of a djinni muse from a parallel world is echoed in the story of one of the foremost 'Udhri poets from the Umayyad era, an early Islamic period from 10661 to 10750 HE. Kuthayyir ibn 'Abd al-Raḥman, also known as Kuthayyir 'Azzah, wrote panegyric poems about his unconsummated love for a married woman, 'Azza. These poems, focused on chaste love, are typical of the style of 'Udhri poetry, which was popularized by and named for the ʿUdhra tribe of eastern Arabia.

When asked how he came to write poetry about 'Azza, Kuthayyir explained that one day, a strange-looking man who turned out be from alam al-ghayb appeared before him and claimed to be more closely related to him than he expected. This story echoes the parallelism of djinn and human worlds, but also calls into question the true origin of Kuthayyir's affection for 'Azza—had she been his love or his djinni double's obsession? It also calls into question the provenance of his poetry. Who was the true author of lines like these?

خَليلَيَّ هَذا رَبْعُ عَزَّةَ فَاعْقِلَا قلوصَيكُما ثُمَّ ابْكِيَا حَيثُ حَلَّتِ

Oh my companions, that is the convoy of 'Azza, so tie your she-camels,
then start weeping where she has camped!

وَمُسّا تُرابًا كَانَ قَد مَسَّ جِلدَها وَبيتا وَظِلاً حَيثُ باتَت وَظَلَّتِ

And [try to] touch the sand, which has touched her skin,
and spend your nights and remain, where she has spent her [nights] and remained.[25]

24 ibn Shuhayd, Abu Amir: *Risalat-al-Tawabii' wa al-zawabi* (Beirut, Dar Sader, 1967).

25 From *Kitab al-Aghani* by Abu al-Faraj al-Isfahani.

Kuthayyir was asked, "When did you start reciting poetry?" He responded, "I did not start reciting poetry until it was recited to me." He went on to describe exactly how his life as a poet began:

> One day, I was in a place called Ghamim, near Medina. It was noon. A man on horseback came toward me until he was next to me. I looked at him. He was bizarre, a man made out of brass; he seemed to be dragging himself along. He said to me, "Recite some poetry!" Then he recited poetry to me. I said: "Who are you?" He said, "I am your double from the djinn!" That is how I started reciting poetry.[26]

Kuthayyir seems to have been inspired by just one muse from a parallel tribe in the djinn kingdom, but shāʿir were often inspired by two djinn. This fact was even used to rebut scathing critique. Once, al-Farazdaq, an eighth-century poet and critic, was asked for his opinion on a poem. He explained that poets have two djinn muses:

> One of them is called Hawbar and the other is called Hawjal. If Hawbar is your inspirer, then your poetry is good, but if your inspirer is Hawjal, then your poetry is bad. Both were your inspirers in this verse. Hawbar inspired the first part of it, and Hawjal inspired the second part of it, and he damaged it.[27]

Kuthayyir and his Islamic and pre-Islamic peers sometimes described memorizing or scribbling down verses recited by their djinn muses or doubles, which seems to make them less like shāʿir and more like rāwī; rāwī sometimes did go on to become full-fledged poets themselves. They often began their careers at the feet of distinguished, elder poets from whom they hoped to learn how to sharpen their craft. Perhaps, then, the greatest human poets have been simply the rāwī of more gifted poets from al-ghayb.

26 If this sounds strange, consider that Milton (English, Christian) called on his Muse, the Holy Spirit, when writing *Paradise Lost*, and petitioned Urania, one of the nine muses of Greek mythology in Books III, VII, and IX.

27 Abu Zaid al-Quraishi, *Jamharat ash'ar al-'arah*. Beirut, 1986.

In the twenty-first century, songwriters and singers such as Adele and Beyoncé describe not knowing the origins of their lyrical gifts. Melodies and hooks emerge from somewhere, but they can't be sure where. There is some mystical depth from which they pull forth sonic inspiration and craft tunes that reverberate between our ears and throughout the world. Music is magical, after all, and scientists still cannot explain why certain songs become "earworms" while others fade into oblivion.

And perhaps you, reader, know this feeling. That surge of inspiration, that idea that seemingly emerges from nowhere and blooms into a fully grown awareness. Perhaps it isn't your brain's neocortex or thalamus in action—perhaps it is your djinniyah muse, a parallel you who is more inventive and artistic and from whom your best ideas have sprung.

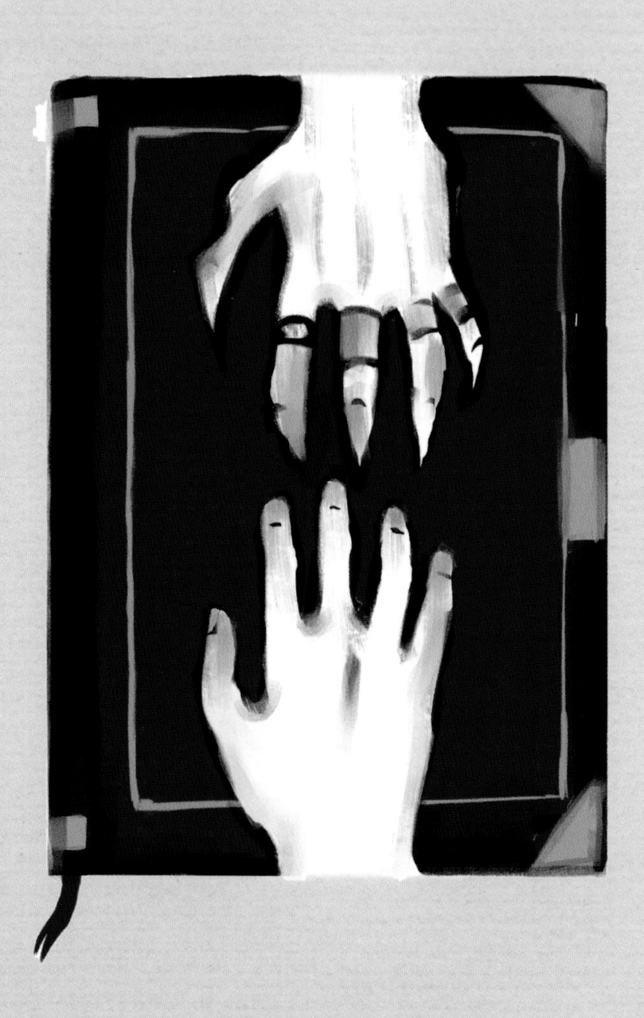

I am a man whose follower is a djinni
I befriended him and he befriended me for life
He drinks from my cup and I drink from his cup
Thanks be to God who gave him to me

—Unnamed pre-Islamic poet

Half of What It Seems

Paris, France, 11997 HE (1997 CE)

Monsieur Margolin was always pushing harebrained ideas. In January, he demoted every single senior editor to associate editor to "inject some desperately needed hunger, drive, and bloodthirsty ambition back into the workforce." In April, he ordered the junior editors to work the jobs of their seniors for half a year to prove to him that they were up to the job; only then would he consider a promotion and a 2.5 percent pay raise.

"So we have to do twice the work for half the pay, and I probably still won't make associate editor, even though I'm twice as qualified as Claude?" Ayyub groaned to Leon. The pair stared at the corkboard outside the boss's office. Every few months it was updated with the latest, painful announcement.

Leon rolled his eyes and opened his mouth to speak but hurriedly poked a sharp elbow into Ayyub's chest and whispered through gritted teeth, "Incoming!"

Monsieur Margolin was hobbling out of the elevator and heading straight for them.

"Dawdling? When this publishing house is drowning in contracts and deadlines?" he said, talking at them while walking straight past them. A woman marched ahead of the boss, opened the door to his office to let him through, but didn't entirely close it behind him.

"Ayyuuuub!" he yelled from behind the half-open, guarded door.

"Yes, Monsieur?"

"Come and see me at half past three. We need to discuss your promotion."

The secretary closed the door, and Ayyub heard a click as she turned the lock.

Ayyub had taken all the right steps on the path from earnest literature lover to persistently junior editor at France's oldest and largest publishing house. An English degree. Unpaid internships in publishing companies every summer. A one-year apprenticeship straight after graduation for very little pay, which he was told would give him "great exposure" and make him "extremely employable and attractive to senior editors." And then here, to Le Livre, through an ethnic minority editors training scheme, for even less pay.

"But we will take you straight to the top," Monsieur Margolin had promised him, jabbing the air during the recruitment drive at Ayyub's alma mater in the fifth arrondissement. Ayyub had been impressed that the CEO of Le Livre would bother to come out to recruit needy brown kids on a Monday evening, let alone take Ayyub by the shoulder and assure him that he would have the kind of job he had dreamed of since he was a nerdy nine-year-old who couldn't sleep unless at least half a dozen books were crammed beneath his pillow.

In one hand, Ayyub clutched the shiny paper folder with Le Livre's promotional materials (featuring one token brown face); he anxiously folded his other arm behind his back as Monsieur Margolin took him by the neck and guided him around the perimeter of the university's wood-paneled grand salon. Ayyub could smell cigars and coffee on the old man's breath. His skin smelled of baby powder. Ayyub examined Monsieur Margolin's right hand, which he was pointing at the oil paintings on the walls. Portraits of ancient white men peered down at Ayyub; they had graduated this same university hundreds of years earlier and had gone on to rule the country.

"That's my great-great-great-grandfather," said Monsieur Margolin, pointing a fat finger at a particularly yellowed figure who must have sat in uneven light for his portrait; only half his face could be seen. The tips of Monsieur Margolin's fingers were also yellowed. Nicotine-stained nails gave way to liver-spotted fingers. But the hand resting on Ayyub's shoulder, the one he could see out of the corner of his eye, looked lighter and cleaner. Maybe the man smoked with only his right hand.

Monsieur Margolin promised Ayyub the world—the publishing world, at least. Within six months he would be promoted to assist a junior editorial assistant; in one year he would *be* the assistant! And by the end of his third year, Ayyub would be an acquiring editor, soliciting manuscripts and signing authors. "We can even talk at that point about you heading up your own imprint, eh?" said Monsieur Margolin, stumbling a little on the uneven floor. His gait was wobbly, as if one leg was slightly shorter than the other.

My own imprint! thought Ayyub. *I could really make a mark in the literary world; really nurture up-and-coming ethnic minority writers. We could fix everything that is broken in publishing.*

It had been five and a half years since he had signed the contract—signed away his dignity, lunchtimes, evenings, and even nights to Le Livre and Monsieur Margolin. The aging man's every whim was entertained; his every want became urgent. An entourage of young female secretaries, assistants, and even a "massage lady" ushered cups of coffee into his hand, draped coats over his back, and rubbed his temples as he barked commands into a speakerphone on international conference calls.

At 3:30 on this particular day, Ayyub knocked on the office door. *Click.* The door was unlatched, and an older woman gestured for Ayyub to enter. The room smelled of latex, baby powder, and espresso.

"Coffee?" the assistant asked Ayyub.

"No time for that," said Monsieur Margolin before Ayyub had time to answer. The boss waved the assistant out of the room.

Ayyub settled into the only available seat.

"I am an old man," said Monsieur Margolin before swinging his chair around so that he had his back to Ayyub. He spoke to the rooftops of Paris: "Really, if I am to be completely honest with you, I am a dying man."

Ayyub sat up straight and gripped both armrests. "Oh my God! Really?" he said to Monsieur Margolin's back. Ayyub inched forward in his seat. Suddenly his mouth felt dry. His head began to buzz.

"Really. And it is because of this place. It is going down, and it is taking me down with it."

Ayyub frowned. "Going down?"

Monsieur Margolin turned sideways to face the wall, his sagging turkey neck silhouetted against the Paris skyline. "No one knows this, Ayyub, but Le Livre will likely not exist in half a year. And neither will I."

Ayyub gasped. How could that be? The grandest, richest legacy publishing house in the country. Poof. Gone. Just like that?

"This is why we have not been able to promote you. We are drowning in debt. Everything is going to ruin, and I have been concealing it all so as to protect the board. To protect you. My only hope is that a young and hard worker such as yourself can help me rescue Le Livre from the debt collectors. And if you can, my dear Ayyub, you will also be rescuing me."

Monsieur Margolin turned to face Ayyub, and for the first time Ayyub noticed that the old man's left eye was made of glass. Or perhaps the eye just looked glassy because he was sitting in a shadow which illuminated only half his face. Maybe the left eye had been replaced because of some sickness spreading through the old man's body.

"I will do anything within my power to help," said Ayyub, trying not to stare into the left eye. "My future, the future of this company, means everything to me."

Monsieur Margolin did not speak. He tapped his right foot on the floor and stared at Ayyub.

"But . . . drowning in debt?" said Ayyub softly. "How could that happen without anyone knowing?"

Ayyub scoured the publishing magazines religiously, followed the industry news, and went for drinks at the bars where assistants and junior editors lamented their fates over Chardonnay. He knew which editor was on their way out of which of the big seven publishing houses; which publisher was launching the writing career of the young, neo-Nazi politician; and which hotshot executive had been poached by a competitor. The industry had been booming. And all this time, he had been ignorant of the rot bubbling beneath his own nose. *I should have been paying more attention*, he thought.

Monsieur Margolin stopped tapping his foot. "I can't get into details right now. I can only say that you can be of great comfort to an old and dying man."

"Anything," said Ayyub as the secretary returned.

"We shall speak again tomorrow," said the boss.

Ayyub marched out of the office and straight to the bathroom to splash his face with cold water.

"Any good news?" asked Leon as he emerged from a stall. He turned on the faucet in the wash basin next to Ayyub.

"I mean, it was bad, but it was good. It might be good. For me. I'm not sure?" Ayyub reached for a paper towel and walked out of the bathroom, his palms dripping water. A puzzled Leon stared at the closing door.

That night, Ayyub's father appeared in his dream. *My dear son*, he said, looking as gaunt as he had on the day he died—but also peaceful. *My dear, dear son. Beware your ambition. Beware those who seek favors. Beware that which is only half what it seems.*

Ayyub woke in a cold sweat and pulled the blanket over his shivering torso. He fell back into a fitful sleep, only to dream of a school trip he had once taken to the north of France. A kayaking excursion that had begun with cheer had ended in tragedy. An eleven-year-old girl, one of his classmates, had tried to help a younger boy whose kayak had overturned near a thick knot of underwater vines. The boy's foot became entangled, and it was only with the girl's help that he was able to kick off his shoe, leaving it caught in the roots. The boy spluttered and huffed as he clambered onto the girl's kayak, and the class clapped from their boats and from the banks. But as he scrambled to safety, the kayak tipped over and the girl became trapped in the cockpit. The boy rocked and rocked the boat as teachers jumped into the water and frantically swam toward them. The girl flailed underwater, but the boat remained upside down. The girl drowned. The boy survived. The boy was Ayyub.

It was a recurring nightmare—his penance, he believed. No amount of therapy or taweez or journaling could banish the vision. He would watch Esme swallow water and thrash in the murky lake over and over and over again for the rest of his life. The same tangled roots that had reached for his ankles had grabbed Esme's braids, pulling the girl deeper into the water.

The warning from his father was new, though. It was the first time Ayyub had dreamed of him since they had buried his emaciated body six months earlier. The three admonitions echoed in Ayyub's head as he listened to coffee percolate on the stovetop the next morning and pounded cardamon pods into a green-black powder. *Ambition. Favor. Half of what it seems.*

Monsieur Margolin wore a dark orange Hermès tie, which he straightened as he limped into his office ahead of Ayyub. His expression was still maudlin; his room still smelled of latex, baby powder, and espresso. The liver spots looked like they were expanding, and, as he sat in his chair, Ayyub noted that his left eye looked glassier than ever. The entire left side of his face looked different from the right. Ayyub put it down to the office lighting.

The boss man had a plan. "I need you to come to my country estate to work on the restructuring mission for Le Livre. The matter has become urgent. My driver will pick you up at seven this evening, and we will begin the rescue work tomorrow morning."

Ayyub felt full of purpose. He rubbed his palms together, bowed his head, and thanked Monsieur Margolin for the great opportunity.

Later that afternoon, Ayyub neatly stacked the manuscripts on his desk and slid them into his satchel. Would he have time to read these in the country? He wasn't sure how long he would be there, but despite the chilling news of Le Livre's—and Monsieur Margolin's—imminent demise, and the urgent task ahead, his editing deadlines still stood. He couldn't call his boss and explain that he was embarking on a clandestine rescue mission with his boss's boss's boss. "What kind of mission?" Claude would have said with his trademark sneer. And Ayyub, typically flustered in front of the half-qualified but doubly paid man, would have mumbled something about drowning and debt. He daren't risk it. Surely the countryside excursion would be an efficient one.

The driver was late. Ayyub waited on the street corner with his satchel and overnight bag for nearly a half hour. The ride north was uneventful except for a glimpse of a lake that reminded him of the school trip. He wasn't fearful of bodies of water. His father had made sure of that. Every summer they had taken a trip back home to Sana'a, where his parents insisted on driving for hours until they arrived at the shore. They would climb into a small boat and sail to Socotra island, the jagged limestone mountains of which poked into the clouds. Ayyub would run along the shoreline where the turquoise waters of the Indian Ocean lapped at sparkling white sands. But it was Detwah Lagoon, with its cool, calm, and crystalline waters, that became Ayyub's favorite place to snorkel. Yellow, orange, and pink fish kissed his toes and skimmed his belly as the boy oohed and ahhed underwater.

It wasn't the water that was scary in Yemen; it was the stories. When the men came back from Maghreb salat—especially on Thursday nights, the Night of Power—they gathered the boys in the courtyard at the back of Ayyub's grandfather's house. The men squatted or sat on stuffed rice sacks, lit stubby cigars, and talked about the ills of society. Amreeka was exploiting the region for oil; the government was hiking taxes, again; and another Nasnās had been spotted by the hospital.

"Always by the hospital," his father said. "Those cowardly animals." He shook his head as he listened to the men lament. It had been the same when he was a child.

Ayyub wanted to tap his father on the arm and ask, "What is a Nasnās?" but he knew the answer would haunt his dreams.

"They stay by the hospital because that's where they can lure the do-gooders who go to volunteer," said an uncle. "That's how they got poor Uncle Ismai'l."

"Uncle Ismai'l? Our old math teacher? Is that what happened?" said another uncle, a cigar dangling from his lips.

"He was my son's math teacher, too," said someone else, tapping each side of his face with his fingertips in a symbol of divine mercy.

Uncle Ismai'l had vanished two months earlier. The old man's disappearance had been a mystery until the week that Ayyub and his parents arrived in Sana'a, when curious townspeople had mostly pieced together the mystery. Uncle Ismai'l was a kind man who had taught algebra to three generations of local boys. In his retirement, he believed he could stimulate the minds of the hospital's infirm and quicken their healing by playing math games with them. The Numbers Man, they had taken to calling him. The nurses plied him with cups of mint tea in gratitude for the tactful way he distracted cantankerous patients. The doctors slapped him on the back and said, "Good man. We need more like you, Uncle." But one Thursday, Uncle Ismai'l stopped knocking at the door of the cancer ward. "Where is Uncle Ismai'l?" the nurses asked. From the canteen to the pharmacy, Uncle Ismai'l's disappearance was the talk of the hospital, and it soon became the concern of the town.

This was the rumored explanation: Ismai'l had been walking across the bridge one evening with his ink-stained sudoku sheets folded beneath his arm and a pencil tucked into his turban when he heard a high-pitched hooting.

"Saeeduni! Saeeduni!" The strangled, pitiful voice was calling for help.

Uncle Ismai'l froze on the bridge and looked around. There was no one behind him. There was no one in front of him. Was there somebody beneath him? He craned his neck over the bridge and sure enough, there lay a frail and elderly figure on his side. The man was slender; his body was pressed into the red dirt of the riverbank, and his leg was contorted at a disturbing angle.

"I'm coming!" said Uncle Ismai'l, flinging his papers to the ground. He walked as fast as he could to the end of the bridge, sat down at the top of the rocky riverbank, and used his hands to guide himself down the red-dirt slope. The elderly man lay panting and sweating on his side, his cries for help diminishing as Uncle Ismai'l rose to his feet and approached. But just as Uncle Ismai'l went to crouch at the man's side, he spotted a snake behind the man.

"Don't move!" said Uncle Ismai'l. Then he leapt up, pulled a spindly stick from the ground, and lunged toward the snake.

But the elderly man on the ground grabbed Uncle Ismai'l's ankle, sending him flying toward the venomous creature. "You fool!" said the old man. "That's not a snake! That's my tail!"

The tail flicked up and to the side, helping the old man gain his balance as he tried to stand. Uncle Ismai'l rubbed his gashed head and gasped. The side of the man that had been pressed into the red dirt was missing, and standing over him, with its long and forked tail twisting this way and that, was a half creature. It had one leg, one eye, one half of a head, one arm, and only half a heart. The creature bent down to grab the stick still clutched in Uncle Ismai'l's hand. He raised his arm high above his half head and clobbered Uncle Ismai'l's skull. Then the creature dragged Uncle Ismai'l into the river and hopped off along the riverbank in search of more gullible prey.

An orderly from the hospital found Uncle Ismai'l's mathematics papers flapping in the wind as he crossed the bridge later that night, but the old man's disappearance had remained a mystery until his body had washed up days later, soon after a teenaged boy swore that he saw a human sliced in half hopping along the riverbank.

After this revelation, one of the uncles jumped to his feet and hopped toward the house, on his way grabbing the head of Ayyub's older cousin and whispering, "I'm a Nasnās and I'm going to eaaattt you!" The teenager laughed, but Ayyub saw that he mouthed a silent prayer as the uncle passed.

"Actually, I heard that you can eat *them*," said an uncle.

"That is true," said Ayyub's dad. "There's a tribe in the east, the Hadhramaut, who were haunted by Nasnās. They got so sick of being hunted that they began to hunt the Nasnās instead. They say the flesh, when roasted, tastes exceptionally sweet."

Ayyub met his father's eyes. "Come here, son," he said, pulling Ayyub's face into his broad chest. "Nothing for you to worry about. You pray ayat al-kursi and it frightens these things away."

Then why hadn't Uncle Ismai'l just prayed? Ayyub wondered as he tried to fall asleep that night. All summer long, half-human beasts with snaking tails chased him in his sleep.

Ayyub awoke to a perfectly bucolic scene shining out from behind an ornately curtained window. Rolling green hills gleamed beneath the kinds of fluffy clouds schoolchildren scribble in the margins of their notebooks.

There was a knock at the door. A maid, an older woman, entered and placed a silver tray on a small table next to the window. "Monsieur is still being dressed," she said. "When he is complete, he will meet you in the orchid greenhouse. Out there." She pointed out the window, past a tennis court, to an ornate glass building.

Ayyub downed his coffee, dressed, and carried his pastry over to the orchid house. Monsieur probably wouldn't be ready yet, but maybe he could take a wander to see how rich people tended to their flowers. He nibbled his croissant as he reached for the door but stopped when he heard voices inside.

"It used to be properly humid in here! It made the rubber softer! Goddamnit!" There was a squelching sound, as if boots were being excised from thick mud. "Pull it. Pull it. No, no, no! You're going to have to pull it all the way off now and put it back on to get it right."

It was Monsieur Margolin barking instructions at some poor soul. Who knew that orchid gardening was so complex? Ayyub stuffed the pastry into his mouth and gently opened the frosted-glass doors. Rows and rows of orchids lined long silver tables. Deep purple and lilac blooms hung upside down from the ceiling. Bright-white flowers extended from tree trunks that dangled from fraying ropes. Amid the epiphytes, peeking out from behind pink, purple, and white petals, stood a wobbly Monsieur Margolin. Ayyub took a step through the doors and quietly closed them behind him.

It was then he realized that Monsieur Margolin was entirely naked. Pink, splotchy skin sprouted crops of scarlet blisters along his spine. He was hopping out of a garment while a woman crouched at his ankle, yanking at the rubbery material. As she pulled the garment completely off the old man and stood to shake it, Ayyub noticed that it wasn't a pair of trousers; it was a rubber bodysuit. A floppy arm splayed across the damp floor. The woman reached for a spray bottle and spritzed the inside of the hollow arm. As she lifted the suit higher, Ayyub saw a dangling leg. When she lowered the suit to slip Monsieur Margolin's foot into the rubber, Ayyub gasped. Monsieur Margolin had one leg and one arm and only half a head. His other arm and leg were made of rubber. Ayyub's jaw dropped, the pastry fell from between his lips, and he stepped backward into the closed door.

The old man groaned as he hopped. "Come onnnn." A saggy buttock jiggled. Tucked along the inside of his one leg was a thin, pink tail. Sad and limp, it didn't look at all like the whiplike serpentine tail that had haunted Ayyub's teenaged nightmares.

Ayyub backed slowly away from the flowers. Forgetting his pastry, he quietly opened the doors and walked out into the summer morning.

He was trapped. He didn't have a car, he didn't have a map, he was in the middle of nowhere, and he didn't know where the nearest train station was. If he tried to escape now, he would be lost by sundown and Monsieur Margolin would surely come looking for him. *Hunting for me*, thought Ayyub, and he shivered beneath the sun.

Inside his room, he gathered his manuscripts back into his satchel, piled his belongings onto the table, and sat on the edge of the bed to plot his escape. Monsieur Margolin had been slowly killing Ayyub for years, crushing his dreams and wringing out of him any remaining passion for literature. But now the old man was literally trying to lure Ayyub to a painful death. And soon. He thought of Uncle Ismai'l and how his good deed had been punished with a blow to the head and a watery grave.

His father's face flashed before his eyes. *Beware your ambition. Beware those who seek favors. Beware that which is only half what it seems.*

Pray ayat al-kursi, his father had said in Sana'a, whenever djinn stories haunted his night terrors. *It frightens these things away.*

Ayyub could barely remember the words after all these years. He scanned the room's high walls and ornate ceiling as he searched his memory for the opening ayah. Somewhere in the depths of his mind were the words that his father said would save him. Ayyub prayed and prayed and prayed and stopped only when Monsieur Margolin knocked at the door and said, "May I enter? You dropped your croissant."

Ayyub froze. Somewhere in the middle of the Qur'anic versions, between *Who is it that can intercede with Him except by His permission?* and *He knows what is before them and what will be after them*, Ayyub's heart stopped. Then it pounded. "I'm not ready! I'll be down in a minute." He listened to Monsieur Margolin shuffle away.

He would have to make a run for it now; there was no way he could wait until this evening if Monsieur had an inkling that Ayyub had seen his true form. He'd follow the long path out of the estate and toward the country road. He could at least remember that the driver had turned left before reaching the locked gates.

When Ayyub arrived in the downstairs dining salon, his satchel over his shoulder, he found Monsieur Margolin looking forlorn and frail. He hadn't yet walked through the doorway when the old man looked up at him, his neck buried in his chest, and began to cry. "It's worse than I thought, my dear boy. The debt collectors are coming tomorrow! Tomorrow! They wish to collect what is owed. Come in. Come in. My heart can't take this. To watch my family's company disintegrate after a hundred and fifteen years in power. Oh!"

The door to the salon had closed behind Ayyub as he entered the room. He waited near the exit as Monsieur Margolin wept. If Ayyub turned and sprinted through the door and out of the house, how fast could a frail, one-legged man possibly give chase?

No one had told Ayyub that even a one-legged djinni possesses great speed. As Ayyub opened the salon door and sprinted to the entrance of the house, Monsieur Margolin was right behind him, weeping while running at great speed. Ayyub slowed only to turn his head and look behind. The old man suddenly slowed, staggered. And feigned frailty. "Why are you leaving me? I need your help!" he cried, stooping with his hands on his knees. His voice became a screeching whine. "Ayyub! I need yoooou!"

Ayyub cleared the front door. He ran around the fountain, along the path leading to the gate, all the while glancing over his shoulder. Monsieur Margolin was still at the fountain when Ayyub approached the locked gate, but as he scaled the wrought iron that was as tall as three humans, the boss inched closer. Ayyub gripped a cherub's head and pulled himself up a few feet. He anchored a foot on an angel's wing just as Monsieur Margolin jumped up to snatch at his ankle. He missed, and Ayyub crouched on the gate like a monkey, eight feet up. His satchel hung at a precarious angle and spilled a few white pages onto a sweating Monsieur Margolin. The Nasnās jumped up and down, his arms outstretched, groping for Ayyub's ankles.

The suit was peeling away from the old man's face. He frantically pressed on his left ear to push the rubber back onto his head. *Slurrrrrp*. Ayyub kicked Margolin's left arm, the rubbery arm, and the rubber half head flopped off. Ayyub pulled himself higher up the gate. He needed to jump down to the other side. As Monsieur Margolin tried to climb after him, pieces of his suit ripped away from his body.

Ayyub kicked down from the top of the railings. He kicked and kicked until his foot connected with the half head. *Thud*. The Nasnās collapsed to the ground. The half creature writhed, and Ayyub almost felt sorry for this pitiful thing with one leg and one arm, its flat side caked in gravel, pieces of silicone dangling off the metal rails. Ayyub clung to the gate and watched as its whimpering quieted and its squirming slowed. Ayyub exhaled. But just as he loosened his grip on the metal to reach higher, a long tail slithered out from beneath the Nasnās and reached up to grab at Ayyub's ankle. Ayyub hoisted himself up and over the gate, flinging both legs in a single move. Somehow he landed on his feet, crouching on the other side of the metal as the Nasnās's skinny tail reached through the metal bars and tried again to grab his ankles. Ayyub ran down the lane as the hungry half creature rattled the metal behind him.

Nasnās

Tales of the half-bodied Nasnās abound in the Persian Gulf states, particularly in Yemen, where I heard of many sightings of these dastardly creatures. Ayyub remained traumatized by his experience, at some points shaking as he recounted Monsieur Margolin's appearance and the creature shedding its rubber disguise while giving chase. His uncles tried to console him as he recounted his tale, while also informing me that Nasnās feed on the energy of human bodies and can live many years by doing so. In this case, however, a company memo was circulated stating that Monsieur Margolin had suffered a massive stroke while at his country estate. Ayyub's uncles said that it was Ayyub's father who had contributed to this positive turn of events. "My brother made sure that his son landed safely even though he jumped from a great height. It is because of my brother's prayers that Ayyub is safe and the Nasnās is dead."

Many believe the Nasnās are djinn, but an alternative theory postulates that they are derived from the original inhabitants of the lost city of Ubar. This lush desert city was ruled by King Shaddad ibn 'Ad at the same time as Queen Sheba's reign. 'Ad was the center of a booming frankincense trade, three thousand years before the birth of the Prophet Isa, back when the sap was used in medicines and religious ceremonies and was more precious than gold. Ubar was also known as Iram of the Pillars when it was home to the ancient tribe of 'Ad. The city was destroyed by Allah as punishment for its citizens' debauchery, their worship of false Gods, and their rejection of the message of a one true deity, which was delivered by the Prophet Hud.

وَأَمَّا عَادٌ فَأُهْلِكُوا بِرِيحٍ صَرْصَرٍ عَاتِيَةٍ

سَخَّرَهَا عَلَيْهِمْ سَبْعَ لَيَالٍ وَثَمَانِيَةَ أَيَّامٍ حُسُومًا فَتَرَى
الْقَوْمَ فِيهَا صَرْعَىٰ كَأَنَّهُمْ أَعْجَازُ نَخْلٍ خَاوِيَةٍ

And the 'Ad, they were destroyed by a furious Wind, exceedingly violent;
Which Allah imposed upon them for seven nights and eight days in succession, so you would see the people therein fallen as if they were hollow trunks of palm trees.

—Holy Qur'an 69:6–7

In the 11990s HE, the lost city was seemingly discovered by a team of amateur and professional archaeologists from Los Angeles. The fifty-three-year-old filmmaker Nicholas Clapp had become fascinated by the lost city after reading *Arabia Felix* by British explorer Bertram Thomas. Clapp studied maps at the Huntington Library in California, including a map drawn by the Greek-Egyptian geographer Ptolemy in 9801 HE, which showed the presence of an old city in what is modern-day Oman.

Clapp approached NASA with a bold request: Could the space agency deploy its special shuttle radar system to scan the earth over Oman from space in search of the lost ruins? Scientists at NASA's Jet Propulsion Laboratory in Pasadena agreed, and satellite imagery revealed the tracks of a long-lost caravan, visible in their entirety only from the sky. These images led archaeologists to a fortress buried twelve meters (almost forty feet) below the sands of Rub' al Khali, a part of Oman so desolate it was named the Empty Quarter.

The eight-walled fortress was as described in the Qur'an. Among the archaeologist's excavations were the remains of towers at each corner of the fortress's sixty-foot-high walls.

أَلَمْ تَرَ كَيْفَ فَعَلَ رَبُّكَ بِعَادٍ

إِرَمَ ذَاتِ الْعِمَادِ

الَّتِي لَمْ يُخْلَقْ مِثْلُهَا فِي الْبِلَادِ

Seest thou not how the Lord dealt with the 'Ad of the city of Iram with lofty pillars, the likes of which were not produced in all the land?

—Holy Qur'an 89:6–8

What the researchers may not have realized–since they attribute the great city's demise to its construction over a limestone cavern and not God's castigation–is that some Arab historians dispute the discovery, claiming the real Ubar remains hidden. The real ruins, they say, are haunted by Nasnās, who are protecting the lost city's sunken riches. The Nasnās of this lore are said to be the former inhabitants of Ubar, and they threaten to attack anyone who seeks to unearth the treasures they are guarding. Perhaps this was Monsieur Margolin's agenda, too? Maybe he had seen in Ayyub a potential helper who could save his company from dire straits. I still wonder: Had Monsieur Margolin's true identity not been discovered by Ayyub, perhaps the company would have survived, and Monsieur Margolin, too.

The Baby

The Cotswolds, Gloucestershire, England, 12005 HE (2005 CE)

First published on the fertility blog Muslimahs T.T.C.

I had been late for the doctor's appointment, which made me late for the notary, which made me late to clock back into work for at least two more hours of data entry, which made me late to arrive home to pick up Sam's "personal specimen" (as he liked to call it), which he had produced late because, as he explained, "I can't do this shit on a schedule, OK? It's not easy for me like it is for you. I have to really, really be in the mood."

Late, late, late all day, which was why I was careening around the sharp bends of the glassy country lanes in the midst of a torrential summer storm. As a watery sun disappeared behind the tops of the sycamore trees, I tried not to think about the anemic models posing spread-eagle on the cover of the magazine Sam still had in his hand as he had given me the specimen. I bounced from one edge of the driver's seat to the other, swerving around tighter and tighter curves, my pelvis still aching from the indignities of the lunchtime procedure. I couldn't slow down now. The medical storage facility closed in thirty minutes and I was at least twenty miles away, navigating roads that looked like shimmering rivers.

I gripped the steering wheel with my right hand so tightly that the tips of my fingers became mottled. Crumbs from a protein bar tumbled down my sweatshirt as I tried to scarf down dinner and navigate the lanes at the same time. The rain was relentless. Sheets of water pummeled the windscreen as the lilac sky turned a dark purple, then crept toward a sooty black. Every few seconds, a bolt of lightning revealed a flash of the dark and winding road ahead.

In the back seat, a bucket-size silver vat fell to its side. I squinted into the rearview mirror. Sam had joked that the contraption looked like a beer keg. It was not the kind of device I would usually drive around with. Liters of smoky liquid nitrogen swirled inside the metal vat, the subzero fumes encircling Sam's specimen, cryogenically preserving the half babies, as I liked to call them, until I—because it was always my job—could deposit the sample at the baby library, our name for the sperm bank.

I swerved on tires that were hydroplaning and craned my neck forward as if advancing my eyeballs two inches closer to the windscreen would make the road ahead clearer. That was when I saw the thing. As I veered around another sharp corner and came onto a straight stretch, a hunched and hooded figure darted into the road. It stopped in the middle of the lane—to stare in my direction, it seemed—then crouched to place something in the road before disappearing into the bushes.

I slowed down and checked the rearview mirror; there was no one behind, no cars in front. I hadn't passed another human for miles. I wiped my eyes with my damp sleeve, mindlessly smudging mascara across my face and dislodging the contact lens in my left eye. I blinked frantically.

My headlights illuminated a small, curved bundle. I slowed down to a crawl. Was it a box? A bucket? A pile of blankets? A bushy plant in a pot? Could it be . . . no, it couldn't possibly be . . . Could it be a baby's bassinet?

The bundle had the same shape and thick upper handle as the bassinet my sister-in-law had enthusiastically wrapped in yellow bows (gender neutral, she had said with a smug grin) and gifted to me late last summer, one week before I would miscarry for the second time that year.

The bundle shook. I considered swerving around it. What if it was a trap? But if it was a baby, well, how could I live with not knowing? The ache in my pelvis deepened as I slammed the brakes and lurched to a stop. The metal vat crashed into the back of my seat. I released my seat belt and rubbed my lower back.

I wound down the fogged-up passenger-seat window to scan the bushes into which the hooded figure had run. But there was no one. Just the bassinet and me.

This is like the scene in the horror film where the White girl gets out of the car—but the sensible Black girl keeps driving till she gets home, I thought as I shook my head and, against my better judgment, lifted the hand brake and turned on the hazard lights. I reached for the raincoat jammed into the holder at the back of my seat, draped the waxy green coat over my head, took a deep breath, and swung open the car door.

The faint bray of a distressed baby reached my ears. It grew louder as I walked through the inch-high water, my jeans growing wetter and heavier the closer I got. I stopped a foot away from what was certainly a gurgling child, although I could see only a white woolen blanket wriggling endlessly. Was that a tiny balled-up fist punching beneath the blanket? The bassinet rocked from side to side beneath the lashings of rain on its hood. I was close enough to reach inside or at least lift back the hood—but I was frozen. *What a silly girl I am,* I thought. *Why is my heart pounding as if it's about to jump out of my chest?* I pressed my palm into the deepening cramps beneath my belly button and took a half step toward the bassinet. *If that's really a baby in that thing, then surely it's going to drown beneath these buckets of rain! Why am I waiting to rescue the poor child? What kind of paranoid monster have I become?*

I looked around again. It was just me, the rain, and the bassinet. I crouched down to lift back the hood and locked eyes with a beautiful baby girl. Big, round eyes blinked up at me with the longest eyelashes I had ever seen. A yellow bow was tied around her head, which was nestled in a white, wooly hood. I cooed. The baby stopped crying. It seemed as if the rain quieted and the headlight beams dimmed as I reached inside the bassinet and lifted out the sopping-wet child.

"Oh baby! Your clothes and your blanket are absolutely soaking. You poor, poooor, poooooor thing!" I cradled the sweet child against my neck and began to stand. But then I stopped, crouched, and looked around once again. There was no one. No furtive figure. No concerned villagers with flashing torchlights. No sirens blaring in the distance. No one but me and a baby in the middle of a country road.

I turned to walk toward the car, my driver-side door still open, headlight beams illuminating us. I let the wet blanket fall to the tarmac and walked steadily, cooing to comfort the child. The baby girl began to cry again; her forehead wrinkled in a furious frown, and her legs kicked at my tender breasts.

What would I say to Sam? *Oh hey, so I was on the way to drop off your specimen thingy, but we don't need to make a baby cuz I found one*?

I could imagine him throwing back his head and howling one of those too-loud guffaws that made me laugh and cringe at the same time. *What are you talking about, habibti?* he would say. *You found a what? Where? Is that how the fertility clinic does it these days? Some kind of newborn treasure hunt instead of IVF?* He would grip my cheeks in both hands and pout before saying, *I swear all those crazy hormones are making you cuckoo. You're even worse than last year.*

The baby kicked again. I stopped a foot away from the car door. This time the kick landed beneath my left breast and dug into the metal underwire of my bra. I clutched the baby tightly and took another step. But another sharp kick stopped me in my tracks. This one dug into my aching lower abdomen. I think I groaned. Another kick, this time a sharp punt to the groin. Then something as hard as rock slammed against both of my kneecaps. I buckled from the pain, lurched forward, and steadied myself against the bonnet of the car. I moved past the driver's-side door, opened the back door, and crouched to lower the baby into the back seat. She kicked me again, sending shooting pains across my knees and toppling me into the back seat. I landed on top of the poor girl.

As I groped across the seat to push myself up, my hands swept over furry, knobbly sticks. The sticks flailed and kicked me in the arm. I gasped and jumped backward into the rain. The knobbly sticks were legs.

Flailing in the back seat of my car was a half-human baby with two freakishly long legs. Gray, hairy, and bony, with heavy hooves for feet. Now the hooves pounded the plastic interior of my car, lashing against the metal keg. They kicked upward, gouging holes in the upholstery that lined the roof, until one leg became entangled in the seat belt. *Bang, thrash, bang, thrash.* I screamed and fell back onto the wet road as the hooved creature flailed its ever-growing limbs.

Should I risk getting back in my car and being confined with this . . . baby? Maybe I could grab its legs and pull it out? I crawled toward the car, scraping my bruised knees on the wet tarmac. I slammed the back door shut, trapping the baby inside.

The baby brayed loudly as it kicked through a window. I ducked. I crawled to the open driver's side door and climbed into the car as the baby wailed, its legs still flailing and thrashing out of control. Rain poured in through the shattered window. I didn't know what to do so I slammed the door shut and put the car into drive. I had found this baby—it was still a baby even though it brayed and kicked its hooves into the back of my seat. I couldn't abandon my baby now.

A loud *thunk* on the roof of the car made me jump. Another *thunk*. And another. Then terrible, angry sounds were all around me.

Crunch.

Thunk.

Screech.

Screeeeeech.

The roof began to cave in. I hit the gas. Hooves scraped angrily against metal as I sped off. An entire pack of creatures galloped behind my car. They screeched and pounded the country lane with their hooves, advancing on us until they crashed through the back window. The baby brayed; I swerved and screamed. A flurry of beasts enveloped the car, jumping on the roof, kicking in the windscreen. Gangly limbs reached in and dragged me from my seat and onto the road. I screamed and screamed, "My baby! Leave my baby!" But there was no one, no human, to hear me cry for help.

The beasts dragged me through the forest, my head smacking against the ground and hitting thick tree roots and sharp rocks. My hair was soaked and plastered across my face. By the time I arrived at the den, I was bloodied and fading in and out of blackness. My contact lenses had been dislodged so I could just about make out the shapes of these creatures. They looked almost like kangaroos—but in the Cotswolds? They were gray and muscular, and they sat upright even though they had four legs. They formed a circle around me; their hooves were neatly folded across their torsos. My baby lay in a corner suckling milk from its mother's nipple.

When I woke up, it was almost light outside, the rain had slowed to a drizzle, and the creatures were still in a circle but they were fast asleep, their limbs overlapping, chests rising and falling slowly. Only the mother lay awake, blinking curiously at me while her tail twitched against her sleeping child. I tried to get up, but my ankles had been bound with a wiry twine that twisted around my damp jeans and cut into my skin. I went to loosen the rope with my hands, but the mother-beast spoke.

"You cannot go until you bear the gift." She said it gently, knowingly.

"What?" I said.

"The most precious gift," said the mother. "We chose you because you put yourself in peril to rescue a helpless, drowning child. For your sacrifice, we have blessed you with a gift."

I rubbed my belly. The ache was still there but it was deeper now, much deeper, and it was moving. I lifted my muddied sweatshirt to look at my stomach. A fist—or was it a hoof?—protruded from my womb and kicked against my insides. I dropped the sweatshirt and gasped. I would be a mother after all.

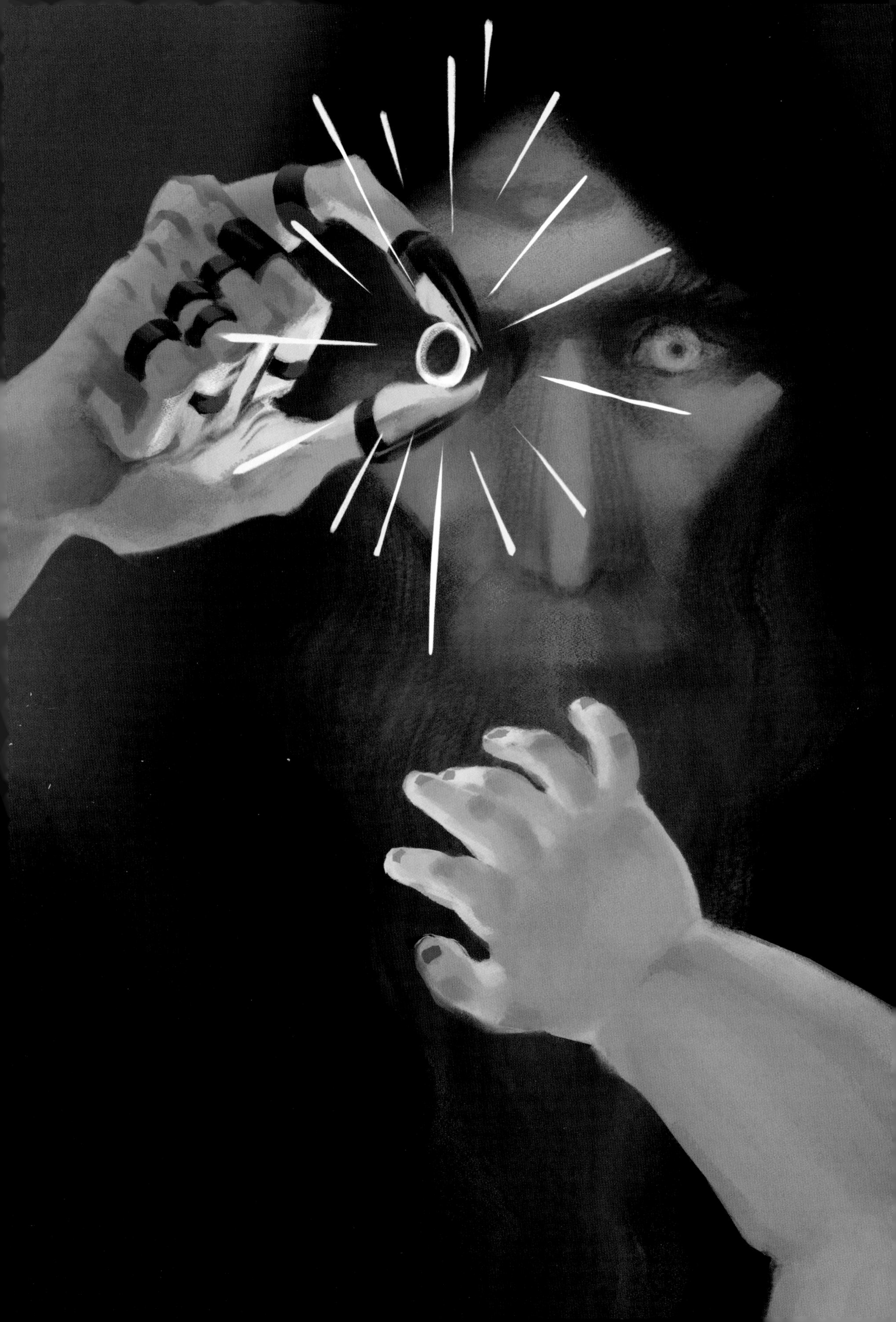

The Sixth Finger

Bogotá, Colombia, 11978 HE (1978 CE)

Mrs. Oslem Mohamet only agreed to go in for the hernia repair because her daughter, Asli Mohamet, refused to eat her food unless the pouch of her mother's bowel was placed back where it belonged.

"But Asli hanam, I can put it back in myself. Look," Mrs. Mohamet said, her eyes rolling up to the kitchen ceiling, her hand disappearing beneath her dress. The pads of her fingers massaged the soft mass of flesh protruding from her abdomen, easing it through the hole in the muscle wall until it disappeared.

"Mama, you know and I know that it will pop out again!" Asli said, pushing the plate of imam bayildi across the dining table and crossing her arms. A flowery bowl of salad, a dish of yogurt with diced cucumber, a plate of warm pita bread cut into halves, and a platter of couscous were jammed onto the wooden table, which was never large enough for the food Mrs. Mohamet cooked when her daughter made time to visit.

The hernia had first popped out the day before the second Eid. When it happened, Mrs. Mohamet had been lifting a large saucepan of boiled milk flavored with rose syrup from where it had been cooling in the corner of the kitchen floor.

She had lifted the pan, perched it on her right knee, pinned the fridge door open with her left elbow, and pushed her chest out as she thrust the pan from her knee to the middle shelf of the fridge. "Ooh!" she groaned, feeling a tug beneath the waistband of her pajamas.

When the fridge door was closed, she pulled her pants down and patted a hand over her softly corrugated stomach until her fingertips settled on a bouncy bulge of flesh in the lower left corner.

After Asli left, Mrs. Mohamet turned her back to the kitchen window, lifted her dress, and felt a fresh delight at the sight of the bulge. It was as if a new friend had come to visit.

The hernia didn't cause her any pain, and Mrs. Mohamet wished she hadn't mentioned it to her daughter. But she had been curious about the growing mass and wanted to show somebody.

At night, she fell asleep with her hand on the escaped coil of intestine that pulsed beneath her skin. The smooth muscle moved like a worm underneath her fingers, and the slow and steady rhythm of peristalsis pushed her into a pleasant sleep.

She dreamed she was riding the train from Istanbul to Ankara, bouncing up and down and side to side in an unpadded seat as the carriage rolled along the tracks. She arrived at the train station, where a horse-drawn carriage carried her up a dirt road to her village.

Her mother, her hair long and loose, was carrying a bowl of green figs into their house. They drank tea at the rickety kitchen table, and when Mrs. Mohamet took a final sip, her mother took the cup from her daughter's hands to read her future. The lacy trail of tea leaves reminded Mrs. Mohamet of the pattern on a dress she had sewn for Asli when she was a baby.

Mrs. Mohamet's mother peered into the cup. Her eyes grew wide. She raised her hand to her mouth and coughed and coughed, pulling Mrs. Mohamet out of sleep and into the overcast Tuesday morning in Bogotá.

Over lunch, Mrs. Oslem Mohamet again demonstrated her ability to push the hernia back into her abdomen. "It's called 'reducible,' Asli hanam," Mrs. Mohamet said. Asli was shaking her umbrella in the entrance to the kitchen. "That is what it is called when you can push it back into you. The childish doctor you sent me to said so."

The doctor had also told Mrs. Mohamet that the escaped loop of bowel could become knotted, trapped outside of the internal cavity beneath the skin, and starved of oxygen, a phenomenon called strangulation. The tissue could die a black death and take Mrs. Mohamet to an early grave.

She didn't mention this to Asli. She couldn't imagine that her body would betray her in that way, that flesh would choose to strangle itself.

Mrs. Oslem Mohamet was born Oslem Aydin in a sky-blue house in a village that faced magnificent rippling hills. The village was a day's ride by horse, two days by donkey, from Ankara.

Her mother, Zeynep, was descended from the great Sheikh Abu Zafar. He had fallen in love with a beautiful djinniyah who had traveled from an island somewhere in the Indian Ocean. They had married during the earliest days of the magnificent Ottoman empire, sometime around 1350. The magical vestiges of this union were said to have dissipated over the generations so that Zeynep was left only with the gift to foresee storms, offspring, and bad marriages. She would hang a spoon over a swollen abdomen and predict the sex of the baby or the number of fetuses growing inside. It was said in the village that this was because the smokeless fire of the djinn flowed through her veins. Zeynep didn't tell them it was because she was able to speak with a nosy djinniyah cousin who told her the secrets of the future (which she had learned from eavesdropping on the angels). "When you see shooting stars in the night sky, those are the missiles the angels fling at me to shoo me away," the cousin said, her amber eyes sparkling with glee.

The day Zeynep's only daughter was born, the midwife counted six fingers on the baby girl's right hand. She congratulated the young parents on the bonus digit and warned them never to remove it.

"Empires will topple. Seas will rise. If this child's finger is ever taken, six great calamities will descend from the heavens," she said, and then she spat an amber mush of dates and figs into the baby's mouth.

A djinni Zeynep met a week later confirmed the news. The shrouded figure stood next to a well at the edge of an orchard. He had his back to Zeynep as she walked through the tall grass with her daughter strapped to her back. He lowered his hood as Zeynep leaned forward, pressing her palms into her knees to catch her breath. When the shrouded figure turned to bless the newborn and her mother, Zeynep noticed there were six fingers on both of his hands. She had never seen this djinni before. "Consider me a long-lost relative," he whispered, sliding a tiny silver ring onto the newborn's sixth finger. He turned around, walked toward the well, and vanished.

And so Oslem Aydin's mother, a sweet woman who enjoyed reading tea leaves and tarot cards, bought her daughter ever larger silver rings to adorn the special finger. On Oslem's tenth birthday, she received a silver band inscribed with surah al-fatiha. On her eighteenth birthday, the ring was wide enough for ayat al-kursi.

Oslem collected the previous years' rings in a silver box painted with turquoise flowers. When she married and moved to Bogotá, the box stayed in a dresser drawer, shrouded in silk scarves. When her husband died and she moved to a smaller apartment near her daughter's medical school, the box sat on her bedside table.

The sixth finger had remained ringless since her husband's death. Whether it was naked or wrapped in silver, Mrs. Mohamet knew her finger was special.

The day of the hernia repair, Mrs. Mohamet made her tea with an extra tablespoon of loose black leaves and no milk. She was half following the hospital's orders to go in for surgery with an empty stomach and half hoping the extra caffeine would jolt her heart into a rhythm unsuited to surgery.

But the nurse peeling the EKG pads from her chest gave her a thumbs-up. A second nurse poked a pink cannula into the crease of her elbow, ready for the milky anesthetic. She pushed Mrs. Mohamet's bed into the vestibule outside the operating room, where a third nurse approached her from behind with a clipboard and asked her to sign another set of consent forms.

Mrs. Mohamet had told the surgical nurse, the phlebotomist, and the anesthetist the very important message. Short of the surgeon, who she had not met, she had told everyone: "This is very important. On no account must my finger be removed."

The surgical nurse had chuckled as she peeled off the sticky pads. The phlebotomist had shrugged. The anesthetist had smiled and patted her on the shoulder. "Why would we do that if you're here for a hernia repair?" said a nameless doctor who stood at her side wearing a gown and mask. She clutched a metal clipboard with yet another consent form that Mrs. Mohamet was made to sign in a language not her own.

"Are you the surgeon?" Mrs. Mohamet asked.

"No," the woman whispered, shaking her head. She took Mrs. Mohamet's raised hand and pressed it down into the bed. "Don't worry about your hand. You're here for the hernia."

Mrs. Mohamet pursed her chapped lips. "In these countries they get rid of anything they think is abnormal," she said. The masked doctor slid the metal clipboard out of Mrs. Mohamet's hand and adjusted the bed so that she was lying flat. Mrs. Mohamet was rolled into the operating room, where the anesthetist looked down at her, his face a pale moon. She watched the moon blinking as she sank into a milky sleep.

She dreamed the hills surrounding her village were wobbling. No, they were shaking. Were they crashing? Rubble descended toward her childhood home and somebody was stroking her feet. Her feet? She was awake. Asli hanam had one hand on her mother's foot; the other held a slim textbook, *A Complete Guide to Obstetrics*.

"They gave me this to rub on the tip of your nose if you feel queasy," she said, waving a small square packet containing a piece of tissue steeped in alcohol. Mrs. Mohamet was not queasy. Her stomach ached. The side of her hand throbbed beneath layers of gauze bound by a long white bandage wrapped around her palm.

When she returned to her flat, she moved the silver box with the turquoise flowers to the bottom drawer of the chest that sat inside the closet. She boiled rice and fried aubergines to make imam bayildi. Asli packed the leftovers to take home. When she had gone, her hands loaded with plastic carrier bags full of food, Mrs. Mohamet stacked the dishwasher, filled the washing machine, set the timers for midnight, and went to bed.

Loud knocking at the door woke her. *Tut tut tut*, as if wood was banging wood. Her alarm clock had not yet sung so it had to be before sunrise, she thought. Mrs. Mohamet slipped an abayah over her head and opened the door.

The short Turkish man who lived in the flat below rushed past her with a mop in one hand and a towel in the other. His thin white beard gave him the appearance of a garden gnome.

He made a beeline for the laundry room. "Must be coming from here. Must be!" he said. The green light of the washing machine was flashing to indicate the load was clean. The linoleum floor sat beneath four inches of soapy water.

"All down my walls, all on my carpet," the man was saying. "Mrs. Mohamet, how can I fix this when I have to lead the Fajr prayers?"

Mrs. Mohamet left the man reaching behind her washing machine in search of the plug and walked to the kitchen, where the phone was ringing. Her socks soaked up more water. The dishwasher lights flashed red and green. Water seeped out of the machine. When she answered the phone, a garbled voice spoke in long, nonsensical sentences.

She called the first number in her phonebook. Asli answered. "Mummy," she said quietly, "I've been vomiting all night. Really bad diarrhea as well. I'm going to miss my exam."

The next week, Mrs. Mohamet took the bus alone to her post-operative checkup at the hospital. The same nurse who had slipped the cannula into her arm ushered her into the examination room. "You'll never believe this," she said with enthusiasm. She lifted the dressing on Mrs. Mohamet's abdomen. "Nobody could believe it." But Mrs. Mohamet already knew what she would say.

The surgeon who had operated on Mrs. Mohamet had collapsed on top of his next patient, right after he had converted a laparoscopic surgery to an open one. The patient's bowels were resting on top of his chest and groin. Damp rags lay over the guts to keep them wet and warm.

"Heart attack," the nurse said. "Was humming along to Brahms one minute, went all wobbly the next, and fell onto the wet rags on top of the poor man's bowels! Turns out he had a bad heart. Your wound looks very good, though."

Three more, thought Mrs. Mohamet as she left the hospital. She considered the two dead cats by the side of her doorstep as she searched her handbag for a key. *Maybe one more.*

It is a mundane thing, the business of waiting for calamity. In the kitchen, Mrs. Mohamet filled a saucepan with water, expecting the faucet to jam or the water to emerge in explosive jets of smelly brown liquid. When she pushed buttons on the fan that refused to work, she wondered if the fuse might blow or if deranged wires would send electricity up her arm and fry her heart like an aubergine.

She drank her tea at the kitchen table, staring at the pink and yellow flower arrangement that Asli had bought for her before she herself had fallen sick. The diarrhea had subsided, but her daughter had retched and vomited for days, missing a whole semester's worth of exams.

She spat the last sip of tea back into the mug and swirled the liquid around. Leaves settled in the shape of a broken egg. She rubbed her hand as she left the kitchen and walked to her bed to take a nap.

When Asli called, Mrs. Mohamet was dreaming about a young woman plucking ripe figs from a short tree, its boughs heavy with fruit. The woman was squeezing the green orbs between her fingers until they exploded in a riot of pink pulp and white sap. The woman howled, flung the crushed figs to the ground, and stomped on them. Then she got on her knees and collected the mess into her lap.

Mrs. Mohamet's brow was clammy, and her belly ached a little as she reached for the phone on her bedside table. Asli said not to worry and that she was fine now, but in the early hours of that morning she had woken to thick clots oozing into her underwear.

Mrs. Mohamet prayed surah al-fatiha and blew through the phone. She told her daughter to drink strong black tea; it would help to expel any remaining tissue. "They took it all, mummy," Asli said. "The doctor took it all."

"I know," said Mrs. Mohamet, rocking back and forth, cradling the handset as if it were her daughter. "I know."

Djinni-Human Offspring

Some human families claim djinn ancestry. They explain all manner of "inherited" peculiarities and seemingly magical traits by way of ancestors from al-ghayb. Two 'alimahs I interviewed in Perth said that, much like the Banu Si'lat, both of their families descended from the pairing of a djinniyah with a man. It was this lineage that gave one of them the ability to commune with djinn and the other the gift of prophetic dreams. (Although, when I referred to this as a gift, the 'alimah said it was really a curse since she had night terrors that predicted only tragedy.)

It was these women who were able to locate Mrs. Mohamet's daughter, Asli. I had learned of Mrs. Mohamet's story a year or so earlier through a case report that Asli published anonymously in a journal about the esoteric. As a practicing physician, Asli offered no clues to her location and did not publish using her real name. But when I mentioned the story and the Mohamets, familial relation to djinn, the two 'alimahs (who also asked not to be named) came back to me days later with Asli's location (she was based in Istanbul) and email address.

This was not the first time this had happened. When I read a report about an older man possessed by a djinn that lived in his phone, I had only the initials of the report's author and the location of the incident (New Jersey). About a year after learning of that case, a message landed in my inbox with A. S-P.'s full name, address, and email. This is when I began to understand that, much like the great poets, scholars such as myself might be guided and aided by djinn. I began to wonder why a djinn would be motivated to assist in the writing of a compendium about its kind, especially since the nefarious agenda of the Sheikh was known to me by then, and so, I assumed, known to my Qareen and any djinn accompanying me on my travels. But time and time again during the research and writing of this book, knowledge from the realm of the Unseen has landed in my inbox, tapped me on the shoulder in airports and souks, and somehow guided me to source after valuable source.

I emailed Asli with the understanding that much like A. S-P., she might be spooked and upset that I had found her. On the contrary, she wanted to speak on the phone and was happy for me to use her and her mother's full names. "I think mama would have liked for her story to be known," she said. "And I'm not worried about repercussions since I work in Turkey now. Everyone believes in djinn here."

Asli was kind enough to flesh out the details of her mother's story, the history of the hernia that should have resulted in a simple repair, and the nonconsensual finger amputation which-and Asli is firm on this belief-led to her mother's death. "Imagine," Asli said. "A healthy-ish woman, active and happy, goes in for a simple inguinal hernia mesh repair and leaves missing a finger. We told them so many times that the finger was not to be touched, but Mama had warned me that the reason she avoided doctors was because at every visit, whether it was to discuss urinary incontinence or a headache, they became enthralled with her finger and asked if they could remove it. I don't know what possessed them to treat Mama like she was some freak of nature who needed 'normalizing.'"

I asked Asli about her own health since her mother's story, as published in the article, ended with tragedy for her as well. She told me she suffered three more miscarriages after that one and had never been able to carry to term. "Mama was convinced I miscarried because her finger had been removed. That warning from her childhood, the one where our djinni cousin said never to harm that finger, she took that very seriously." Mrs. Mohamet died seven weeks after the surgery.

I learned of Nafisa's story during an internet search that led me to the piece she published on a blog for women trying to conceive (T.T.C.). She was easy to track down *without* any djinn intercessions since she included her contact information on the blog. Nafisa agreed to elaborate on her story, and we met in Gloucester to talk about the night that she was taken from her car. She walked into the café with an eight-year-old boy in tow. Ma'ez looked at me for all of half a second before he looked back down at his mother's iPad. He shared no physical similarities with his mother, but that's how genetics work, don't they? I have cousins who don't look like they belong in our tribe but are in fact our flesh and blood.

As boys are apt to do, Ma'ez remained glued to the iPad for the duration of our conversation, which lasted nearly two hours. But my eyes were glued on him. Were his eyebrows preternaturally bushy? Were his eyes green or turquoise? His hair was an unusual shade of brown, almost ash gray, and much lighter than Nafisa's jet-black locks. I asked to see a photo of Sam, assuming that he might be a light-skinned brother or even a White man. But when Nafisa scrolled through her Instagram account to show me photos of Ma'ez's recent birthday celebrations, she explained that Sam was short for Samir. The proud father beaming next to Ma'ez and his Batman birthday cake was as dark-skinned as Nafisa and shared her Somali features.

It was only when we were walking out of the café and toward our cars that either one of us addressed the elephant in the room. It was Nafisa who spoke. "I know what you're thinking. And yes," she said. She put her hand on the boy's shoulder and angled him toward me, although his body was facing the car and his nose was almost touching the screen. "Allah works in mysterious ways."

Later that week I spoke to Nafisa's imam, who confirmed that he had been present when she gave birth to a djinni. Although the djinn clan apparently offered her the child as a reward for her kindness, they took Ma'ez away from her a day after his birth and only returned him to Nafisa and Sam six months later. The imam said that in these instances, djinn might use a human to create a hybrid child with non-djinn characteristics. "Nafisa has no children of her own," he said. I beg to disagree.

MORE THAN A WOMAN, LESS THAN A DJINNIYAH

The Qur'an tells only a single story of an independently prosperous and formidable woman. She is never mentioned by name, much like the twenty or so women who appear in the Holy Book (only Maryam, mother of Isa, is ever named). But this woman is the only one who is described independently of her relationship to a man. We do not meet her as a wife, a mother, or a daughter; she is identified by her status as a sovereign, the only female head of state in the Qur'an: the Queen of Sheba.

We come to know of her as Bilqis through Islamic folklore, which melded with Yemenite tales over the centuries. We learn more about her through Jewish stories, Ethiopian legends, and Javanese accounts. She is known as Makida in the *Kebra Nagast*, the Ethiopian book of kings. Some scholars trace the word *Bilqis* to the Hebrew *pilegesh*, meaning "concubine." But while the Prophet-King Sulaiman oversaw an infamous interfaith and interracial harem of concubines and wives, the Queen of Sheba (in some tellings) adopts Islam, becomes his faithful wife, continues her role as a just and wise leader, and is never taken into the harem.

Before we arrive at the Bilqis of folklore and her connection to the world of the djinn, let us remind ourselves of the brief and inconclusive story of the Queen of Sheba as it appears in the Qur'an.

One day, the great King Sulaiman, son of King Dawud (David in the Bible), was presiding over his vast army when he noticed his hoopoe was missing. Sulaiman threatened to punish or even slaughter the missing bird. The all-knowing king, who was blessed with enormous knowledge and the power to commune with animals and djinn, was stunned when his hoopoe returned with a revelation.

إِنِّي وَجَدتُّ امْرَأَةً تَمْلِكُهُمْ وَأُوتِيَتْ مِن كُلِّ شَيْءٍ وَلَهَا عَرْشٌ عَظِيمٌ

Lo! I found a woman ruling over them, and she has been given (abundance) of all things, and she possesses a Mighty Throne.

—Holy Qur'an 27:23

The hoopoe is referring to the queen of a land called Saba (Sheba), thought to be in Yemen or in Axum, Ethiopia, thousands of miles from Sulaiman's Palestinian palace. The queen, the hoopoe tells the king, reigns over a technologically advanced queendom and possesses great wealth. Her throne is made of silver and gold, embellished with rubies and pearls, and draped in curtains crafted from the finest silks.

The queen's single flaw: She worships the sun. Shaytan has blocked her blessings and hindered her from knowing the one true God. Hearing of the queen's magnificence and ignorance, King Sulaiman sends a brief missive via his avian emissary, inviting the queen to worship Allah.

أَلَّا تَعْلُوا عَلَيَّ وَأْتُونِي مُسْلِمِينَ

Be ye not arrogant against me, but come to me in submission.

—Holy Qur'an 27:31

Armed with immense weaponry and an expansive, species-spanning army, Sulaiman also possesses great might and mystical powers, including the ability to summon the wind and travel in one night the distance most traverse in a month. He can also turn the wind against those he wishes to conquer. Sulaiman has deployed these capabilities in the service of subjugating other kingdoms, and now, perhaps, will turn them upon a queendom.

وَلِسُلَيْمَانَ الرِّيحَ غُدُوُّهَا شَهْرٌ وَرَوَاحُهَا شَهْرٌ وَأَسَلْنَا لَهُ
عَيْنَ الْقِطْرِ وَمِنَ الْجِنِّ مَن يَعْمَلُ بَيْنَ يَدَيْهِ بِإِذْنِ رَبِّهِ
وَمَن يَزِغْ مِنْهُمْ عَنْ أَمْرِنَا نُذِقْهُ مِنْ عَذَابِ السَّعِيرِ

And We subdued the wind to Solomon: its morning course was a month's journey and its evening course was a month's journey. We gave him a spring flowing with molten brass, and We subdued for him djinn who, by his Lord's permission, worked before him. And whoever of them deviated from Our command, We made them taste the torment of the blaze.

—Holy Qur'an 34:12

Ever mindful of the king's propensity to invade and conquer, and intrigued by his use of a hoopoe as emissary, the queen sends messengers bearing gifts to defuse the threat and elucidate whether Sulaiman is perhaps more than a king, and possibly a prophet. Medieval scholars tell us the gifts included camels laden with gold, spices, frankincense, and riddles.

Sulaiman receives advance warning that the queen's courtiers are bringing gifts and so he gathers his troops to welcome the envoys. The army stretches for three miles and includes subservient tigers, lions, and djinn. The gift-bearing messengers walk past this impressive display and step into a palace made of sandalwood and gold. When they offer their gifts, Sulaiman refuses them.

فَلَمَّا جَاءَ سُلَيْمَانَ قَالَ أَتُمِدُّونَنِ بِمَالٍ فَمَا آتَانِيَ اللَّهُ
خَيْرٌ مِّمَّا آتَاكُم بَلْ أَنتُم بِهَدِيَّتِكُمْ تَفْرَحُونَ

ارْجِعْ إِلَيْهِمْ فَلَنَأْتِيَنَّهُم بِجُنُودٍ لَّا قِبَلَ لَهُم بِهَا
وَلَنُخْرِجَنَّهُم مِّنْهَا أَذِلَّةً وَهُمْ صَاغِرُونَ

When the chief-envoy came to him, Sulaiman said, "Do you offer me wealth? What Allah has granted me is far greater than what He has granted you. No! It is you who rejoice in receiving gifts. Go back to them, for we will certainly mobilize against them forces which they can never resist, and we will drive them out from there in disgrace, fully humbled."

—Holy Qur'an 27: 36–37

The queen is intrigued by the rejection. She pays Sulaiman a visit, but as she makes the journey to Palestine, Sulaiman asks from among his djinn if there is one who can bring Sheba's magnificent throne to him before she arrives. Her throne, which is thirty yards tall, forty yards wide, and eighty yards long, is enclosed within seventy walls.

From among the djinn, a mighty one responds: "I will fetch it for you in the twinkling of an eye." In a flash, the Queen of Sheba's throne stands before Sulaiman in Palestine. To test her acuity, Sulaiman alters the throne.

When the queen arrives, she is stunned by the beauty of Sulaiman's temple and the shimmering pool she must cross to enter the palace. She lifts her dress only to learn that it is crystal, not water, that she must walk over. The Queen is awed by Sulaiman's wealth and acumen. She tells him that his refusal of her gifts and his acquisition of her mighty throne is proof enough that he is not only a ruler but a prophet. She submits to Allah and asks the denizens of her queendom to do the same. The fact that she has recognized her altered throne proves to Sulaiman that she is a wise woman who has witnessed his ability to command miracles.

The Qur'an says no more about the couple's fate or the Queen of Sheba's lineage. Prophetic narratives and medieval Muslim scholars fill in the gaps, perhaps to make sense of these two contradictory themes: A powerful sovereign is a woman, according to the Qur'an, but women cannot be successful rulers, according to the sayings of the Holy Prophet (p.b.u.h.). And so the non-Qur'anic story goes that Bilqis was not fully human. She was born to King al-Hadhhadh, the mighty ruler of Yemen, and a nonhuman mother.

One day, the king was hunting when he saw two creatures fighting. In some accounts the animals are a white serpent and a black serpent; in other stories they are deer. In any case, one serpent was poised to kill the other, or one of the deer was in danger of being killed, until King al-Hadhhadh saved its life. The animal was grateful, for not only was its life spared, but also its curse was lifted and it was able to resume its natural form. After transforming from a serpent or a deer into the djinni king Sakan, the formerly cursed sovereign offered the Yemeni king a reward: Al-Hadhhadh could marry the djinni king's daughter, Raihanah Bint As-Sakan. When the king consummated his marriage, Bilqis was born, the daughter of a human king and a djinniyah princess.

Bilqis possessed supernatural powers, as such chimeric children do, and grew up mastering the arts of metamorphosis and magic. She was thirty years old and unmarried when King al-Hadhhadh died and his kingdom was usurped by an unscrupulous man. The new king was a misogynist who raped women while their husbands watched. So the brave and brilliant Bilqis hatched a plan. She married the man, got him drunk, and chopped off his head. The Yemenites rejoiced at the death of their despotic leader and hailed Bilqis as the Queen of Sheba.

Rumors circulated that the half-woman, half-djinniyah queen had the legs of a donkey, and here we return to the Qur'an: the Queen of Sheba's arrival at Sulaiman's palace and the explanation from folklore as to why she was made to lift her skirt and step onto King Sulaiman's shimmering palatial floors. The floor was a test: If the Queen of Sheba lifted her dress, the king would see if she had the legs of a human or the donkey legs of a half-djinniyah being.

Rumors and negative characterizations of Bilqis in Islamic folklore and legend stand at odds with the queen's Qur'anic portrayal as a powerful, independent woman beloved by her people. But when another queen is mentioned in the presence of the Holy Prophet (p.b.u.h.), this time a queen elected to rule the people of Persia, the Prophet says, "Never will succeed such a nation as makes a woman their ruler."[28]

Folklore helps to make sense of the contradiction. The djinniyah legend persists as a convenient bridge between both versions of her story. Bilqis, it is said, must be more than a woman in order to be a wise and formidable sovereign.

28 From Sahih al-Bukhari 7099, Book 92, Hadith 50.

The Girl in the Purple Hijab

Rome, Italy, 12009 HE (2009 CE)

There once lived a teenaged girl who wore a purple hijab. Every day, the same color. The ignorant ones with skin a different hue to hers would sneer, "Why do you wear that silly thing on your head? Don't you know women here are free?" Her face stayed expressionless, but into their lavender-oat-milk-double-shot-extra-foam lattes, she poured milk in the shape of a frowning face.

The ignorant ones with skin the same shade as hers would say, "Why do you wear the same one every day? Don't you know there are so many different fabrics and colors and styles now? Even H&M does halal fashion. Dolce has halal couture, if you can afford it." As they waited for the women's side entrance to be unlocked for Jummah prayers, she would look down at her feet, and with the tip of her ballet flats she would push the dusty stones in the mosque yard until the gravel formed a maudlin expression.

Her mother wore a purple hijab; her grandmother, great-grandmother, and all of her aunts and great-aunts had worn one, too. She came from a long line of purple hijab–wearing women—women who had lived century-spanning lives in Rome since at least the time of Caesar. Before that time, they were healers in a land called Kush, where they had lived even longer. The color purple was a family tradition. It was believed that wearing it would heal and protect, not to mention accent the glints of amber in their otherwise dark eyes. Even when the emperor staged public executions of anyone who dared to wear the regal color, her ancestors, she was told, bravely held on to tradition. For centuries, this conviction, paired with their ability to catch and crush the rarest insects to make the longest-lasting purple dye, had been their secret weapon.

She thought about the strong women who had lived before her as she hopped over a puddle on the cobbled street. The rain slowed; she pressed her back into the yellowing plaster of a church next to the bus stop. A gaggle of White girls spilled out of a souvenir store, looked in her direction, and erupted into laughter. She stood stone-still and remembered how purple had protected so many ancestors. The girls turned and walked in the opposite direction.

In a lecture the next morning, her sociology professor made the class watch a YouTube video of an attack in Mogadishu days earlier. Her cheeks burned when the professor paused the video and repeated, "Ala . . . hua-ukbhaaar," or something like it, in a terrible accent. "Listen to what they are saying. They are inciting—no, inflicting—deathly violence because of their God." The professor looked around the hundred-seat lecture theater, transmitting her disdain. "How does this make us feel?" she asked. "Disgusted," a young woman said. Students whispered when the lecture was finally over. They backed into the walls and made space so the girl in the purple hijab could exit.

On Saturdays, she worked as a medical scribe in the emergency department. On this particular afternoon, an elderly lady with a forehead gash that would not stop oozing blood requested the doctor use a different scribe. "But why?" said the doctor, a drop of anesthetic dripping from the needle in his hand. He spoke with all the enthusiasm of a sleepy child as he poked the long needle into the woman's forehead. "She wears the thing," said the patient. "But she is only here to help us," he said. The woman clucked her tongue. "I don't like it, doctor. Makes my heart feel funny." The doctor shrugged. "I think that is your angina, Mrs. Bianchi."

Outside the hospital, three magpies stopped drinking from a fountain and cocked their heads in the girl's direction. Clouds heavy with water drifted over the hospital and merged into one gray mass. The birds flew away.

Since it was threatening to rain, she walked the mile to the Piscina delle Rose. The weather would scare away swimmers at the outdoor pool, she thought, but when she arrived, rows of pasty limbs flanked the water's edge. She unfurled the bundle of Lycra at the bottom of her satchel and smoothed the wrinkles inside a changing cubicle. Mama had lovingly sewn the lilac burkini with a tight hood to keep her head dry and her purple hijab secure.

"Those things are illegal in Varallo Sesia," said the lifeguard when she emerged. He scratched his hairy calf with the toes of his opposite foot. "They should be banned in Roma as well." She slunk into the pool and sliced the water with her hands. Heads turned right to left, left to right as she swam her laps.

Home had been happier these days, ever since Mama's herbal offerings had eased the growth of Papa's cancer. Papa smiled and kissed his daughter's cheek when she entered, his wrinkled hands full of roots, vines, and a rolled-up newspaper. "Running errands for your Mama," he said, winking. Mama was in the kitchen, balancing on an upturned wooden crate, peering over a pot big enough to bathe two babies. She stirred the dark water with a thick stick until a vortex spun in its middle.

No, she couldn't stay and eat, the girl told Mama. She had a shift at the café starting in just forty minutes, and it would take at least a half hour to get there in traffic. "Well, at least let me give you this new hijab I made for you," Mama said, ushering her into the pantry. There hung a freshly dyed purple triangle. They closed the door and carefully made the switch. When she emerged from the pantry, she felt fresh and new, like she had slept for eight uninterrupted hours. Mama conjured a snack bag seemingly out of nowhere and pressed the brown paper filled with dried apricots and cashews into her precious daughter's hand.

The Mogadishu attack was still front-page news. She read the tourist's newspaper upside down as she poured his Americano. Three Italians were among the dead, so the story demanded ink for at least two more days. The Italian prime minister was promising to "purge" the land of evil, beginning with a moratorium on the building of new mosques and expanded surveillance of those groups "inclined to acts of terror." The tourist looked at the newspaper, looked at her, and retrieved the folded bill he had dropped into the tip jar.

She took a less efficient route home that evening. A longer walk down a narrower alley to a lonelier bus stop, where a less frequently running bus would drop her at a spot farther away from home. When the bus finally veered around the corner, its wide front almost scraping the fifteenth-century courthouse, it carried on past the bus stop. She jumped back as huge tires splashed a dirty puddle across the pavement and onto her feet. She could swear the driver was smiling. But the flash of teeth might have been the glare of headlights reflected through the puddle.

Her ballet flats squelched water between her toes as she arrived at the corner of the winding alleyway, the spot where the local boys revved engines and spun their mopeds in tight circles. Her feet were cold, her hijab was damp, and her jaw was tense and aching.

The first boy drove his red Vespa along her left side. The second hopped his scooter onto the pavement and followed behind her, his engine revving and braking so that the putrid smell of diesel mixed with the acrid stench of burning rubber. The boy on the red Vespa reached out an arm and tugged at her hijab above her left ear. She yanked her head to the right. He lost his grip and grabbed again, clenching the purple fabric in his fist. She pulled away harder, so hard that she smacked her right temple on the side of a building. The street became blacker. She staggered for a moment, steadying herself against the wet brick. The boys howled.

A third boy approached from her left and spun his moped in front of her, stopping with his front wheel almost touching her toes. He reached over the handlebars and grabbed the lip of the purple fabric where it skimmed her forehead. She pulled her head back. She felt the boy behind her tug at the end of the hijab that Mama had wrapped around her neck and tucked into her denim jacket. From the front, from the back, from the side, they grabbed at her hijab.

"STOP!" she yelled. The boys let up for a second, bemused by her protest, and immediately began to tug again. She wrapped her arms around her head, her right palm cradling her left ear, her left palm cradling her right. She twisted and turned, her elbows poking into the dark spaces, but the boys dodged her sharp edges. They pulled and tugged. They laughed and yanked.

"Stop!" She said it more quietly this time. She could feel her insides loosening their grip, a sensation similar to how she had felt hours earlier, when Mama had gently lifted and replaced her hijab in the pantry. She had felt airy and soft, then safe and warm. Mama's hands had gently peeled back the fabric, cradled her head, and raked her fingers through her hair. Then Mama had draped this new hijab over her head, knotted it tightly at the back, and secured the ends inside her jacket while whispering seven supplications for safety.

The boy behind her pulled at Mama's knot, his fingers wriggling to unravel what had been secured with prayers. The boy in front towered over her. He spoke to the boy behind her as if she weren't there, grunting and jeering. The pack tightened, enclosing her in its triangle. The pulling descended into something more aggressive. Their grunts deepened as they jerked her head back and forth and to the side.

"Stop," she whispered. Then in her quietest voice, "Stop, stop, stop." The boy in front pushed forward on his scooter, driving the wheels over her feet and into her shins. She yelped and crumpled to the ground. "Oh shit!" she heard them say.

That's when the blood drained from the tall boy's face. His cheeks went from pink to pale. In his right hand he gripped the top of her hijab—her unrelenting, immovable purple hijab. Its soft cloth and secure knots cradled her blinking, severed head.

"I told you to stop," said her head as her body lay on the pavement. She unwedged her torso from between the two mopeds. "Now, don't you dare drop my head," she said as she wiped her knees. The boy opened his mouth. No sound emerged. He too blinked as if he were the one who had been recently decapitated. But his surly head remained attached to his brutish body, if only for a moment longer.

The girl stood, retrieved her head from his grip, and reattached it with a squish and a click. She straightened her hijab on her head, reached for a loose end, and held a length of fabric between two fists. "Now," she said, "be silent." And although the tall boy with his neck conveniently at her eye level followed orders, the boy behind her fainted, and the boy to her left unleashed an unearthly sound. Back and forth, she sliced through the tall boy's neck with the purple cloth, the soft cotton suddenly as sharp as cheese wire. Blood spurted from his arteries and pooled on the ground. His head lolled where a piece of muscle hung on for dear life. She pulled the fabric back and forth against the flesh with a flourish. His head snapped off and fell to the ground with a satisfying *thunk*. "Now," she said, turning to the boy on the red Vespa. "Your turn."

"Hail Mary, full of grace, the Lord is . . ." She waited so he could finish. She swiped her ballet flat through the bloody puddle, dragging a red trail into a smiley face while he mumbled. But the boy was a quivering wreck; he couldn't complete his prayer. As his voice trailed off, she wrapped his neck in a length of purple fabric and pulled the two ends. His eyes remained open as his head rolled down the cobbled street. She turned to the boy behind her, who was slumped over his handlebars. She would spare one witness, so that he could spread the oft-whispered but rarely believed rumor. *More people should believe*, she thought as she tied her hijab and tucked the bloodied ends into her jacket.

HEADLESS DJINN

Years ago, on a research trip to the underground Catacombe dei Cappuccini in Sicily, I walked among the twelve hundred or so mummified bodies of the island's former inhabitants, entombed there since the 11500s HE. Back then, the dead were dehydrated, bathed in vinegar, and either laid out in crypts or hung from the cave's walls. There was a baby girl seemingly asleep in a glass coffin, her mummified corpse dressed in a white baptism dress, a red rose at her side, its stem as long as her body. A postman's remains were pinned to the cave's dimly lit wall, his skeleton shrouded in a traditional uniform and a satchel. I was in search of cemetery-dwelling ghul, but found none. Instead, a young woman sweeping at the tomb's entrance led me to the story of the girl in the purple hijab.

I had not mentioned my research on djinn to anyone in Italy, nor did I appear as a researcher with notebook and pen in hand. I was simply another foreign visitor to Sicily, enjoying a walk through the macabre tourist attraction. But the girl, who had barely glanced in my direction on my way in, blocked my exit from the inner chamber by kneeling on the floor to pick something off the ground. She stood to face me and spoke in Italian. "Mi scusi, inglese o arabo," I replied in my limited Italian as she reached for my hand. "Catacombe di San Callisto" is all she said, in a whisper. She pressed a fragment of soft, purple fabric into my palm and closed my fingers around it, before turning away. I was confounded, but between my lack of Italian and her disappearance into the tombs, my questions were left unanswered.

Back in Rome, I headed to the Catacombs of Saint Callixtus, the site the young woman had quietly mentioned, on the assumption that she was recommending a different (better?) set of tombs. Indeed, this necropolis was older, dating back to the second century; deeper, with twenty meters of underground crypts, extending over twelve miles; and home to many more bodies. Among its half million decedents are sixteen popes and ten martyrs.

Perhaps there would be ghuls here, or at least traces of their presence, I hoped. By now, I was deeply entrenched in the supernatural, in the power of possibility-the belief that anything could happen anywhere. And this was to be just one of *many* encounters during my period of djinn research when a stranger serendipitously led me on a voyage of discovery.

I walked down to the first floor of the tombs and instinctively reached inside my bag as I looked up at the skeletons hanging from the wall. I fumbled for the purple fabric buried somewhere in the satchel. And in the manner of a fainthearted tourist who has no business walking among a half million dead bodies, I unleashed a high-pitched howl. But it wasn't the mummies that caused me to cry out; it was a blade in my satchel that had sliced my palm. A blade that appeared out of nowhere. As I had fumbled around for the scrap of material, something sharp had cut me. But when I dropped my satchel to the ground, pulled out my bloodied hand, and wrapped the scrap of fabric around it to staunch the blood, there was nothing inside the bag but the notebook, pens, lipstick, hand cream, and wallet that I had placed there earlier.

As luck would have it (and there was much "luck" experienced in the course of writing this compendium), a pediatrician on holiday from Nigeria came over to where I was kneeling. She said my gash was deep enough to warrant antibiotics and possibly a dozen or so stitches. The doctor in the ER was not as concerned. He said stitches across the palm were a nuisance and instead he fobbed me off to a nurse who washed the cut and closed it haphazardly with sticky white strips. I walked out of the hospital with a bandaged right hand and a stained piece of purple fabric, which I couldn't bring myself to discard for some reason.

She spotted me before I saw her: the girl in the purple hijab. It was the fabric in my hand that she fixed her gaze upon, not me. She was resting against a fountain near the hospital's entrance, eating from a pouch of nuts and fruit. "Where did you get that?" she said. So I told her the story about the catacombs in Sicily and my trip to Rome, and before I knew it, I was regaling her with my belief in intuition and providence, how at every twist and turn of this journey into the realm of al-ghayb, I had been met by those who offered clues and new directions, and who helped me see the Unseen.

"She must have trusted you," she said. "The sweeping lady. To give you this fabric. She must have sensed that you can stomach these truths." And that's when she told me. Without hesitation or emotion or a break between sentences to catch her breath. At the end of the story, she took the fabric from me and stuffed it into her pocket.

During the French Revolution of the 11700s HE, and especially during the two-year Reign of Terror, the efficiency of a new and supposedly gentler method of execution led to the beheadings of an estimated forty thousand people. From those days of Madame Guillotine emerged the story of the Girl with the Velvet Ribbon. Sometimes the ribbon is green, and sometimes it is red or black, but the story almost always begins with a man intrigued by a woman who wears a ribbon around her neck.

The man falls in love with the beguiling woman and asks why she insists on wearing the ribbon. But the woman refuses to give him an answer. So the man asks whether she'll remove the ribbon if they marry. The woman says she might, but that he'll be sorry. Eventually they marry, and the husband asks his wife every day if she will remove the ribbon. "You'll be sorry," she says again. When he attempts to untie the ribbon, it unravels endlessly, as if it has no end.

One night the husband waits for his wife to fall asleep. He creeps up to her with a pair of scissors and cuts the ribbon in two. Her admonitions had been right all along. As the ribbon falls to the ground, so does her head. Terrified, the man flees while his wife's head cries, "I said you'd be sorry."

Alternate versions of the story end with the woman untying the ribbon herself or the ribbon never coming undone. In any case, it became fashionable after the French Revolution for women to tie a red ribbon around their necks where the guillotine would have left them headless.

Another decapitated woman features in the horror stories of the Tower of London and other sites frequented by King Henry VIII and his six wives. The king's second wife, Anne Boleyn, gave birth to a female heir, Queen Elizabeth I, and later a stillborn child-but not the male heir the king desired. For her failure to birth a son, and so that he could marry his third wife, Jane Seymour, Anne was charged with treason, incest, and adultery, among other false accusations. She was beheaded by a French swordsman in 11536 HE. (The king and Jane married a few days later.) Nowadays, Anne is seen drifting through the courtyard of the Tower of London with her head tucked beneath her arm.

Although the story of the Girl in the Purple Hijab unfolds in Rome, with a girl who hails from the Horn of Africa and whose head is (mostly) attached to a human-looking body, it reminds me of the creatures known as *penanggalan* in Malaysia, *manananggal* in the Philippines, and *kra-sue* in Thailand. In Malay, the name *penanggalan* originates from the world *tanggal*, meaning "to take off or remove," since the creature is able to remove its head. Penanggalan floats through dark streets, her disembodied head trailed by her spinal cord and the organs still attached to her. Some say the woman is a witch who only appears headless at nighttime; during the day, her head is attached to her body. But others say she is a djinniyah who ties her hijab tightly to secure her detachable head.

The Mermaid Djinniyah of Java

Java, Indonesia, 11300 HE (1300 CE)

Once upon a time, there was a divine being who had only one desire: to give all the love blooming inside her ever-growing heart to a deserving and capable companion. This mighty queen, for she ruled all of the South Seas, swam through forests of kelp, scaled underwater volcanoes, traversed coral reefs, and engaged in battle with ferocious and disobedient marine beasts while in search of her true love.

She swam east to west, she swam north to south, she swam up and down the differently colored layers of the seas, from the ocean's darkest depths to the cool and shallow pools of aquamarine lagoons. She danced with demersal creatures and sang with pelagic fish. She even ventured outside her queendom to consult with the djinn queens and kings who inhabited the underwater caves in empires neighboring hers.

The queen eyed sailors and mermen, surveyed merchants and tradespeople, and contemplated fellow kings and queens. She even considered giving her love to a kindly angel shark who once guided her through a stretch of mangrove trees lining one edge of her queendom. But everywhere she went, the beautiful ones looked away, for the queen was mighty and breathtaking, and her love was overpowering and tremendous.

The queen amassed more love inside her heart with every passing tide, until one day, while she was floating near the beach at sunset weaving white flowers into her hair, her heart began to pound. She could feel the chambers fluttering beneath her breast, the muscle pulsing fervently against flesh. The organ was swimming inside her ribcage, desperate to break free.

The waves grew taller, and the surf smashed into the beach. The queen swept aside her hair to watch the quivering skin across her breast. She cried to the moon. She wept and wept, and the oceans rose and rose until great floods drowned the low-lying islands.

When enough sorrow had escaped the queen, she plunged deep into her ocean and took shelter in a cage made of glittering coral. She fell asleep dreaming of the love she had witnessed between her father, a powerful king, and her mother, a half-djinniyah queen.

The next day, the queen resumed her search. She swam beneath islands, she swam over mountains, she swam between caverns, and she swam around forests. That night, her aching heart beat so feverishly that a great wail escaped her throat and her tail flapped ferociously. A magnificent tsunami swept across the queendom. Forests were ripped apart, coral reefs were smashed, and marine mammals were swept onto rocky shores. The queen surveyed the damage and tried to still her beating heart. When more grief had left her flesh, she lay down in her coral cage and fell asleep.

News of the queen's distress, her ever-filling heart, and the string of destruction it was causing spread across the queendom. The next morning a merman arrived with his entourage of crabs and fish. He was the queen's former lover, whose face she did not desire to see. This merman had not recognized the depth of the queen's love nor the ferocity of the queen's heart. He did not know how to receive love fully, nor did he know how to fully love the queen.

The merman offered his greetings, respect, and condolences. He was sure that the queen missed him; in fact, he was sure that it was him she was seeking. Staking his seven-pronged trident into the sandy seabed, the merman declared that the queen could love him if she so desired. He would allow it. Together they held the power to calm the seas.

The queen took in the merman, his trident, and his entourage. She licked her lips and flicked her tail and wondered if she could again love him. The truth was, she had never stopped loving him. But it was a foolish game to go back to the one who had bounced her abundant love into the ocean because he was too feeble and inexperienced to receive it. The queen bid him farewell, turned her back, and swam away. She wept and wept, the seas rose and rose, and a third tsunami stretched from the bottom of the sea to the ocean's waves. A tsunami bigger than the world had ever seen.

The flume of water reached for the sky, where it met the tip of a cyclone. Where water kissed air, where sea caressed wind, where ocean spray danced with the breeze, the queen met her love, Mataram. For while she had been searching the world she knew, swimming from low

ocean to high seas, her great love had been searching for her in the skies, dipping from the heights of the earth's atmosphere to the breeze that caressed the waves. The queen learned all of her love's names. He was Sirocco and Mistral and Chinook and Cape Doctor and Khamsin and Santa Ana and Harmattan and Pampero.

The queen was elated. Her big heart swelled. Now her heart could empty each day. Her love fed winds and was spread all over the world by the one who could carry it far and wide.

The queen still lives in the ocean, and Mataram still lives in the sky. But where sea meets air, where birds graze white foam, where whales breach the ocean's surface, where you feel a coolness against your cheek and the taste of salt across your lips—this is where the two convene to profess their undying, everlasting love.

The Islamification of Lore

I was told this story by a group of seamen who sailed trade routes around the Arafura, Banda, and Java Seas. They told me that some call the Queen of the Southern Seas by an ancient Javanese name, Nyai Roro Kidul. *Nyai* is the term used for an elderly woman, although the Nyai of this legend is a young woman with white flowers in her hair, a fish's tail, and a woman's upper body, which is sometimes draped in green silks. When Islam spread to this region, the mermaid queen came to be known as the djinniyah daughter of King Sulaiman and the Queen of Sheba.

The Nyai Roro Kidul of Javanese and Sundanese legend is a violent and beautiful creature, half woman, half fish, who preys on handsome young men on the beach. Her story may originate with animistic beliefs about a female deity of the Indian Ocean from pre-Hindu-Buddhist times. The Pajajaran kingdom was founded in West Java in the early 11500s HE and was conquered by the Islamic kingdom of Mataram, which originated in Central Java. Prabu Siliwangi was the ruler of Pajajaran before the Muslim conquest, and the story goes that in one of his harems lived a beautiful bride who gave birth to a beautiful girl, Dewi Kadita. Dewi's and her mother's immense beauty gave rise to jealous conspiracy theories. Eventually, the pair were cursed, so that their bodies appeared mutilated and disfigured. Prabu Siliwangi expelled his wife and daughter from the harem, and the vagrant mother died. Dewi Kadita wandered in her grief until she reached the shores of the Indian Ocean. A dream inspired her to jump into the ocean to expunge the curse. When she emerged from the water, she was once again beautiful, but she was no longer human.

The supernatural Dewi Kadita became sovereign of the Southern Sea, known to all as Nyai Roro Kidul. To exact revenge on her callous father and to avenge her mother's death, she married her father's rival, King Senapati of the Mataram state. It is this queenly figure who is said to police the seas and snatch the souls of men walking along the shore. They are feared dead by their loved ones, but in fact they have been transformed into eternal deep sea companions for Nyai Roro Kidul.

The love story told to me by the sailors reflects a Muslim extrapolation of the pre-Islamic Javanese and Sundanese tale. It is symptomatic of the arrival of Islam to the region and the melding of ancient folklore with the new(er) religion's beliefs. Senapati, the king whom Nyai Roro Kidul married, was the founder of the Muslim state of Mataram.

The Queen of the Southern Seas continues to inspire fear in Indonesians of all faiths. Seaside hotel resorts still dedicate a suite to the mermaid, decking out the room in white and green to appease her appetite for destruction, while asking visitors to avoid wearing the same silky green robes as the queen.

SORCERY AND THE STATE:
DIVISIVE DJINN AND MAGICAL CRIMES

The wolf's head was wrapped in lingerie. Within its severed skull, possibly jammed between its locked jaws, lay a curse which trapped an entire family in a series of wretched and damning events. Luckily for the family, they lived in a country with an anti-sorcery hotline. Officers were hurriedly dispatched from the Anti-Witchcraft Unit of Saudi Arabia's Committee for the Promotion of Virtue and the Prevention of Vice (Hai'a). The Anti-Witchcraft Unit broke the spell, and the family was freed from the wolf's bloody curse.

The Anti-Witchcraft Unit was established in 12009 HE and expanded to nine nation-spanning bureaus in 12011 HE. Its growth speaks to the Saudi Arabian government's belief in and disdain for magic, feelings not equally shared by all Muslims. The Ummah (the global Muslim community) is not a monolith. Even when "proof" appears in the form of decapitated evidence wrapped in a negligee, belief in the occult varies across the Ummah. Geography, age, ethnicity, culture, political ideology, and other factors inform a Muslim's belief in these phenomena.

In a survey of Muslims in more than two dozen countries, ranging from Russia to Thailand, and Tunisia to Pakistan, more than half affirmed that djinn exist. Nearly 9 out of 10 Muslims in Morocco believe in djinn, as do half of Iraqi Muslims.[29] In Kosovo, only around 1 in 4 Muslims admitted to believing in djinn, while 3 in 4 Muslim Malaysians said djinn exist. Muslims who observe the mandate to pray five times a day are more likely to believe in djinn compared to those of us who are not so observant.

But belief in witchcraft, sorcery, and the evil eye (negative energy or a curse that can be transmitted through a malignant glare) is considered more contentious and is less broadly accepted among Muslims. Almost 90 percent of Tunisian Muslims believe in witchcraft, while only 14 percent of Palestinians admit to the same. In Tanzania, 92 percent of Muslims say witches roam among them, while fewer than 10 percent of Bangladeshis think sorcery is real.

Those who believe might point to a number of Hadith and Qur'anic verses that confirm the legitimacy of evil eye.

وَإِن يَكَادُ الَّذِينَ كَفَرُوا لَيُزْلِقُونَكَ بِأَبْصَارِهِمْ لَمَّا
سَمِعُوا الذِّكْرَ وَيَقُولُونَ إِنَّهُ لَمَجْنُونٌ

The disbelievers would almost cut you down with their eyes when they hear you recite the Reminder, and say, "He is certainly a madman."

—Holy Qur'an 68:51

There is more explicit description of the evil eye in Hadith, which includes the story of a young girl who appeared with black stains on her face. The Holy Prophet (p.b.u.h.) told the girl that these stains were a result of the evil eye and that she could be cured with the help of an incantation (Sahih Muslim 26:5450).

Ibn 'Abbas reported Allah's Messenger (p.b.u.h.) as saying: "The influence of an evil eye is a fact; if anything would precede the destiny it would be the influence of an evil eye, and when you are asked to take bath (as a cure) from the influence of an evil eye, you should take bath."[30]

29 Pew Research Center, "The World's Muslims: Unity and Diversity," August 9, 12012 HE, https://www.pewresearch.org/religion/2012/08/09/the-worlds-muslims-unity-and-diversity-4-other-beliefs-and-practices.

30 From Sahih Muslim 2188, Book 39, Hadith 56.

The geographic, generational, and cultural diversity of belief in djinn and sorcery reveals how Islamic scripture is interpreted through a layered stack of historical, ethnic, geopolitical, and typically patriarchal prisms. People's relationships with that which cannot be seen are informed by those who wield power over them. The state can permit its citizens to blame a sorcerer for a run of bad luck or detain a witch for putting designs on another woman's husband.

In Saudi Arabia, this power dynamic is primarily defined by two particular strands of Islam. Salafism, an eighteenth-century conservative movement within Sunni Islam, promotes an absolute monotheism and warns against ascribing power to any entity besides God (including djinn). Salafis take their name from *al-salaf al-ṣāliḥ*, the Arabic term for the pious predecessors. This refers to the first three generations of Muslims, beginning with the Holy Prophet (p.b.u.h.). Salafis advocate for a return to the teachings of these originators, who they say epitomized a pure form of Islam. This means that literal interpretations of the Qur'an and a close reading of the Hadith are among their prescriptions for modern-day Muslims.

Wahhabism, an ultra-conservative movement which is the national religion of the Saudi state, considers it heretical and polytheistic to use incantations, talismans, or amulets, or to access otherworldly powers through djinn intercessors. Salafism and Wahhabism are connected ideologies: the kingdom of Saudi Arabia was created in the mid-eighteenth century through the collaboration of Muhammad bin Abd el-Wahhab, the founder of the Wahhabi movement, and Mohammed bin Saud, the chief of the house of Saud. All Wahhabis are Salafis, although the converse is not true.

Wahhabism banishes fetishes and talismans, accoutrements of idolatry which harken back to the pagan, pre-Islamic era. This is meant not only to promote Islam but also to foster nationalism. Abd el-Wahhab waged war against religious polymorphism because the diversity of practices that existed among the tribal groups of Arabia were an impediment to the rise of a unified Saudi kingdom.

Both Salafi and Wahhabi adherents support a literal reading of the Qur'an. Sorcery is portrayed in Qur'anic verses as a God-given portent, offered to humans as a test of faith. In a passage about angels teaching humans how to access magic, the Qur'an warns of the dire consequences for those humans who meddle in magic.

وَٱتَّبَعُوا۟ مَا تَتْلُوا۟ ٱلشَّيَـٰطِينُ عَلَىٰ مُلْكِ سُلَيْمَـٰنَ ۖ وَمَا كَفَرَ سُلَيْمَـٰنُ
وَلَـٰكِنَّ ٱلشَّيَـٰطِينَ كَفَرُوا۟ يُعَلِّمُونَ ٱلنَّاسَ ٱلسِّحْرَ وَمَآ أُنزِلَ عَلَى
ٱلْمَلَكَيْنِ بِبَابِلَ هَـٰرُوتَ وَمَـٰرُوتَ ۚ وَمَا يُعَلِّمَانِ مِنْ أَحَدٍ حَتَّىٰ يَقُولَآ
إِنَّمَا نَحْنُ فِتْنَةٌ فَلَا تَكْفُرْ ۖ فَيَتَعَلَّمُونَ مِنْهُمَا مَا يُفَرِّقُونَ بِهِۦ بَيْنَ ٱلْمَرْءِ
وَزَوْجِهِۦ ۚ وَمَا هُم بِضَآرِّينَ بِهِۦ مِنْ أَحَدٍ إِلَّا بِإِذْنِ ٱللَّهِ ۚ وَيَتَعَلَّمُونَ مَا
يَضُرُّهُمْ وَلَا يَنفَعُهُمْ ۚ وَلَقَدْ عَلِمُوا۟ لَمَنِ ٱشْتَرَىٰهُ مَا لَهُۥ فِى ٱلْـَٔاخِرَةِ
مِنْ خَلَـٰقٍ ۚ وَلَبِئْسَ مَا شَرَوْا۟ بِهِۦٓ أَنفُسَهُمْ ۚ لَوْ كَانُوا۟ يَعْلَمُونَ

They instead followed the magic promoted by the devils during the reign of Solomon. Never did Solomon disbelieve, rather the devils disbelieved. They taught magic to the people, along with what had been revealed to the two angels, Hârût and Mârût, in Babylon. The two angels never taught anyone without saying, "We are only a test for you, so do not abandon your faith." Yet people learned magic that caused a rift even between husband and wife; although their magic could not harm anyone except by Allah's Will. They learned what harmed them and did not benefit them—although they already knew that whoever buys into magic would have no share in the Hereafter. Miserable indeed was the price for which they sold their souls, if only they knew!

—Holy Qur'an 2:102

Some Hadith offer a different perspective on magic, suggesting that spells and charms *can* be used in certain circumstances.

Imam Malik ibn Anas reported that he had been granted sanction to use an incantation as a remedy for the sting of the scorpion, curing small pustules, and dispelling the influence of an evil eye.[31]

But Wahhabis and Salafis point to particular Qur'anic verses to support their anti-sorcery dogmas, such as this "besides Allah" phrase in the Qur'an's tenth chapter:

31 Sahih Muslim 2188, Book 26, Hadith 5448

وَيَعْبُدُونَ مِن دُونِ اللَّهِ مَا لَا يَضُرُّهُمْ وَلَا يَنفَعُهُمْ وَيَقُولُونَ
هَٰؤُلَاءِ شُفَعَاؤُنَا عِندَ اللَّهِ قُلْ أَتُنَبِّئُونَ اللَّهَ بِمَا لَا يَعْلَمُ فِي
السَّمَاوَاتِ وَلَا فِي الْأَرْضِ سُبْحَانَهُ وَتَعَالَىٰ عَمَّا يُشْرِكُونَ

They worship besides Allah others who can neither harm nor benefit them, and say, "These are our intercessors with Allah." Ask them, O Prophet, "Are you informing Allah of something He does not know in the heavens or the earth? Glorified and Exalted is He above what they associate with Him!"

—Holy Qur'an 10:18

Seeking help from an entity or power other than God is heresy to Wahhabis and Salafis. They say that offering a gift at the grave of a saint; clinging to or keeping pieces of the black cloth that hangs over the Kaaba in Mecca; or invoking djinn, prophets, and saints all typify the warning highlighted in these verses from the tenth chapter.

Despite the Saudi government's anti-sorcery stance, some regional leaders are said to favor working *with* sorcerers. These allegations have fostered hatred and even incited violence against Muslim minorities such as Shi'ite Muslims.

Former Iranian president Mahmoud Ahmadinejad is reported to have colluded with two sorcerers, including one who was his chief of staff. These staffers invoked djinn and used supernatural powers to advance policy efforts and overpower Iran's Supreme Leader Ayatollah Ali Khamenei. One presidential sorcerer, Seyed Sadigh, confirmed to the *Wall Street Journal* that he gathered intelligence on djinn "who work for Israel's intelligence agency, the Mossad, and for the US Central Intelligence Agency." Sadigh said, "We have had a long battle to infiltrate the Israeli Jinn and find out what they know."[32] Questions posed to djinn by the presidential informant included: What does Israel have on Iran's nuclear program? And are Arabs polluting Iran's water?

If this sounds archaic or triggers Islamophobia, consider that Ronald Reagan's presidency was informed by a stargazer who interpreted horoscopes and shifted the presidential calendar accordingly. Negotiations between the American president and Mikhail Gorbachev, among other leaders, were scheduled according to the positioning of the planets.

Saudi Arabia's Anti-Witchcraft Unit, which was established expressly to protect the Gulf from the dangers of evil magic, would not be happy

32 https://www.wsj.com/articles/SB10001424052702303657404576357323069853958

to know that sorcerers had infiltrated the upper echelons of its neighbor's government—although they may have been unsurprised to learn that American politics was ruled by astrology.

Domestically, Saudi's religious police have established an immense workload. In their first two years on the job, officers of the Anti-Witchcraft Unit apprehended close to six hundred perpetrators of magical crimes. Many were executed. Once, a female agent of the Anti-Witchcraft Unit entrapped an elusive witch by requesting a spell that would turn her husband into an "unquestioning, obedient man." But oftentimes the tactics of Anti-Witchcraft Unit officers are kept secret. The Kingdom will neither confirm nor deny whether its law enforcement officers use incantations and magical rituals to protect the Gulf from the dangers of illegal spells.

INVESTIGA
FEET

The DDU

Simi Valley, California, USA, 12002 HE (2002 CE)

He liked being Muneeb. He liked the way Brylcreem smoothed his hair into a glossy wave, and the way three spritzes of hairspray elevated that wave into a subtle but jawbone-elevating puff. He flattened the puff a little with the palm of his hand. He needed to look suave, but not so perfect as to arouse suspicion. He chose the black-and-gold aviator sunglasses and popped a loop of mother-of-pearl rosary beads into his back pocket.

It was Thursday, and he was headed to the Islamic Center in Simi Valley. The center's youth missionaries had done a superb job of recruiting tweens in the late eighties. Those kids were in their early twenties now, chain-smoking blunts and cigarettes from the stress of lugging around names like Ahmed or Hamid. Their foreheads were knitted with the fear of what hatred might stagger into their bearded fathers' gas stations during the graveyard shift.

"I get it," Muneeb said to Anwar. "My uncle works at the Exxon on Lavell. Those rednecks bust through the door and be like, 'Hey, Mo-ham-hed? Got an uncle called Osama?'"

Anwar cackled and lit another cigarette.

"Easy on those cancer sticks."

Anwar held the cigarette at arm's length and surveyed it as if for the first time. He dropped the cigarette on the ground and stomped it out.

Muneeb had quickly picked up the language of the youth missionaries. Cigarettes were cancer sticks. Sexy kuffar girls were sharmutas. Wifey-material Muslim sisters were Maryams, and racist Islamophobes were crackers, a term appropriated from their African American brethren. Muneeb couldn't be accused of cultural appropriation, he liked to say. He transcended racial categories. He thought everyone did. "We are all one race. The human race," he would say, pointing his finger around the center's dedicated youth room, where all the faces were the same shade of milky tea.

There was a rumor circulating throughout the congregation that Fat Sal (short for Salahuddin) was an undercover CIA operative. "No, not CIA. *FBI*," said Anwar to Muneeb, who was looking at his watch and pretending to be disinterested. "Whatever it is, he's definitely a Fed. Have you seen that tape recorder he brings in every day? Like, what are you doing, bro?"

"Isn't he recording the imam's sermons?" said Muneeb as the pair walked into the center.

Anwar shrugged. "That's what he says. And then he sits outside the mosque in that stupid white van for an hour after Jummah watching everybody drive away."

The Fat Sal rumor suited Muneeb. An unintentional decoy was a blessing. He straightened his aviators and patted his hair. "Time to preach some sense into the boys."

Anwar unfolded a long picnic table and loaded it with bottles of Mecca Cola, Sprite, and packets of Lay's Potato Chips. The young men trickled into the room, neatly arranged their Jordans by the entrance, and filled their plastic cups. Muneeb watched the door for a teenager named Haani. But by the time seventeen pairs of sweatpants had filled seventeen chairs, Haani was nowhere to be seen. Anwar noticed the absence, too. He whispered to a gangly kid named Ilyas and shook his head when Ilyas whispered back.

"He's staying at home. Bit shaken up still," Anwar reported back to Muneeb.

"But they've got nothing on him!" Ilyas said unexpectedly. "Absolutely nothing! Straight up lies, man."

Haani had been up to something. Muneeb knew all about it, even if these knuckleheads hadn't worked it out. Haani's after-school activities were enough for the local FBI office to pay him a visit during third period art class. The burly White agents dragged the paint-spattered kid away from his still life of a bruised apple and barked questions that they were certain would spook him.

It was all thanks to their new and elusive colleague, who had appeared at their field office four months ago and had been visiting the Simi Valley Islamic Center every Tuesday and Thursday since. Muneeb had quickly befriended the garrulous Haani and his friends. To the other agents' chagrin, Muneeb was able to extract the kind of intel they had been unable to gather over the course of a year, despite their best attempts.

The FBI had long suspected that young men in the valley were being lured into terror cells. New laws empowered the agents to act on paranoid hunches with even less scrutiny than before. Haani wasn't connected to any kind of terror cell, but he was bold enough to be pro-Palestine and bookish enough to link the "War on Terror" with, according to the pamphlet he'd typed up in his bedroom, "the war on Vieques, the continued occupation of the West Bank, and countless other struggles around the world and throughout history."

"Connect the dots, my people. Unite, and we can conquer the Oppressor," the pamphlet continued. It had caught the eye of Mr. Telent, the general manager of the Kinko's on Central where Haani had misguidedly printed the pamphlet in bulk.

Haani's pamphlet was faxed to the LAPD by the store's general manager. Three days later, Muneeb was flown in to do his thing. *Suspect could not organize a piss up in a brewery, let alone plan an act of terror,* he typed in his weekly report, happy at his use of a human idiom for incompetence. He scratched it out. Sometimes he messed these things up and they landed badly. *Suspect does not pose a threat to national security,* he typed. But then he scratched that out, too. Haani's father was a belligerent drunk, and Muneeb didn't want to abandon the kid before teaching Mr. Abadi a lesson.

It had taken all of one millisecond to deduce that Haani was a good kid, making this Muneeb's sixth useless mission. He had grown accustomed to the fruitless pursuits assigned to him in the FBI (or DDU). Still, he liked floating through this earthly realm, even if it meant he had to write "FEET" on his human wrists to remind himself that toes pointed ahead of you, not behind you; and even if it meant having to listen to the bald agent in boot camp declare: "Most acts of terror in the United States are perpetrated by White nationalists." *Then why are my first seven assignments spying on American Muslims?* Muneeb had thought as he eyed his schedule.

The day after the youth center visit, Muneeb was Omar, a light-skinned Black man with a whispery laugh and a thin goatee. He brushed his chin hairs with a boar bristle brush and straightened the collar of his white shirt. He looked down to make sure his loafers were pointing in the right direction.

Friday's target was a twenty-two-year-old engineer who had recently graduated magna cum laude from UCLA. Lateef Hawkins was handsome, witty, and popular; the human FBI agents despised him. When they had first accosted Lateef in the engineering school's gym, they had sneered at the stack of engineering books he was balancing. Lateef's girlfriend, Mel, shuddered as the agents lobbed insults at her man.

American-born science majors (there were a few thousand of them that year) with an interest in Islam (which was everybody after 9/11) and a reason to turn against the American government (applicable to any non-White person) were deemed potential terror suspects worthy of interrogation. Lateef's father was Muslim, so Lateef liked to attend the Muslim-Bruins Mixers from time to time. Every Ramadan, he fasted for at least ten days, including the first and last days of the holy month. Engineer? Check. Muslim? Check. Black? Check. The FBI thought they were onto something.

Omar had absorbed the 270-page file on Lateef in half a second. *Pleeease*, he had thought, dumping the binder on his desk. *A few more pages and this kid will have a dossier the length of Reverend King's.* A moment later he had brushed his beard and was at the mosque watching Lateef wash his feet before prayer.

"Salaam," Lateef said, passing Omar on his way out of the ablution room. "Salaam, brother," said Omar, pretending he was on his way in. He would track the kid for a few days, but his gift of intuition told him what he had already guessed: The agents had picked on this kid because they envied his brains and brawn.

Omar's real name was Abd al-Rahman al-Jabr. He had initially been assigned to work with another special agent, Yasin Anwari, but the pair had been separated and told to work independently after 9/11. There were twenty-five thousand more special agents like them in the Djinn Detective Unit. The FBI had begun its djinn recruitment drive in the summer of 1940, when the Brooklyn Boys, a neo-Nazi terrorist organization funded by Hitler himself (with money funneled through American churches and into the pockets of congressmen), had threatened to bomb Congress and overthrow the United States government. The seditious plot was foiled one week before the bombs would have detonated. But the real scandal was the trial. Helmed by the Department of Justice, the government's attempt to take down America's deadliest White supremacist terror unit had fallen apart in spectacular fashion. All of the terrorists were acquitted.

Among other failings, the Department of Justice had underestimated the level of support for the Brooklyn Boys among the local community. Even that moniker, the Brooklyn Boys, was a term of endearment, a popular stand-in for their actual name, the Christian Front. With funds from Hitler and the rallying cry of Father Charles Coughlin and his radio audience of thirty million Americans, the Christian Front had managed to infiltrate and radicalize the upper echelons of American law enforcement and the military. Hence the acquisition of enough explosives and assault rifles to take down the federal government.

The Department of Justice was humiliated. The government had egg on its face. So emboldened were the fascists that minutes after the judge read the verdict acquitting the Christian Front, the terrorists walked directly from the docks to the judge and demanded their weapons. Which they were summarily handed.

Guy T. Helvering looked on in horror. If only the justice department knew what he had known for decades: The only way to cement the FBI's success was to recruit otherworldly agents. He had been doing the same as IRS Commissioner since 1933, when Pressly R. Baldridge had handed him the reins and explained how things really worked. The IRS had been carrying on this tradition since its inception. How else could one government entity know the incoming funds and the outgoing expenditures of nearly three hundred million people? How did Americans think their secret mattress stashes were unearthed and their clandestine gambling spoils tallied? *Technology* was a euphemism for *djinn*.

Helvering knew the average man off the street would cry *Fake!* so the details of his Djinn Diligence Unit were kept secret. Simple minds couldn't comprehend it. What he could not understand was why the DDU was kept secret from his counterparts in intelligence. Helvering decided then and there that he would take it upon himself to make the details known to J. Edgar Hoover, the man who had founded and steered the FBI since 1924—but had yet to figure out how to gather intelligence effectively.

He wouldn't deliver the news himself. As storied as his position was as IRS Commissioner, he knew the best way to demonstrate the power of the DDU was via Al Saidi, his most treasured asset. It wouldn't be a hard sell; everyone knew that Hoover was unscrupulous in his quest to surveil anyone espousing anti-American values. Hoover had deployed those tactics to protect himself after he was spotted kissing his lover, Clyde Tolson, in New York's Stork Club. Every journalist who made reference to their affair was threatened with the publication of deeply researched defamatory material. Helvering felt certain Hoover would be open to the idea of the DDU as soon as he recovered from the shock of watching Al Said appear and vanish in a puff of smoke.

So it was under Hoover that the Djinn Diligence Unit became the Djinn Detective Unit. The DDU was instrumental during the Cold War. In the 1970s, the Americans deployed their most sophisticated assets in a program called Directorate D, in which DDU agents posed as everyday Russians and gathered invaluable intelligence. It was too bizarre to be believable, even if the KGB knew something was at play. Anyone spreading rumors that the Americans were employing "an alien species" in their intelligence units was branded a conspiracy theorist.

Abd al-Rahman al-Jabr had a cousin who had been employed by the FBI back then. Joining the DDU had been frowned upon by some tribes at first. They deemed employment by humans to be humiliating, since a djinni needed neither a job nor a purpose. But possessed of free will, some djinn were open to the encouragement of older relatives and peers who advocated for this interspecies alliance. There were tribes, Abd al-Rahman's included, who felt it a noble endeavor in the vein of the much-celebrated djinni muses who inspired the so-called greatest human poets. Abd al-Rahman's great-grandfather had told him stories of a bloody djinn war that took place many millennia before humans were created. "If this work can bring peace to their world, then it is noble to assist in that effort," he had said. "If there was someone outside of our kind who could have helped to stop our conflict, we would have welcomed it. Instead, the Almighty sent the angels to punish us."

Abd al-Rahman couldn't help but feel that his work was not fostering peace. The humans were paranoid, and he was being deployed as a tool of their unreasonable mistrust. It was now his sixth day as Omar and his second time trailing Lateef out of the ablution room and around the prayer hall. As they stood in line to pray, Omar felt Lateef's eyes on him for an uncomfortable duration. Even as the imam said, "Allahu akbar," and the men all raised their hands to their ears to declare that God is great, Omar could tell that Lateef's head was angled in his direction.

After prayers, Lateef asked Omar if they could talk outside. "Are you working security?" he said, his lips pressed into a straight line. He folded his arms across his chest. "I don't want to cause a scene here, but has Mel hired you as a private investigator? I'm not cheating! Tell her *that*!" And he stormed off.

Omar turned the corner and walked toward the garbage cans in the alleyway. He stood between them, looked around, and disappeared.

"Maybe being private investigators would actually be more useful?" said Yasin when Abd al-Rahman explained the confrontation. "'Cuz they have me gathering intel on a sixteen-year-old in Akron who can't even spell terrorist." The pair shook their heads.

The day that Abd al-Rahman handed in his notice of resignation to the DDU, he was asked if he would sit down for an exit interview. "After you've worked your mandatory two weeks of notice and completed the necessary paperwork, of course," said the chief of staff to the division's director. Abd al-Rahman opened a filing cabinet, took out a box, and emptied a stack of documents onto the desk. From his pocket, he took a gold pen, which he placed carefully atop the pile of papers.

Abd al-Rahman had decided to appear as Salim that day, an older gentleman with a neat white beard and gold-rimmed spectacles. Salim straightened the knot of his tie, cleared his throat, and said he would do neither. *These humans*, he thought as he dissolved into the carpet tiles of the DDU building. *They know so little about intelligence.*

Djinn-Human Collaborations

There are many stories of benevolent djinn who guide weary seafarers to shore, offer helpful insights into the future, or simply help humans escape tragic circumstances. This story, however, was confirmed to me during off-the-record conversations with a number of FBI officials who sought to shut down the DDU. The djinn might be benevolent, they said, but their intelligence-gathering efforts were rousing suspicion among enemy nations and amid the FBI's own ranks.

They felt blindsided, it seemed, by their own inability to interpret and truly understand the DDU agents' motives and methods. The agency felt it would be safer, in the age of high-tech surveillance modalities, to rely on methods it could actually explain during congressional hearings. One official recalled blundering a response during one high-level testimony, when he was asked to explain how intelligence agents in sixteen countries had been able to gather information so deep and triangulated that nothing like it had been documented before. He said he used the sentence, "In the interest of protecting national security, I cannot expound on those methods," so many times that the committee eventually gave up on asking further questions.

But beyond those frustrations, there was concern that djinn could not be trusted, even if they hailed from families with long histories of supporting human peace, as was the case with Abd al-Rahman al-Jabr.

Here is where I will share, reluctantly, a little more about my relationship with the Sheikh who first invited me to compile this compendium. This entire endeavor arose because the Sheikh had contact with Abd al-Rahman al-Jabr. The Sheikh's version of the story claims that the djinn presented himself by possessing one of the Sheikh's high-ranking lawyers. Abd al-Rahman didn't realize that

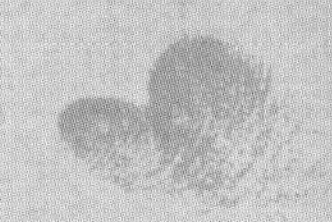

among these men was a cleric highly adept at sniffing out djinn. Abd al-Rahman was exorcised in a covert and lengthy ceremony, an ambush really, during which the imam threatened to curse the djinni's entire clan if he refused to divulge state secrets from the United States and become a double agent. Abd al-Rahman refused and was cursed and trapped in a bottle.

Abd al-Rahman tells the story differently. (I was able to interview him only once my ability to speak with djinn didn't make me lightheaded and too jittery to be of any use.) Abd al-Rahman says that he began to work as a private investigator for people concerned about their safety. He was abducted by a cleric who worked for the Sheikh and threatened with a generational curse and imprisonment if he didn't also work for the Sheikh. Abd al-Rahman refused and was imprisoned. His great-grandfather, however, learned of this horror and intervened to release his descendent. This was done at great cost to their family (they would not tell me what was sacrificed to protect Abd al-Rahman).

The Sheikh categorically denies any allegations of djinn abduction. But I learned that the intent behind this compendium was not the scholarly search for knowledge, but a plan to harness djinn to advance nefarious human agendas. I told the Sheikh I wanted no part in this venture-that I would continue to collect this data since I was many years into this research, but that the final result would be made available to all-open access is a hallmark of my approach to academia. The Sheikh was furious. This is when the threats began. If I disappear upon publication of this book, you will know what happened to me.

But I have felt strangely (naively?) protected since that time. I wonder if it is Abd al-Rahman al-Jabr, his great-grandfather, or another one of their clan who circles my bed when I sleep. How else can I explain the breeze that flutters my sheets when the windows are closed and the fan is turned off? What else could explain the way every stumble results in a warm cloud lifting me back to my feet before my knees can graze the ground?

The Husband

Beypore, India, 11866 HE (1866 CE)

On the morning of her fiftieth birthday, Bibi woke to the sound of her husband chewing loudly next to her in bed. Neither of them knew it was Bibi's birthday, born as she was without a birth certificate, but it was to be a special day anyway, because for the first time since their wedding, they would be receiving guests.

Bibi soaked basmati rice and orange lentils in copper bowls, stacked sweet samosas crammed with shredded coconut onto her best platters, and chilled glass jugs in cold water before filling them with green, salty lassi. Special silver plates had been purchased from a widow in the next village. Bibi's husband had transported them back to their home.

Their pistachio-green bungalow sat at the edge of a mango orchard. Bright-orange garlands of marigolds hung near the entrance. Bibi had woven the flowers together herself, such was the occasion. Two more garlands waited on the dining table, ready to adorn the necks of the couple who would be arriving by train from Tirur later that afternoon. Bibi's husband would meet them at the station with a wagon to bring them and their suitcases to the bungalow.

The guests were two of her childhood friends from the village by the sea. Bibi had moved up in the world: Now she lived even closer to the ocean, next to a less seaweed-strewn stretch of beach. Bibi rubbed her round cheeks with freshly ground turmeric root mixed with oil, as she had done the day before her wedding. She admired the henna patterns she had drawn on the palm of her right hand. But her fingers tingled with such excitement that the pallu of her green and pink sari escaped her grip over and over again as she tried to arrange the pleats neatly around her waist.

Amina and Arif had married around the time of Bibi's first wedding. They still lived in the village that Bibi had fled after her first husband's funeral. Bibi had found love and a new life in a different fishing village. She met her second husband one early spring evening while she was bathing in the ocean. She shrieked when she first saw him. He was sniffing around the pile of clothes she had piled neatly next to a coconut tree, sifting through her garments.

"Hey, you! Leave my things alone!" she had wailed from between the waves. But the mysterious creature ran away with her sari blouse, and a naked Bibi staggered onto the beach, arms clamped across her chest, knees awkwardly knocking as she tried to conceal her womanhood. The creature scampered between the coconut trees, dragging her blouse and frolicking, pleading with her to give chase. So she did. It was the very first day that she had emerged from the house after four months of ritual mourning. And this—this felt like destiny. A dark and playful stranger had chosen her, and she could swear that she had been too busy praying for the repentance of her deceased husband to even think about asking Allah for a new man.

Bibi skipped after the creature as he dragged her sari blouse through the sand. She chased him between thick tree trunks and jumped over vines that scratched her smooth, brown skin. Bibi didn't care. She was

lost in the moment, giggling like a schoolgirl. The pair collapsed on the sand and lay cheek to cheek, huffing and puffing and laughing. The sky had turned black. Bibi pulled the first brightly colored sari she had worn in months over their bodies.

Bibi told anyone who would listen, "It was love at first sight. When you know, you know." To the young women who sold marigolds by the temple, she would say, "When you put aside expectations of how you think your perfect spouse will look, smell, and act, *that's* when you'll find true happiness."

Her second wedding had been a small affair, as was the custom for a widow: only two fisherwomen to bear witness, and an imam to officiate the union. Her first husband's death, caused by choking on a fish bone, had rattled her. She was relieved that her second husband refused to eat spined creatures of any kind.

By the time the guests pulled up to the house in the wagon, it was filled with the aromas of Bibi's cooking. Biryani, idli, masala dhosa, and three kinds of dhaal were arranged on the table. Bibi pushed a serving spoon into a platter of pilau rice scattered with strands of saffron and topped with flaked almonds and plump raisins.

"Come in! Come in!" Bibi said, standing at the entrance, two garlands bouncing in her hands. "You made a looooong journey. I'm so glad you found Babu. I was worried you would walk past him at the train station. He can be too quiet for his own good."

"But where was he . . . we weren't sure?" said a quizzical Arif.

"Well, you got here, so everything worked out perfectly," replied a grinning Bibi. She laughed and ushered her guests over the threshold. They ducked to receive the floral necklaces. "Now be careful and don't bend over," Bibi said, patting the marigolds against Amina's bosom. "Sometimes Babu gets carried away and likes to nibble."

She showed the silent couple to the table, where she lifted cloths and plates to reveal the fragrant feast. She had expected at least a few compliments about her house and her cooking. But when she turned back to look at the pair, their eyes were as white as coconuts and as wide as tea plates. "Yes, yes!" said Bibi. "I made *all* this food for you!" She watched their eyes grow wider as Babu trotted into the house and sat by the door to catch his breath. "Very special guests have come to meet my very special husband. Now please, won't you sit?"

Bibi stroked her husband's hair and picked strands of hay from his beard, flicking them into the air. "I should have made a garland for you," she said, giving him a peck on the cheek. Bibi picked up a cloth sack that sat near the entrance, hoisted the burlap over her shoulder, and walked to the table with Babu at her heels.

Babu settled into his usual position at the head of the table. Bibi emptied the cloth sack directly onto the tablecloth in front of him and poured him a glass of green lassi. Arif stared at the food. Amina shook her head. "I'm sorry, but we won't be able to stay tonight," she said.

"Areh, what talk is this?" said Bibi. "You only just got here! Babu helped me to prepare the guest room for you. How many husbands help their wives with such chores, eh?" She dished out a puddle of orange dhaal onto Arif's plate.

He looked at Amina, who was mouthing something slowly. "This is enough!" he said. The pair turned their heads and rudely stared at Babu. Babu looked up from his hay pile and let out a faint *baaah*.

"What do you think, Amina? I did good, eh?" Bibi said, and giggled. "For an old woman like me, I am so lucky." Amina coughed. Bibi handed her a cup of lassi to clear her throat.

Babu didn't speak. He chewed and grunted and eventually spit brownish wads onto the floor. A long silence followed the expulsion of the last chunk of cud, and then a burp, for extra flourish. "Oh hoh, Babu!" Bibi sighed. "This is why I gave you the big napkin." She shook her head and looked at Amina. "I never understood how husbands are always so disgusting. How do we cope, eh?"

Amina and Arif moved food around their plates. "Eat, Arif. Eat!" Bibi insisted. Arif scooped fingerfuls of dhaal into his mouth and talked with his mouth full, the orange lentils muffling his voice as he said, "We have to go." He glared at his wife, and Amina stood and walked toward the shoes she had left by the front door. Babu had nibbled on the leather soles on his way in.

"Oh! Bhai! But I haven't given you masala tea and samosas yet!" Bibi cried, clutching her dupatta to her chest. "You *must* stay. Babu, take them to the divan. What's that? Yes, I can see it, too. They are very tired."

Babu excused himself from the table and began to clear up the spit wads from the floor. He cocked his head and looked at the guests through long, curved eyelashes. Bibi nudged him in the direction of the divan and their guests followed. Arif sat on the small chair closest to the door. "Not there, Arif," Bibi said. "That's Babu's chair."

In the kitchen, ginger-scented puffs of steam condensed on Bibi's round face as she stewed black tea in a steel pot with cardamom and slivers of unpeeled ginger root. She arranged sweet samosas on a silver plate and carried the treats to the guests. They were sitting in silence.

Babu was still chewing. "I feel so lucky," Bibi said. She handed the samosas to Amina and Arif and placed cups of hot tea on the table. "I never thought I could have a husband who is so quiet, so loving."

Bibi poured tea into a silver bowl and held it to Babu's mouth. He puckered his lips, unfurled a thick tongue, and slurped the tea. Bibi stroked her husband's head. "Tell him about your business, Arif," Bibi said, nodding her head. "Babu is *very* interested in the import-export trade."

"Really? I mean, I *really* think we should be going," Arif said. He placed his teacup on the table and stood. Bibi walked over and gently pushed him back down into the chair. "Babu can take you to the station anytime, but there is no train until tomorrow," she said quietly.

What did it matter what her husband looked like? So what if he didn't speak the same tongue? So what if he didn't eat the same food? Could they not see that she was happy? Did a woman's contentment mean nothing? Bibi crossed and uncrossed her arms. She stood to refill Arif's teacup, pouring from the pot until it reached the brim and spilled into the trembling man's saucer. "I said, tell him about your business."

Arif explained to Bibi that he bought long-grain rice from a distant village, transported it by donkey to Tirur, and sold it at twice the price. "No, tell *him*," Bibi said, pointing her chin in Babu's direction. Arif turned to Babu, opened his mouth, and closed it.

Babu scratched his face. "That means he is very impressed," Bibi said. She turned to Amina. "But with all that hard work your husband does, I bet he doesn't have much time for you, not the way my husband has time to cuddle and play with me!" Amina nodded silently.

Bibi sipped her tea and told them about the beginnings of her love affair. The night of the beach encounter, after Babu had licked her cheek and disappeared into the bush, Bibi knelt on the sand and prayed to Allah that she be blessed with a spouse as playful and affectionate as the creature she had danced with at sunset. Her first husband had been a debt collector with a capricious demeanor and chronic bowel troubles. Sometimes the gas escaped from his mouth, other times it emerged from the back end. Either way, Bibi said, she felt that her life had been engulfed in a constant miasma of stink.

The very next day, Bibi's prayers were answered. She spotted Babu at the grain market. Her hair was still dripping wet from that morning's ablutions—an indecent, besharam way in which to leave the house, she knew. Mother had warned against it ever since Bibi was a young girl. "Wet hair attracts djinn," Amma had said. "If a girl walks outside with wet hair, especially beneath trees and especially at Maghreb, the djinn will sniff you out and follow you home."

At the market, Bibi let the thin pink dupatta slip from her head to reveal the glistening locks beneath. She wandered through the bazaar in her rose-pink kamees and spotted Babu's head peering at her from between two burlap sacks. His nostrils quivered as he caught Bibi's scent. His eyes tracked her as she moved between mountains of powdered spices. She knew it was him instantly: that solid frame, those long, thick eyelashes. He was excited to see her again.

"Two pounds of chapati flour," she said to the old man sitting at Babu's side. She eyed Babu as the man poured flour into a cloth bag and held the bag out for Bibi to take. "You want him?" he said, looking from Bibi to Babu and back to Bibi again. "If you want him, you can have him." The man jiggled the bag and pointed to the coins in Bibi's hand.

"Sometimes love really is *that* simple," Bibi said. "You wouldn't believe how easily true love can fall into your lap." Amina listened with parted lips. "The very next week, we were married in that mango orchard," Bibi said, pointing out beyond the open door, where a golden sun was melting into the mango trees. "We built this house with money my first husband had stashed. Sorry I couldn't invite you to the wedding, but you understand these things. That is the custom for a widow. Small wedding. No fuss."

Arif nodded his head. Amina stared at the floor.

It would be dark soon, and Babu liked to take a leisurely stroll before bedtime. "Helps him digest," Bibi explained, patting her belly. She stacked the teacups on a tray, carried them to the kitchen, and returned with her hands dripping water.

Bibi crouched in front of Babu and gently combed her fingers through the wiry hairs sprouting from his chin. When his beard was clean, she lay her warm, damp hands over his hooves and picked at the fibers jammed between his toes. She pecked her husband on the nose and stroked his cheeks until he sighed.

Djinni Spouses

This story reminds me of the hundreds of tales I have unearthed about amorous djinn who take animal form, often appearing as deer, to conceal their true identity. (The word *djinn*, after all, comes from the root word for "cover" or "hide.") But in Bibi's story, Babu maintains his animal form, as if he and his lover are comfortable with and comforted by his bestial qualities—the muteness, the grateful slurping of tea, the stroking followed by an appreciative sigh. The less savory details-chomping, burping, grunting, and spitting-are not dissimilar to the habits of certain human men. (And how many married women have warned their female friends to not bend over in the presence of their husbands?)

A few questions remain, though: If Babu was a djinn, did he possess the capacity to shape-shift into human form? If so, did he choose not to do so because Bibi's first marriage put her off human men forever? An elder from her fishing village, responsible for djinn exorcisms, informed me that some djinn can assume only certain animal shapes, among them deer, black dogs, parakeets, large spiders, snakes, and invasive parasites. I asked if Babu might have been an animal possessed by a djinni as opposed to the alternate form of a djinni itself. The elder said it was possible.

Tales of interspecies love usually involve the transfer of skills from djinni/yah to human, skills such as weapon-making or the science and art of healing. In the story of Bibi and Babu, however, there seems to be no material exchange, only a relationship that provides Bibi joy and comfort-more joy and comfort than she enjoyed with her human husband.

But is this story real, or is it a tale told loudly by women to their daughters in the hopes that boys and men will overhear and be reminded that they can be replaced by equally grubby but less talkative (and more grateful) creatures?

I scoured local records in search of clues. The Beypore masjid ledger confirms that an Imam A. S. Bora officiated a nikkah ceremony between a Bibi Hussain Amerjee and a Babu (last name blank) on April 19, 11866 HE. (There is a thumbprint where the wife's signature or marking is required, and a smudge where there is space for the groom's.)

If local birth and death records are accurate, the marriage did not result in offspring. Bibi's death is recorded in the 11913 HE village register (although her birth was not listed in the register in Tirur). I visited her grave at the cemetery by the beach, but I could not find any public notice of Babu's passing nor find a gravesite marked with his name in the vicinity of Bibi's.

If Babu was a djinn in animal form, as the families who live by what was once Bibi and Babu's mango orchard told me, this would make him a tab'i. *Tab'i* (masculine) and *tab'iah* (feminine) are Arabic words for "follower," derived from the trilateral root T-B-ع, meaning "to follow." These words have been used since pre-Islamic times to describe djinn in animal form who follow and fall in love with humans.

Islamic and pre-Islamic folklore, oral histories, prophetic narratives, and published tales are replete with djinn-human love stories. But are these interspecies, interdimensional marriages permissible under Islamic law? Most Shariah jurists would answer *no*, pointing to Qur'anic verses such as this one, in which *yourselves* is said to highlight the otherness of djinn:

وَمِنْ آيَاتِهِ أَنْ خَلَقَ لَكُم مِّنْ أَنفُسِكُمْ أَزْوَاجًا لِّتَسْكُنُوا إِلَيْهَا وَجَعَلَ بَيْنَكُم مَّوَدَّةً وَرَحْمَةً ۚ إِنَّ فِي ذَٰلِكَ لَآيَاتٍ لِّقَوْمٍ يَتَفَكَّرُونَ

And one of His signs is that He created for you spouses from among yourselves so that you may find comfort in them. And He has placed between you compassion and mercy. Surely in this are signs for people who reflect.

—Holy Qur'an 30:21

Yet, it's not atypical that Bibi and Babu were able to find an imam to officiate their union. The Qur'an does not expressly prohibit the intermarriage of djinn with humans. (Although I noted the two witnesses were women, which is prohibited in most interpretations of Shariah law, when researching this rule, I discovered that, in the state of Colorado, a dog can act as official witness to a wedding, its paw print serving as an official signature.)

Over the centuries, stories conveyed by men with authority usually cast aspersions on the hybrid babies a djinni/yah-human pairing might produce. (Perhaps Imam A. S. Bora agreed to perform the nikkah because of Bibi's advanced age and unlikelihood of producing offspring?)

I found a story about the highly respected cousin and companion of the Holy Prophet (p.b.u.h.), Alī ibn Abī Ṭālib, which points to how these chimeric offspring have been perceived. One day, Ali inquired about a child who was acting strangely, and he was pointed in the direction of the child's mother. "Who is the father?" he asked the woman. "I don't know," she replied. "One day I was pasturing the sheep for my parents—this was before Islam—when something in the form of a cloud mated with me. I became pregnant and gave birth to this child."

Another respected scholar, Ibn Malik bin Abas, said, "It is not against the religion, but I hate to see a woman pregnant from marrying a djinni, and people would ask, 'Who is the husband?' and then corruption would spread among Muslims."

Djinni/yah-human love stories are so common as to follow a formula and feature typical motifs. The swan maiden tale is one blueprint. In this enduring legend, a hero (who might be a hunter or voyager) arrives upon a body of water (perhaps it is a lake, perhaps it is a fountain) where he is struck by the beauty of a bathing woman. But the woman is not human; she is a mythical creature. Our hero learns this when he discovers her swan coat discarded by the shore. The so-called hero steals the swan maiden's coat and refuses to return it to her unless she marries him. The swan maiden agrees, takes the coat, transforms into a swan, and takes her captor to her father's house. It is here that she resumes human form.

But her subjugator takes back the coat to keep her in bondage as his wife, housekeeper, and child bearer. One day, when the husband is out hunting or foraging or busy with some other business, the swan maiden finds her key to transformation. She dons her coat, becomes a swan, and disappears to another world, never to be trapped again.

This story is seen over and over again across time and terrain. In some versions, a hunter, nearly always a man, refuses to shoot an animal after it speaks out to him and reveals itself to be a djinniyah. They fall in love, marry, and have children, only for the mercurial and volatile djinniyah to fly away, leaving the husband bereft. Sometimes he embarks on a yearslong voyage to find his love; sometimes he is successful.

There is no man holding Bibi hostage, no father whose permission she must seek, although she does find an imam to make her union sacrosanct. From what I learned, there was no fickle will-she-stay-or-will-she-go element to their love story. Bibi was content, even if her friends could not bear witness to her joy. And who knows? After the dissatisfaction of her first marriage to a human, perhaps she set out for the beach and the grain market, with her wet hair and dupatta slipping, intent on enticing a lover from the spirit realm.

The Djinniyah in the Perfume Bottle

Shanghai, China, 11969 HE (1969 CE)

There is a Me that lives happily ever after with Him. A Me that has babies with Her. A Me that brings home a puppy and gifts it to Our blended brood. A Me that builds a home with Them. There's a Me that is alone—but never lonely. Single and free. No tethers, no cuffs. Space for all of my books, vinyls, leather jackets, shoes, tea collection, labeled spices, and filing system.

I wanted All of It and None of It at the same time, which is why I was drawn to flea markets. A fish kettle for the Me who cooks with Him. An antique accordion for the Me that serenades Our children. A vintage Dior robe for the Me that dances for Her; a crystal nineteenth-century perfume bottle to scent the fragile kaftan. I scattered the artifacts around my home, lifting each one as my elbows and toes collided with reminders of my wants, the accoutrements of my Possible Other Lives.

It's a superpower, this imagination. It's also a portal for those who prey on unchained desire. The wants, some say, take on the shape of long, unruly snakes whose hungry mouths snap open and shut in the ether. Always hungry, always in search of satiation. That's how otherworldly creatures come to know of us, of people who possess extraordinary creativity. We are the special ones who can See farthest into other places, and visualize other ways of being.

It was twilight. I slid into the kaftan, twirled over to the record player, and dropped the needle on the vinyl. I was nothing if not loyal to character, married to the details of each possibility. I waltzed to the powder room and squeezed the black bulb of the antique perfume bottle, aiming the nozzle at my collarbones. That's when she appeared.

Purple haze seeped out of antique crystal, coalesced in the shape of a fairy, and landed on my marble countertop.

"Be careful," I said. "That's Italian marble. It can probably only take so much weight."

She pressed her small hands into the cool stone, lifted herself off the edge, and hovered above its surface. "Don't you want to know why I'm here?" she said.

"Alright," I replied.

She looked at me quizzically. Her purplish atoms rearranged into a small tornado and then a question mark which grazed my bronze faucets. "I've been trapped in that bottle for hundreds of years," she said, widening her curve. "You have rescued me."

"Fancy that," I said. "Now you can live the life you want."

"Well, not exactly," she said. Her question mark dissolved into a puddle that spilled over my basin. Out flew a hummingbird to dance near my nose. "Not yet. First, out of gratitude, I must make three of your dreams come true. Tell me, what do you desire?"

I balanced on one foot and then shifted my weight to the other. I bit my bottom lip and wondered about my Possible Other Lives. "Is there a way you . . . I don't suppose I . . . What if we . . ."

"Spit it out," she said. "I haven't got too much time. I'm itching to explore and make my own dreams come true."

"Well, it's just that there's so much I could ask for, but you're only granting three wishes. Couldn't I use one of those wishes to ask for three more?"

She turned into a pair of large eyes with drooping lids and sagging bags. The eyes rolled. "Booooring. And no. That's not allowed. Now tell me what you want."

I thought and I thought as I stood in vintage Dior before this purple haze. Jazz from the 1920s played in the living room. "How about . . ." The haze amassed into a tall, thin column. "No, that would be . . ." The haze collapsed into a cloud that cooled my itchy feet. "Well, I suppose I've always wanted . . ." The haze hovered in the shape of a witch's wand. "Mmm, maybe I don't want that as much as I think." The haze became a fog that filled every inch of my powder room.

She spoke from somewhere up in the corner. "For Allah's sake! I've been trapped for centuries! I have neither patience nor time. Now make up your mind, woman!"

"I wish you would stop rushing me!" I said. And *poof*, just like that, one of my wishes was gone. That was sixty-four years ago. She's lived in my guest room ever since, her purpleness drifting from corner to corner, wafting over a typewriter, settling on a rocking horse. Sometimes she plays the abandoned accordion, sometimes she tinkers with a mismatched tea set. All the while trapped by unspoken desires. Still waiting to hear what I wish.

PRAYERS FOR PROTECTION

The Qur'an and Hadith abound with prayers that protect against malevolent djinn. I grew up reciting these and found myself drawn to them as I embarked on this journey into the realm of al-ghayb, particularly as I navigated places like the snake-filled Well of Barhout (the Well of Hell) near the borders of Yemen and Oman or the djinn-infested lost city of Ubar.

But I came to learn that in my case—perhaps because I recited these prayers, or perhaps because of my ancestor's incantations, which were cast forward to shield future generations—it was not djinn who would hurt me. As the Sheikh's agenda became clear and then as my refusal to comply with the inner circle's orders led to escalating threats, I found myself praying these surah for protection not against djinn—but against vindictive men.

I offer these rituals and prayers to you in case—as is feared by some ulama (although I respectfully disagree with those esteemed scholars who hold this belief)—the possession and recitation of this book serves to conjure djinn into your home. Of course, there will be those who use the book as a talisman to do exactly that. I strongly advise against it.

Most famous among the prayers of protection is ayat al-kursi, also known as the Throne Verse. That term refers to its exaltedness because it declares the greatness of God above all others. The Holy Prophet (p.b.u.h.) said: "Whoever recites the Verse of the Throne after every prescribed prayer, there will be nothing standing between him and his entry into Paradise but death."[33]

33 Al-Mu'jam al-Kabīr 7406

Recite, write, and wear these prayers to protect against all types of evil. (The last method might invoke the ire of certain authorities, depending on your location.)

Ayat al-Kursi, the Throne Verse

اللّهُ لاَ إِلَهَ إِلاَّ هُوَ الْحَيُّ الْقَيُّومُ لاَ تَأْخُذُهُ سِنَةٌ وَلاَ نَوْمٌ لَّهُ مَا فِي السَّمَاوَاتِ
وَمَا فِي الأَرْضِ مَن ذَا الَّذِي يَشْفَعُ عِنْدَهُ إِلاَّ بِإِذْنِهِ يَعْلَمُ مَا بَيْنَ أَيْدِيهِمْ
وَمَا خَلْفَهُمْ وَلاَ يُحِيطُونَ بِشَيْءٍ مِّنْ عِلْمِهِ إِلاَّ بِمَا شَاءَ وَسِعَ كُرْسِيُّهُ
السَّمَاوَاتِ وَالأَرْضَ وَلاَ يَؤُودُهُ حِفْظُهُمَا وَهُوَ الْعَلِيُّ الْعَظِيمُ

Allah! There is no god worthy of worship except Him, the Ever-Living, All-Sustaining. Neither drowsiness nor sleep overtakes Him. To Him belongs whatever is in the heavens and whatever is on the earth. Who could possibly intercede with Him without His permission? He fully knows what is ahead of them and what is behind them, but no one can grasp any of His knowledge—except what He wills to reveal. His Seat encompasses the heavens and the earth, and the preservation of both does not tire Him. For He is the Most High, the Greatest.

—Holy Qur'an 2:255

These additional verses are also prayed to protect oneself from possession and djinn meddling.

آمَنَ الرَّسُولُ بِمَا أُنزِلَ إِلَيْهِ مِن رَّبِّهِ وَالْمُؤْمِنُونَ كُلٌّ آمَنَ بِاللَّهِ وَمَلاَئِكَتِهِ وَكُتُبِهِ وَرُسُلِهِ
لاَنُفَرِّقُ بَيْنَ أَحَدٍ مِّن رُّسُلِهِ وَقَالُوا سَمِعْنَا وَأَطَعْنَا غُفْرَانَكَ رَبَّنَا وَإِلَيْكَ الْمَصِيرُ

The Messenger firmly believes in what has been revealed to him from his Lord, and so do the believers. They all believe in Allah, His angels, His Books, and His messengers. They proclaim, "We make no distinction between any of His messengers." And they say, "We hear and obey. We seek Your forgiveness, our Lord! And to You alone is the final return."

—Holy Qur'an 2:285

لَا يُكَلِّفُ اللَّهُ نَفْسًا إِلَّا وُسْعَهَا لَهَا مَا كَسَبَتْ وَعَلَيْهَا مَا اكْتَسَبَتْ رَبَّنَا لَا
تُؤَاخِذْنَا إِن نَّسِينَا أَوْ أَخْطَأْنَا رَبَّنَا وَلَا تَحْمِلْ عَلَيْنَا إِصْرًا كَمَا حَمَلْتَهُ
عَلَى الَّذِينَ مِن قَبْلِنَا رَبَّنَا وَلَا تُحَمِّلْنَا مَا لَا طَاقَةَ لَنَا بِهِ وَاعْفُ عَنَّا
وَاغْفِرْ لَنَا وَارْحَمْنَا أَنتَ مَوْلَانَا فَانصُرْنَا عَلَى الْقَوْمِ الْكَافِرِينَ

Allah does not require of any soul more than what it can afford. All good will be for its own benefit, and all evil will be to its own loss. The believers pray, "Our Lord! Do not punish us if we forget or make a mistake. Our Lord! Do not place a burden on us like the one you placed on those before us. Our Lord! Do not burden us with what we cannot bear. Pardon us, forgive us, and have mercy on us. You are our only Guardian. So grant us victory over the disbelieving people."

—Holy Qur'an 2:286

In some traditions, these verses might be whispered over a cup of water, perhaps holy Zamzam water, which is stored in the fridge for imbibing at times of distress or an uptick in djinn activity. They can also be prayed and blown over an afflicted person, or written and bound in cloth or silver amulets and worn. But beware ascribing protective power to the words and talismans themselves. Protection comes from the God who is revered and whose shelter is invoked through these prayers, not the ink or silver.

Ayat-i-ruqyah

أَعُوذُ بِاللَّهِ السَّمِيعِ الْعَلِيمِ مِنْ الشَّيْطَانِ الرَّجِيمِ مِنْ هَمْزِهِ وَنَفْخِهِ وَنَفْثِهِ
حَسْبِيَ اللَّهُ لَا إِلٰهَ إِلَّا هُوَ عَلَيْهِ تَوَكَّلْتُ وَهُوَ رَبُّ الْعَرْشِ الْعَظِيمِ

Allah is sufficient for me. There is none worthy of worship but Him. I rely on Him alone, He is the Lord of the Majestic Throne.

Surah al-Fatiha

الْحَمْدُ لِلَّهِ رَبِّ الْعَالَمِينَ، الرَّحْمَٰنِ الرَّحِيمِ

مَالِكِ يَوْمِ الدِّينِ، إِيَّاكَ نَعْبُدُ وَإِيَّاكَ نَسْتَعِينُ

اهْدِنَا الصِّرَاطَ الْمُسْتَقِيمَ، صِرَاطَ الَّذِينَ أَنْعَمْتَ عَلَيْهِمْ
غَيْرِ الْمَغْضُوبِ عَلَيْهِمْ وَلَا الضَّالِّينَ

In the Name of Allah—the Most Compassionate, Most Merciful. Master of the Day of Judgment. You alone we worship and You alone we ask for help. Guide us along the straight path, the path of those You have blessed—not those You are displeased with, or those who are astray.

Final two ayat of Surat al-Baqarah

آمَنَ الرَّسُولُ بِمَا أُنزِلَ إِلَيْهِ مِن رَّبِّهِ وَالْمُؤْمِنُونَ كُلٌّ آمَنَ بِاللَّهِ وَمَلَائِكَتِهِ وَكُتُبِهِ وَرُسُلِهِ
لَا نُفَرِّقُ بَيْنَ أَحَدٍ مِّن رُّسُلِهِ وَقَالُوا سَمِعْنَا وَأَطَعْنَا غُفْرَانَكَ رَبَّنَا وَإِلَيْكَ الْمَصِيرُ

لَا يُكَلِّفُ اللَّهُ نَفْسًا إِلَّا وُسْعَهَا لَهَا مَا كَسَبَتْ وَعَلَيْهَا مَا اكْتَسَبَتْ رَبَّنَا لَا
تُؤَاخِذْنَا إِن نَّسِينَا أَوْ أَخْطَأْنَا رَبَّنَا وَلَا تَحْمِلْ عَلَيْنَا إِصْرًا كَمَا حَمَلْتَهُ
عَلَى الَّذِينَ مِن قَبْلِنَا رَبَّنَا وَلَا تُحَمِّلْنَا مَا لَا طَاقَةَ لَنَا بِهِ وَاعْفُ عَنَّا
وَاغْفِرْ لَنَا وَارْحَمْنَا أَنتَ مَوْلَانَا فَانصُرْنَا عَلَى الْقَوْمِ الْكَافِرِينَ

The Messenger firmly believes in what has been revealed to him from his Lord, and so do the believers. They all believe in Allah, His angels, His Books, and His messengers. They proclaim, "We make no distinction between any of His messengers." And they say, "We hear and obey. We seek Your forgiveness, our Lord! And to You alone is the final return." Allah does not require of any soul more than what it can afford. All good will be for its own benefit, and all evil will be to its own loss. The believers pray, "Our Lord! Do not punish us if we forget or make a mistake. Our Lord! Do not place a burden on us like the one you placed on those before us. Our Lord! Do not burden us with what we cannot bear. Pardon us, forgive us, and have mercy on us. You are our only Guardian. So grant us victory over the disbelieving people."

Surah al-Ikhlas

قُلْ هُوَ اللَّهُ أَحَدٌ

اللَّهُ الصَّمَدُ

لَمْ يَلِدْ وَلَمْ يُولَدْ

وَلَمْ يَكُن لَّهُ كُفُوًا أَحَدٌ

Say, O Prophet, "He is Allah—One and Indivisible; Allah—the Sustainer needed by all. He has never had offspring, nor was He born. And there is none comparable to Him."

Surah al-Falaq

قُلْ أَعُوذُ بِرَبِّ الْفَلَقِ

مِن شَرِّ مَا خَلَقَ

وَمِن شَرِّ غَاسِقٍ إِذَا وَقَبَ

وَمِن شَرِّ النَّفَّاثَاتِ فِي الْعُقَدِ

وَمِن شَرِّ حَاسِدٍ إِذَا حَسَدَ

Say, O Prophet, "I seek refuge in the Lord of the daybreak, from the evil of whatever He has created, and from the evil of the night when it grows dark, and from the evil of those witches casting spells by blowing onto knots, and from the evil of an envier when they envy."

Surah an-Nas

قُلْ أَعُوذُ بِرَبِّ النَّاسِ

مَلِكِ النَّاسِ

إِلَٰهِ النَّاسِ

مِن شَرِّ الْوَسْوَاسِ الْخَنَّاسِ

الَّذِي يُوَسْوِسُ فِي صُدُورِ النَّاسِ

مِنَ الْجِنَّةِ وَالنَّاسِ

Say, O Prophet, "I seek refuge in the Lord of humankind, the Master of humankind, the God of humankind, from the evil of the lurking whisperer—who whispers into the hearts of humankind—from among djinn and humankind."

INSTRUCTIONS FOR EXORCISMS

The Arabic word *ruqyah*, meaning "spell," "charm," "magic," or "incantation," is used to describe the process by which djinn are exorcised and removed from persons or buildings. *Ruqyah* derives from the trilateral root R-Q-Y, which occurs four times in the Qur'an to denote words that relate to ascension and cure.

Over the years, ruqyah has come to be viewed as a magical process through which spirits are invoked and sorcery employed. This is perhaps what led to ruqyah being banned by the militant group Daesh, also known as the Islamic State, whose ideologies incorporate Salafism and Wahhabism. Daesh mostly outlawed ruqyah as it took over parts of Iraq and Syria, allowing very few elderly clerics to continue the practice of exorcising djinn from women. (It's always women, since Salafi and Wahhabi doctrine purport that women are weaker and less intelligent than men and therefore more susceptible to djinn. In fact, according to Salafi and Wahhabi scholars, a woman's so-called weak spirit and lower intelligence might even invite possession by a wicked djinni.)[34]

Besides the misogyny, this interpretation of ruqyah belies a deep misunderstanding of the process. Recommended in the Hadith as a mode of healing, ruqyah is at its core a way of supplicating to Allah. It should be used when seeking relief from disease, sorcery, malevolent djinn, and in my case, malicious men. Ruqyah can be performed by oneself or by a cleric

34 Judit Neurink Mosul, "Driving Out Demons in Mosul," DW, last modified February 2, 2019, https://www.dw.com/en/mosul-where-demons-women-and-islamic-state-met/a-47319908.

who can perform the rituals in your presence or via the internet. There is typically no charge for ruqyah, but some clerics will ask for the reimbursement of expenses.

Instructions for Ruqyah

First, perform ablutions and offer two rak'at nafil salat. Second, set your intention to banish evil and bring peace to yourself and your surroundings. Third, give money to charity. Fourth, affirm your belief in one true God and ask for God's mercy and help. Finally, be prepared to repeat the process below for a number of days or weeks, depending on the potency and wickedness of the djinni you seek to banish.

- In the following order, read:
  - Ayat-i-ruqyah, seven times.
  - Surah al-fatiha, three times.
  - Ayat al-kursi, three times.
  - The final two verses of surah al-baqarah, three times.
  - Surah al-ikhlas, surah al-falaq, and surah an-nas, three times each.

- Cup both of your palms, read ayat-i-ruqyah, and blow into your hands. Rub your palms over your face and over your body.

- Blow into a bottle full of water. Drink from this bottle of ruqyah water morning, noon, and night. You can also fill a spray bottle with this water and spray the corners of your home or the affected areas of a building.

Nightmares, fatigue, muscle aches, and pains can occur during and following this process.

Bibliography

al-Alusi, Mahmud Shukri. *Bulugh al'arab fi ma'rifat ahwal al-'arab*. Cairo: al-Matba'a al-Rahmaniya, 1924.

al-Andalusi, Abu 'Amir ibn Shuhaid al-Ashja'i. *Risalat at-Tawàbi' wa z-zawabi' (The Treatise of Familiar Spirits and Demons)*. Beirut: Dar Sader, 1967.

Bubandt, Nils, Mikkel Rytter, and Christian Suhr. "A Second Look at Invisibility: Al-Ghayb, Islam, Ethnography." *Contemporary Islam* 13, no. 4 (2019): 1–16.

Chodkiewicz, Michel. *An Ocean Without Shore, Ibn 'Arabî, the Book, and the Law*. New York: State University of New York Press, 1993.

al-Damiri, Kamal al-din. *Hayat al-hayawan al-kubra*. Beirut: al-Maktabah al-Islamiyyah, n.d.

Disney, A. R., ed. *A History of Portugal and the Portuguese Empire: From Beginnings to 1807. Volume 2: The Portuguese Empire*. Cambridge: Cambridge University Press, 2007.

Ghanim, David. *The Sexual World of the Arabian Nights*. Cambridge: Cambridge University Press, 2018.

al-Isfahani, Abu al-Faraj. *Kitab al-Aghani (The Book of Songs)*. Baghdad, tenth century.

Khayyam, Omar. *Rubaiyat of Omar Khayyam*. Translated by Edward Fitzgerald. London: Bloomsbury Books, 1984.

Laycock, Joseph P., ed. *The Penguin Book of Exorcisms*. London: Penguin Random House, 2020.

Lebling, Robert. *Legends of the Fire Spirits: Jinn and Genies from Arabia to Zanzibar*. Berkeley: Counterpoint, 2010.

al-Mas'ūdī, Abū al-Ḥasan ʿAlī ibn al-Ḥusayn ibn ʿAlī. *Murūj aḏ-Ḏahab wa-Maʿādin al-Jawhar (The Meadows of Gold and Mines of Gems)*. Tenth century.

McCleery, Iona. "Both 'Illness and Temptation of the Enemy': Melancholy, the Medieval Patient and the Writings of King Duarte of Portugal (r. 1433–38)." *Journal of Medieval Iberian Studies* 1, no. 2 (June 2009): 163–178.

Mittermaier, Amira. "The Unknown in the Egyptian Uprising: Towards an Anthropology of al-Ghayb." *Contemporary Islam* 13, no. 1 (Apr. 2019): 17–31.

Ogunnaike, Oludamini. *Deep Knowledge: Ways of Knowing in Sufism and Ifa, Two West African Intellectual Traditions*. University Park, PA: Pennsylvania State University Press, 2020.

Rodrigues, Vitor Luís Gaspar. "The Portuguese Art of War in Northern Morocco during the 15th Century." *Athens Journal of History* 3, no. 4 (October 2017): 321–336.

Sassi, Samir. "The Interaction of the Unseen and the Witnessed in the Tunisian Revolution." *Al-Jazeera*. August 3, 2011.

Seale, Yasmin, trans. *Aladdin: A New Translation*. New York: Liveright Publishing Corporation, 2019.

al-Shiblī, Badr al-Dīn. *Ākām al-marjān fī aḥkām al-jānn (The Hills of Precious Pearls Concerning the Legal Ordinances of the Jinn)*. Lebanon, eighth century.

Stetkevych, Suzanne Pinckney. "Poetic Genius and Poetic Jinni: The Case of Ibn Shuhayd." *International Journal of Middle East Studies* 39, no. 3 (August 2007): 333–335.

Wadud, Amina. *Qur'an and Woman: Rereading the Sacred Text from a Woman's Perspective*. Oxford: Oxford University Press, 1999.

Yeats, William Butler. *Fairy and Folk Tales of the Irish Peasantry*. London: Walter Scott, 1888.

El-Zein, Amira. *Islam, Arabs and the Intelligent World of the Jinn*. Syracuse: Syracuse University Press, 2009.